Publisher: SmithWrite Publishing Ltd
Co Regn No: 16165805

ISBN: 9781917888011
First Paperback Edition published in 2025
First Printed May 2025.

hello@smithwrite.co.uk
Theonewton.co.uk

Instagram @TheoNewtonBook

Book one Theo Newton Destiny
Available in
Paperback ISBN 9781917888004
And as an E-Book.

# BOOK TWO

# THEO

# NEWTON

# DECEPTION

## MARK P. SMITH

*Dedicated to my wife, my best friend of the past 15 years.*

# FOREWORD

The universe, in 2025, remains a mysterious phenomenon that is far from being fully understood. Scientists have been examining the clues, endeavouring to piece together a jigsaw of information, one in which we do not know how many pieces make up the complete puzzle. One in which the pieces may not even be the correct shape to fit together. One in which the image on a piece may not correspond with the developing picture.

I consider these unusual pieces *out-of-place* observations or, to use an idiom, as '*A bolt from the blue*'. They can trigger an even deeper desire to understand the universe, which pushes forward scientific enquiry. Across the multi-disciplinary fields of science, there is not just one jigsaw but several, each complete jigsaw being another piece of a larger jigsaw building our understanding of everything in the Universe.

Through rigorous research and study, repeated independent observations, and peer review discussion, science ever so slowly discovers the correct pieces and through making sense of an image, builds the bigger picture, often also discovering that a piece fits into multiple different puzzles.

Occasionally, science incorrectly throws a piece away that it later considers important. Einstein's *Cosmological Constant* is such a piece. He even referred to it as his biggest blunder, not knowing that it was, with some change, correct.

This leads to the fundamental issue with the jigsaw. As an example of how little we know about the universe, one jigsaw piece suggests the composition of the universe is between 1-10% normal matter (baryonic matter) the stuff that makes up stars, planets, you and me, your coffee, the air, and so on. If you dig a little further, you may see a figure for baryonic matter that states it makes up 4-5% of the universe.

But what makes up the rest? Science will tell you it does not know exactly, but observations suggest it has an idea: the remaining 95-96% of the universe falls into two categories - Dark Matter at 23-30% and Dark Energy at 65-73%. Interestingly, in the 1990s, observations of the accelerated expansion of the universe led to the resurgence of Einstein's Cosmological Constant, which is now associated with Dark Energy and believed to be an unknown force, driving this acceleration.

What is Dark Energy and Dark Matter? Science is trying to figure that out. Experiments in particle colliders such as the Large Hadron Collider and the Super Proton Synchrotron at CERN, amongst others, are helping us understand the fundamental particles and forces that may indirectly shed light on these mysteries. Meanwhile, astrophysical observations and specialised experiments continue to probe the nature of Dark Matter and Dark Energy.

So, how does any of this fit into Theo Newton? As a Science Fiction author, I can use imagination together with a grounding in science to create a universe where the results of science can be cherry-picked. By taking aspects of what we know or think we know, together with some assumptions and fiction, I have constructed a universe with laws and rules, very much like our own.

At the back of this book, I have included a section explaining this universe, a canon of those rules and laws, explaining how the universe works. A basis for perhaps expanding the book series, further adding to the canon. As I do not know what I do not know, I must determine what to include - this is the spirit of scientific curiosity.

# PROLOGUE

A month after the Aelioxar transported him to their homeworld, Genetrix-7X, in the Pleiades Cluster, Theo returned home. The Aelioxar were an ancient race of extraterrestrials. They had visited Earth several times over the millions of years of the planet's history. Masters of genetics, they encouraged life to take hold and thrive.

However, they could not stop themselves making one last change after discovering primates. Eventually, their perseverance paid off, their reward, Homo sapiens. But even then, the humans intrigued them. So they made more adjustments to the human DNA. And in one last experiment, they added their entire genome as 'partially' dormant instructions to the human's active DNA.

This gave rise to a stronger and more intelligent sub-species of human, who in history came to be known as Atlanteans. Today, their descendants carry the mysterious **ΧΩ** (*X-Omega*) blood group, a mutation of millennia of environmental influence.

Theo discovered he is carrier, but his destiny was to follow a different path to others of his kind. On Genetrix, the Aelioxar disclosed the truth about humanity and the gift he carried. Without his consent, they activated the alien genome within his DNA, bestowing upon him superhuman abilities. He is 'The One'.

On his return home, he was to find *The Order of the Etheric Veil*, and then with their counsel, discover and put an end to the deception, which was taking hold of humanity.

But unbeknownst to Theo, the forces of evil were already aware of his presence, plotting and scheming for his ultimate downfall and that of humankind.

# CHAPTER 1 OBSERVE

## SEPTEMBER 15 2021

*10:32 a.m. MDT - (Mountain Daylight Time)*

*5:32 p.m. BST - (British Summer Time)*

*Montana, USA.*

The wheat field stretched far across the horizon, the undulating waves of grain swaying in the breeze. Above, the brilliant blue sky was cloud free and seemed to extend on to infinity. The peace marred only by the distant hum of approaching helicopters. Their mechanical noise cut through the serenity, casting shadows over the sun-kissed earth.

"This is gold, leader. Bird two, you have your orders. Bird three, commence with multispectral imaging. Over."

As they approached the field's boundary, they split formation, each of the three helicopters taking a different path to survey the land beneath them.

The helicopter on the midfield route slowed, then hovered, before making a slow and steady descent, its rotors kicking up dust and chaff.

Settling onto the ground, the black paint gleaming in the sunlight. Its rear door, marked only with the initials 'G.A.R.D', slid open, revealing three figures.

Only then did the two accompanying helicopters make their approach, one climbing to a higher altitude, hovered. The second made a low pass, then climbed once more before heading towards the closest building, a diner, 10 miles away.

As the blades slowed, the occupants of the landed helicopter emerged from the side door. They wore matching jumpsuits, displaying the emblem of the Genetic Anomaly Research Division (G.A.R.D). Their boots crunched on the dry soil as they fanned out, each carrying specialised monitoring equipment.

The leader, Dr Marcus Kane, raised his hand, signalling the others to halt. His eyes scanned the field and then back to the instrument he was carrying. "This is it!" he shouted. "The residual energy signature matches the satellite data."

His team spread out, setting up sensors and probes. They drove stakes into the ground, attaching wires and cables. The air seemed charged and more unsettled here. As they worked, their movements were precise and purposeful. Dr Kane knelt, pressing a palm to the earth, feeling the latent energy thrumming beneath his skin and causing his hair to stand.

"Do you notice how there are no insects? What do you think caused this?" asked Agent Rodriguez, wiping sweat from his brow.

Dr Kane stood, his expression grim, "Not sure yet. But whatever it was, it's powerful. Exajoules don't lie. Rodriguez, grab some more jars. Take a sample every couple of metres within the boundary, then for 10 metres beyond. We will analyse for microbes."

Dr Kane pulled a device from his pocket, pressed a button and waited. He turned 90 degrees and pressed the button again, repeating after another 90-degree turn.

"The compass is spinning erratically." Returning the device to his pocket, he rolled up his sleeve; his skin prickled, and the hairs on his arm immediately stood.

"Fascinating," he murmured under his breath.

"Agent Patterson, take off your cap."

Without questioning the order, the 3rd man carried out the request. His hair mimicked Dr Kane.

"Thank you, Agent. We best grab some core samples, metre depth, random distribution."

The team tirelessly surveyed the 25-metre circle of damaged crops. Taking photos and extracting samples of wheat and earth. Combing the scene with forensic procession for any clue.

Dr Kane pulled out his radio. "Bird Two. This is Gold Leader. Over," the radio crackled, "Gold Leader. Awaiting your orders. Over."

"Rendezvous with Bird Three. We are about to commence harmonic response analysis. Stay off the channel for at least 10 minutes. We require zero electrical interference. Over," the radio crackled once again before the response came through, "10 minutes, Roger that. Heading to Bird Three. Will await further instructions. Over." The second helicopter moved off toward the third helicopter.

Within a minute, the only sound was the wind whistling through the field of wheat and the occasional crunch of the earth beneath boots.

"Ok, guys. Get back on the bird. I am about to initiate the harmonic response analysis."

As Dr Kane surveyed the crop circle, memories of previous energy events flashed through his mind. He was certain they connected to the multiple events in London. But why Montana? Secrecy was paramount in his mind. No trace of G.A.R.D's presence or involvement could remain once they had finished.

The group leader looked back, making sure everything was in order and that none of the sensitive equipment had moved.

Once on board the helicopter, they placed their helmets back on and lowered their visors. Dr Kane pulled the door closed and flicked a switch on his handheld monitor. A series of low rumbling tones was being emitted from the equipment that surrounded the flattened crop. As the sound amplified, its frequency began gradually to change from low to high. As the gauge on Dr Kane's monitor hit 1.21 terahertz, there was a blue electrical flash from the centre of the circle of the damaged crops, followed by the slow but steady appearance of steam from the ground. The sound stopped, and the quantum cascade laser powered down.

Dr Kane "It worked, the resonance frequency of 1.21 terahertz has induced an electromagnetic response in the latent energy signature. Hopefully, the data recorders captured everything. We will leave the equipment running for the moment. Pilot take us up."

Ascending, the full extent of the damaged crop became apparent. The centre of the shape was a perfect circle measuring twenty-five metres across, surrounded by an elaborate geometric pattern of semi-circles, lines and smaller full circles.

"Sir. Do you see that?"

"Yes, Agent Patterson, it looks like a cymatic pattern," the Dr acknowledged. "With the rate of energy dissipation, we were fortunate to capture any data at all. Without the readings, the pattern itself would be meaningless, a mere crop circle without context. But paired with the recorded measurements, it provides a critical insight into the energy source." The Dr was acutely aware that whatever had caused their readings possessed capabilities orders of magnitude greater than the annual combined energy usage of Earth.

After a brief final survey of the field, the helicopter moved off to regroup with the others.

### 11:30 a.m. MDT / 6:30 p.m. BST

### Montana Diner

The scene at the diner car park was an unusual one. Amongst a couple of battered pickup trucks, a big rig, and a motorbike, there were two black helicopters. Four men were walking about the site with electronic equipment, measuring latent electrical discharge, radiation, and exotic emissions. Three other men stood with automatic rifles, guarding the helicopters.

The third helicopter came into view, descending rapidly before touching down on the highway, blocking any traffic that may need to pass.

Two of the men who were surveying the site joined with the three men who had just landed, the rotor blades of their vehicle slowly losing momentum.

"Agent Smith, what is the situation?" Dr Kane looked towards the entrance of the diner, where three confused men were standing. One particular individual was sporting a bandage wrapped across his nose.

"Sir. We have taken readings from the parking lot, indications suggest a low-frequency electromagnetic anomaly, possibly linked to ion imbalance, at 6.5 Hz," Agent Smith continued, "If I may, Sir," Dr Kane nodded. Agent Smith shouted over to one of his colleagues, "AGENT CARTER."

The man who was standing near a wall by the parking lot stopped what he was doing and looked at his colleague. "Can you demonstrate for Dr Kane?" Agent Smith requested.

"Sure. Let's give everyone a laugh. Why not!" Agent Carter walked over to the wall. As he approached, the hair on his head stood on end in every direction, as if he was touching a Van de Graff generator.

"Thank you, Agent Carter. Carry on." Dr Kane turned his gaze back to the men standing by the diner. "Have you spoken to them yet Agent Smith?"

"Not yet, sir. Although Agent Jackson has taken some samples of the broken glass from the diner and the gas station."

"I think it's about time we discover what happened here. Agents Rodriguez and Patterson, with me"

Dr Kane and the two agents walked towards the men standing at the diner entrance. All the windows were shattered. Outside the building, shards lay on the ground. However, most of the broken panes were inside, indicating significant outside force.

"Good morning gentlemen. I am Dr Marcus Kane, I work for a special joint operations division of the US Government and US Military. With me are Agents Rodriguez and Patterson. Your co-operation is your patriotic duty. We expect nothing less from you."

"I will talk to you. But not that gutter trash." The man pointed towards Agent Rodriguez. The agent stood expressionless.

"Agent if you don't mind, switch with Agent Smith, please."

"Sir." Agent Rodriguez jogged over to his colleague; there was a brief exchange before Agent Smith joined his superior.

"Is he more to your liking?" Directing his attention to the replacement.

"Yeah, I guess he will do, he looks American. What do you want?" The man replied.

"Can we go inside? The agents here will look around."

The man with the bandage across his face nodded as he turned and entered the diner.

"May I take your names and what you do?" Dr Kane asked. Meanwhile, Agents Patterson and Smith began assessing the interior of the diner.

The man who had spoken first outside, again, was the first to speak.

"My name is James White. I haul big rigs." Standing about 5 foot 9 inches, had thin, receding blonde hair, maybe in his mid to late 40s. Wearing a red check shirt and jeans, which appeared to have recently been wet. He pointed to the man with the bandage. "We have Al Miller, this is his diner and Art Nelson he has a ranch not too far from here."

"Arthur Nelson is my name. But you can call me Art."

"So who wants to start?" Dr Kane Asks.

"**I WILL**" The shout came from a short, rotund woman, a cigarette hanging from her mouth, "I am Marge Miller and this is our diner."

"Finally, someone with a bit more about them. Please take a seat at one of your booths. Al, since you haven't spoken, grab me a cola drink," Dr Kane grabbed a chair from a table and placed it at the end of a booth. One by one, the trucker, rancher, and Marge took a seat. Sitting down, Dr Kane continued, "So, Marge, what happened here?"

"Well. It was like this. In walks this young fella, I can tell you right away, that he was not white. His kind is not welcome in our establishment. They cause nothing but bother and disrupt good folk's breakfast."

"How was he dressed?" Dr Kane asks.

"Well, he wore jeans and a black 'Bobcats' hoodie. He were tall."

"And how old would you say? You said he was young?"

"Hard to tell, they can always be older than they are, Ain't that right!" Snorting out a laugh that was more reminiscent of a pig squeal.

"Quite. Care at a guess?" Dr Kane requested.

"Marge, I would have said he was maybe 25," Arthur suggested.

"I guess," she continued, "He was a big build. I mean, he wasn't fat like Al. He had muscles."

Dr Kane let out a laugh.

"So. To confirm your description. Tall, muscular build, maybe 25 years old and not white. Care to be more specific? Did he look like he was from the Far East, India or Africa?"

There was an uncomfortable silence. Dr Kane looked at his watch and let out a sigh.

"Marge, just say it. He was dark-skinned. A black man." Arthur finally revealed.

"So help you, James. You know I don't like..." Dr Kane interrupted Marge, from what was inevitably going to be a racist rant, "Ok. I get the point. So, did he give a name? How did he sound? Did he speak English?"

Al had returned from the kitchen with a pitcher of cola and five glasses of ice, placing it on the table.

She continued, "He sounded kinda posh. He spoke English, but he was no American. Wearing our bobcats, damn disgrace." Marge turned her to look at the floor, hacked up, and then spat something green onto the floor.

"Charming," Dr Kane said with a look of disgust, "And what did he say?" He questioned.

Al tried to speak, but he just winced in pain, glancing at James, while directing his head toward Dr Kane.

"Er, well," the trucker was stumbling to get his words out, "It was like this. He came in demanding a coffee and something to eat, he said he didn't have any money. So Marge, Well, she said if he couldn't pay, he wasn't getting served."

Seeing the opportune moment, Marge takes over, "So I said he wasn't getting served. He got real angry. Threatening like. He picks up Art's beer and smashes it against the wall. James gets up to show the man the door, but he picks up a knife and thrusts it a James."

"I fell backwards to avoid the blade," James adds.

"Al, my husband comes out from the kitchen to see what the commotion was. Seeing the foreign guy kicking off. Well, you have seen him," She looks up at Al. "He may be fat, but he is big, used to be a wrestler back in the day. Anyways, Al approaches the guy and tells him to leave. This is when my husband ended up with a busted nose. With no reason, he punched my Al!"

"Is this correct?" Dr Kane looked at each person in the group, receiving confirming nods.

"Right then," he continues, "You have been most helpful. But one last thing. How did the windows break?"

Each of the friends stares at one another, shrugging their shoulders.

"I see. Care to venture a guess?" Dr Kane asks.

"Bunch of cowards," Marge directing her comment at the group. "I don't suppose you would believe me if I said the guy slammed the door on his way out?"

"And that caused the gas station windows to shatter also?"

"Well, I don't know. Maybe he smashed them too," she adds. "Who is going to pay for this damage?"

"Have you called the Sheriff?" Dr Kane asks.

"We tried but it looks like the lines are down." She replies.

"That is good," Dr Kane raises his right hand to shoulder height and points his index finger to the air, moving his hand in an anti-clockwise direction.

Agent Patterson walks over to the table and, without warning, pulls out a suppressed SIG Sauer P226 pistol, dispatching a bullet into the forehead of the three sitting at the table. Agent Smith takes out Al with a rear headshot.

"They were lying and I don't think they got the memo, there is no place for racism in America," Dr Kane stood and walked over to the phone that sat at the end of the counter, "Seems she was right. The phone is out!"

One by one, the helicopters spin up their rota blades.

Dr Kane takes one last look around before climbing aboard.

# CHAPTER 2 IDENTITY

## SEPTEMBER 15 2021

*2:23 p.m. BST - (British Summer Time)*

*7:23 a.m. MDT - (Mountain Daylight Time)*

*Dunthorpe, London.*

Theo stood at the front door to his home and pressed the bell. He heard the bell ring, but no other sounds came from inside the property. He instinctively knew no one was home. Stepping back, he materialised his backpack as if out of nowhere. Bending down, he unzipped a pocket and pulled out his keys.

*'There goes the dramatic return,'* thinking to himself.

He unlocked the door and pushed it open. The hallway seemed smaller than he remembered, but it was a welcome sight.

On the welcome mat were several mail items, the postage dates showing they were a couple of days old.

*'They must have gone away,'* he thought as he entered his home, picking up the letters and closing the door behind him.

Entering the kitchen, there were no notes left for him. Checking the fridge, it contained nothing that could spoil.

*'They must be away for a few days,'* considering where they could have gone.

He pulled out a bottle of water, downing the contents in one go. Next, he went into the living room. The blinds were closed. He noted that someone must have recently cleaned the room, since dust hadn't settled on the mantle or picture frames.

*'They went away very recently,'* thinking to himself.

Heading upstairs, he turned on the shower and went to his room to undress, hanging his super-suit on the door. Before going to wash, he remembered he needed to charge his phone.

While in the shower, he could hear his phone beep and ping, 35 days' worth of notifications all requiring his attention.

'*How many will be from Dad?*' he wondered. Showing no concern that his father and Louise had gone away. Theo could sense where Theodore was. He also knew his emotional state. His father was confident, intrigued, perhaps annoyed, and slightly apprehensive, but not worried about Theo. He felt his dad was on an adventure.

Theo stepped out of the shower, dripping with water. About to reach for a towel, he considered a different approach. He pushed open the windows to help vent the steam.

Closing his eyes, he focused for a moment. The water clinging to his body vibrated, and slowly, the liquid lifted away. Theo opened his eyes, watching as the droplets coalesced into a ball of water the size of a grapefruit. He gazed at the open gap in the window as the water shot out, instantly turning to steam as it went.

'*This is taking some getting used to, but wow.*' Thinking as he ran his fingers through his now-dry hair. A smile on his face as he looked at his reflection in the now steam-free mirror. He sprayed himself with some deodorant. Holding the can, he had another thought: '*I don't need to use this anymore. Ah, what the hell, it smells good.*'

Re-entering his bedroom, he switches on the TV. A sports news channel plays. He pulls on a pair of sweatpants and a T-shirt, then sits at his desk and grabs his mobile. '*So many notifications,*' he thinks to himself. He starts with his messages.

'*Theo, where are you? You should have been here by now x Dad*'.

*'I'm getting worried. I'm heading towards your last location x Dad.'*

*'Hey Theo, I am sorry, but I don't think I will be able to visit as soon as I had hoped. Work is still crazy. Love Mei.'*

*'Theo I am worried for you son. I have found another event site. Message me when you can. Please! Love Dad.'*

He scrolled further.

*'We have been unable to collect payment for your mobile contract on 30/08/2021. We will try again in 7 days.*

Theo decided against reading any more messages. He got the picture. He had been missing and people were worried about him. He made sure he paid his phone bill and checked his emails before heading downstairs.

In the kitchen, he looked for something to eat but couldn't find anything he fancied. It was approaching 4 p.m. and he craved fish and chips, but the *chippy* wouldn't be open for another hour.

Looking for inspiration, he headed out the door. While mask-wearing, for COVID reasons, was no longer mandatory, Theo decided, for anonymity, he would take one, as well as a baseball cap.

The walk took only five minutes. As soon as he rounded the corner onto the high street, he put the mask on.
Unfortunately, there weren't too many 6 foot 6 inch individuals around and he realised he stood out. He hoped no one recognised him, however; he was now a celebrity, something he often forgot.

Across the road was a cafe. He could see it was still busy, which was something he wanted to avoid. Then, a few doors down, a coffee shop, 'Coffee and cake', he thought, 'That will have to do.'

He jogged across the street and entered.

"Can I help you?" the lady behind the counter asked

"Can I have a large caramel latte to go, 3 shots of espresso and 2 pumps of caramel? I will also take a chocolate muffin please."

The lady smiling in reply. For a moment, Theo thought she recognised him, as she seemed to hesitate. Instead, her response was more natural as she spoke.

"That will be £7.50, please. Cash or card?"

Theo pulled out his phone, showing he wished to pay contactless. 'So far so good' he considered. However, his day was about to change. While he stood waiting at the end of the counter, two men wearing balaclavas entered. One was holding a cricket bat, the other a handgun.

"LISTEN bitch. Give me all the money from the till. **NOW**" The man with the gun pointed it directly at the lady behind the counter. Meanwhile, the man with the bat stormed into the office,

"Empty the fucking safe. **NOW**." He shouts.

Theo was considering his options. He wasn't ready to reveal his powers yet. He certainly didn't want to give away his identity. Figuring the criminals would panic and run if he employed his plan. With a simple thought, he made the safe and the drawer to the till, jam and the firing pin and trigger to the handgun lock.

"Hurry the fuck up with the money," the man with the gun shouted.

"I am trying, but it's jammed. It won't open," the lady now panicking, "Why won't it open,"

"You stupid cow." The man went to fire the gun, but nothing happened. He tried to adjust it, but the firearm refused to work.

From the office, the other man shouted to his associate, "Harry, this bitch won't open the safe, she said it's jammed."

"No names! I told you, you fucking idiot." The man with the gun replies.

"It seems like today isn't your day. You best leave," Theo looked directly at the man with the gun, who just stared back. He motioned towards the man, who, taking in the stranger's stature, reconsidered his actions.

"Gerry. We better go. **NOW**," The man with the gun turned to the door and ran. Gerry soon followed.

Theo walked to the door shouting after them, "Harry and Gerry, I will see you around. Keep a look out for me."

Turning, he went back to the counter.

"Are you OK?" Asking the lady

"I think so. I don't know what happened to the till, it genuinely wouldn't open." She was still shaking.

"Do you need any help?" Theo asked.

"No no. Thank you. I think we had better phone the police and consider closing for the day." She moved from behind the counter and into the office, Theo followed.

"Are you OK, Sue?" she called out, seeing Sue slumped on the floor, crying. "They have gone now. The till jammed. Fortunately, they didn't take anything."

For half an hour, Theo assisted the ladies with cleaning up and then closing the cafe. Wanting to leave before the police arrived.

*'That was my first, superhero intervention,'* he thought to himself. *'I need to speak to Dad.'*

Arriving home, he remembered the mail he picked up earlier. Scanning the addressee of each letter, he found only one was for him. It was from the University of Central London. Tearing it open, he read the letter. Sent by the head of Archaeology. Theo was to have met with the professor to discuss his proposed area of research for his doctoral study.

*'I was off planet. I would never have been able to attend.'* It occurred to him how bizarre that thought was: *'I was off planet.'*

He considered his options, should he continue with his PhD, after all, he was now a superhuman and he no longer had anything to prove, but then, with research, he could show via archaeological evidence, that what the Aelioxar had told him was true, he, himself, could be exhibit A, how could they disprove 'him'.

'*I need to speak to Dad. I need his guidance,*' he thought again.

Theo went back to his room and changed into his super-suit. The fit was perfect; it was comfortable and flexible. It felt like it was part of him. Back downstairs, he locked the front door, placing his key on a hook in the passage. Then into the kitchen, he drank another bottle of water. '*Dad. It is time to introduce the new me.*'

Not wanting anyone to see him, he turned invisible, then walked through the closed back door between the kitchen and the garden. He soared skyward. Looking down at the ground beneath him, he could see his garden gradually become smaller, then the row of houses on his road. More streets and rooftops came into view. Then, the lush green of Fryent County Park. Climbing higher, Brent Reservoir and Wembley Stadium could be seen.

He stopped ascending one mile into the air and hovered, taking in the view across London. Flying at just below the speed of sound and allowing the physics of altitude, pressure and air temperature to affect him, it would take a little over 12 minutes to reach his dad. He could instantly teleport, but this would use more energy and while his energy reserves were impossibly massive, Baruch warned him to be mindful of how much he used unnecessarily. He remained uncertain of exactly how much energy he would expend in any activity. '*It isn't like I have a charge meter.*' Laughing to himself.

Theo guided himself south towards Hammersmith and Fulham, then dived towards the Thames, slowing as he approached two meters above the river surface. Flying at only 30 mph, he took in the views of the riverbanks, occasionally having to dodge river craft.

He counted seven bridges that he passed under by the time he reached Battersea Park, the recognisable four chimneys of the former power station now in view as he regained altitude. The river was busier with traffic here. He loved flying. It was exhilarating, the sensation of weightlessness, the speed, the views. It was freedom beyond any other measure. And the cherry on the top was that, for the time being, no one else knew what he could do. He would savour the experience before he became public knowledge.

'Enough now' he thought as he accelerated to 700 mph heading in a generally easterly direction, his dad's location fixed as his bearing. In very little time, he had crossed Kent, then the Strait of Dover. Just for fun, he dropped his altitude to 20 meters above the sea and increased his speed as he approached a giant container ship.

The surrounding air compressed into a shockwave, radiating a sonic boom in all directions, causing violent ripples and waves to cascade across the water's surface.

The ship shudders as the shockwave hits, causing the containers to rattle, forcing the crewmembers to brace themselves against the unexpected turbulence. Beneath, the water churns, causing the ship to rock violently.

"Oops. Maybe I was too close. SORRY," he shouts back. If anyone had heard him, they would be at a loss where the voice came from, since he was under a cloak of invisibility.

Slowing below mach one, he returned to his previous altitude. He learned that even though he was a relatively small object in the sky; he needed to be mindful of his power, he couldn't just drop in at high speed like superhero movies portrayed. He imagined what a 'close' proximity ultrasonic landing would do to a child if he didn't counter the force with matter-energy manipulation.

Belgium was now in view. Oostende disappeared behind him in a blink. In the ever-closer distance, he could see his target, the city of Bruges. Dropping his altitude, he closed in on 'Markt'. He could see his dad with Louise standing near the statue of Jan Breydel and Pieter De Coninck. The market square was teeming with people. Customers packed the outdoor seating at the bars and restaurants.

He chose the closest establishment to where his dad stood. Using intangibility, he passed through the building's walls, entering an empty cubicle in the male toilets. Returning to visibility, he flipped the hood on his suit and in an instant he was wearing jeans and a black hoody with a poster for 'In Bruges' printed on the front.

### 6:11 p.m. - CEST / 5:11 p.m. - BST

### Bruges, Belgium

Exiting the toilets, he walked through the cafe and into the square, jogging over to where his dad and Louise stood, their backs to him.

"Hi, Dad." Theodore spun around to see his son's arms out, waiting for an embrace. Theodore grabbed his son, a tear rolled down his cheek.

"Theo, where the hell have you been? I have been beside myself with worry." Releasing his son, Theo embraced Louise.

"Hi Mam," kissing him on the cheek, tears welling in her eyes.

"Where have you been, son? I found the site of the 'Event'. You have been missing for over a month." Theodore's eyes were red.

"Sorry, Dad. I can't wait to tell you, but not here. It is too public and I think you will both need to sit when I do."

Arriving back at their holiday rental, a small apartment close to Markt. Theodore and Louise prepare themselves for the news by taking a seat on the sofa.

"Are you ready?" Theo asks, "Do either of you want a drink? This may take a while." His parents shook their heads.

"OK." Acknowledging their response.

Theo spoke for almost an hour uninterrupted, beginning with the Aelioxar, how they were 'Masters of genetics' and their influence on human evolution. Reciting stories of Atlantis and the downfall of the ancient and advanced civilisation. He even hadn't mentioned the most important part of the story before his dad could no longer hold back his questions.

"Sorry for interrupting, but this is amazing. Do you know where it is? Atlantis?"

"Atlantis wasn't just a single place. The Atlanteans had several cities. They were all destroyed following the comet impact which resulted in the Younger Dryas. And yes, I know where they are."

"Where?" His dad, wide-eyed, asks

"Their principal city, as described by Plato, is what we now know of as the *Eye of the Sahara* or the *Richat Structure*, in modern day Mauritania. Then they had a small trading post off the coast of Egypt and near the City of Alexandria. Another was in the Adriatic. The final two cities were in the Atlantic. One is at the Ampere seamount, located southwest of Portugal. And another was an island close to Lanzarote. They were all destroyed by a Tsunami. The Atlantic cities fell into the depths of the ocean."

"Incredible. And I thought Atlantis was only one city." Louise adds.

"The story follows that records of Atlantis were believed to have been destroyed or hidden. I may come back to that a bit later. I haven't even covered the major revelation yet. Maybe we should have some food first."

The family headed down to the square for an evening meal. Louise kept staring at Theo. She couldn't put her finger on it, so had to ask, "Theo, there is something different about you. But I can't for the life of me say what it is!"

"I have changed, but I'll explain when we get back to the apartment." Followed by one of his cheeky winks.

"While you were away, I had a phone call from a mystery woman, she identified herself as the Registrar, who was first to see your mam after her event. Anyway, I meet up with her and she tells me I must contact this man," Theodore pulls the card from his pocket. "Do you know who Theo R Derotev is?" Pausing, he handed the card to Theo. "We have searched his name but..." Theo interrupts.

"It's not a man. It is a secret order!" He replies.

"I said, didn't I? The Order of the EV," Louise added with an amazed expression.

"It's the *Order of the Etheric Veil*. This isn't the place to talk about it. Trust me when I say, we need to keep this to ourselves," Theo's tone was direct but hushed.

"Can we change the subject. How are things at DexBox?" Theo asks.

The family stayed for another hour, talking about the charity, the fallout from 'The Games' and then Theo's disappearance and the resultant conspiracy theories that ensued.

Back at the apartment, Theo continued to explain what had happened to him on Genetrix-7X, revealing his true destiny. Theodore and Louise sat mouths agape, taking in everything their son was telling them until Theodore stood and looked out of the window. Raising his arms to his head, he roughly wiped his eyes and then placed his hands on the back of his head.

"I am sorry Theo, I need proof of this. Like what kind of things can you do?" Theodore paced back and forth. The revelation that his son was superhuman made him question everything. He was in disbelief, but was about to be in shock.

"Dad, stop pacing," Theo pleaded as he continued. "I can do pretty much anything. Where do I start? I can fly. I have highly tuned senses. All my senses are turned up to eleven and then some. But I can modulate the frequencies I receive so I don't get overwhelmed."

Theodore stared at his son like he was being told the most impossible lie. "Now come on Theo, people can't fly. Where are your wings?" He turned and stared at his wife, expecting her to say something. She looked at him, words failing her. Instead, all she could offer was a shrug of her shoulders.

"I flew here. When I returned to Earth, Baruch put me somewhere secluded. I found myself in a field, in Montana."

"Montana? As in the USA Montana?" Theo interrupted.

"Yes," Theo answered. "After a brief racist encounter at a nearby diner, I flew home. I climbed into low earth orbit passing over the USA and the Atlantic in a few seconds…"

Theodore's mouth was wide open. Finally, he could feel that his son was telling the truth. Louise, however, stared at Theo like he was insane, but she had to know.

"How fast can you fly?" She asked.

"As fast as I want. As I explained, when my true genetic makeup was activated. I was told I would appear as a god to everyone. But I don't consider myself to be a god, I am still me. I can control matter and energy. I can manipulate the fabric of space and time, I can slow time, even make it stop. I can travel to distant worlds instantly. If I wanted, I can even break the laws of physics, although there are some things I cannot do." Theodore slumped down onto the couch, looked at Louise, and then held her hand. He was going to say something, but he couldn't get the words out. He **was** now in shock.

"I know this is a lot to take in and you will have questions. But I need advice."

He looked at his dad, who on hearing his son, a god, asking for help, sat back up and leant forward.

"Going back to The Order of the Etheric Veil. We are the descendants of Atlanteans. The final genetically changed humans, that was, until the Aelioxar returned and I was the result. Dad, you and I are their descendants. But Mam was also a descendant."

Theodore looked at his son. A tear welled in the corner of his eye before rolling slowly down his cheek.

"The Aelioxar instructed those final enhanced humans to keep their secret. To only pass their story to their male offspring before reaching adulthood. This secret was important and needed to be passed on because like grandad, like you, a trait could activate. You and Grandad shared the same trait, clairvoyance.

Called The Order of the Etheric Veil because they were a community of people protecting the secret of their genetic story. They, or rather, we, exist to this day. They are predominantly men, however, over the generations, more women have inherited the traits. My birth was an event the Aelioxar did not foresee happening.

The Order is to be my counsel. There are many members distributed across the world, in government, military, science, education and even medicine. They know of my arrival and will instruct me on my purpose."

Theodore was beginning to understand, but he had a couple of personal questions. "This all makes sense now, but I have two questions, Did your Grandad know and if he did why did he not tell me? And did your mam die knowing any of this? Was she sacrificed by these aliens so you could be born?" Theodore's tears did not abate. They kept rolling and soaked into his shirt. Louise held his hand tighter as she leaned in to comfort him.

"Your dad, my Grandpa Levi knew. But was killed before he could tell you. I don't know if Mam knew, they never mentioned that, but she **WAS** sacrificed for me." Theo, with an expression of remorse, looked at his dad and without speaking, he knew his dad understood his meaning. He was sorry.

"They say there are plans for me. They say that things are happening now, across the world that has to be stopped and there will be things happening soon that only I can stop. Without me, humanity will end and our planet will be destroyed. There is a

24

massive deception unfolding, it has consequences for us all. So I need to meet with *The Order* soon."

Theodore's eyes, while still red and sore, finally had closure. The mystery of his Izzy finally revealed. Twenty-one years of not knowing had ended.

"Just know this son. IF I EVER MEET THIS BARUCH, I WILL HIT THEM HARDER THAN I HAVE EVER HIT BEFORE." His feelings were in turmoil. On one hand, he had his Theo back, but he was no longer only his. He had to share his son with the world.

Theo could see and feel the pain his dad was experiencing. He knew in time his father would recover.

Eventually, regaining his composure, Theodore continued,

"Deception? What kind of deception?"

"I don't know the full details. But what I do know is that I will be vilified and deemed the most dangerous person in history. Governments will probably have to fall. We will all be targets."

"MY GOD." Theodore looked at his wife, their mouths wide open. It took a few moments for their disbelief to subside. The emotional strain was taking its toll.

Louise finally asks the question which had been their minds for the past five days.

"How do we contact 'The Order' there is no number on the card?"

"There is. The name codes the number; however, you can ignore the letters O and T in Derotev. We need to call 0843 6733738."

"Your dad found that O and T weren't circled when we looked at them with a UV light. How did you know the number?"

"It uses a simple T9 text input found on mobile phones, since all numbers start with a leading 0, that was not included. The answer was in your hand the whole time!"

"You have got to be kidding me! John told me not to ring from the UK as he suspected the USA was monitoring," Theodore exclaimed, pulling out his burner phone.

"The USA? How?" Theo asks.

"John recovered some video footage of you during *the event*. I haven't seen it myself, but he described an ethereal light enveloping you and then you were gone. The UK Secret Service confiscated the footage, his last understanding was that it was now in American hands."

"Shit. That puts an end to the guidance I was going to ask for."

"I don't understand. What guidance did you need?"

"I don't know how to reveal myself to the world or even if I should. I did not enjoy being in the spotlight during *the games*, the press showed no boundaries and to them, everything was fair game. But now there will be people in the US government who have questions about me. I have concerns for the safety of both of you. I suspect they will come for me. They can't possibly know what they are about to encounter, however, if they get you, they have leverage."

Theodore stands and embraces his son.

"Theo, I don't think you need to be so concerned for us."

"Dad, I can't let them harm you."

"Who says they can or will? Just answer this. How did you find me? How did you know I was in Bruges?"

"I could sense where you were, we have an irrevocable bond through our X-blood."

"So son. If you could find me once, you can find me again. And if you have the powers you say, who will be able to defeat the mighty Theo Newton?"

"Still, Dad they may not take you. They may instead kill you. Kill people I love to force me to do their will."

"Theo, I think what your dad is trying to say, even though he hasn't said it, is, that we don't know what the Americans want, they may   have questions, want information, who knows, but you cannot instantly assume they have malevolent intentions."

"She is correct Theo. We don't know what we are dealing with. And I emphasise **WE.** You are not alone."

"Thank you" Theo embraced the pair. "We need to contact 'the order'. What superhero name should I use?"

Theodore looked at his son as if he was crazy.

"You still haven't showed us your powers"

# CHAPTER 3 G.A.R.D

## SEPTEMBER 16 2021

*12:23 a.m. EDT - (Eastern Daylight Time)*

*5:23 a.m. BST - (British Summer Time)*

*Massachusetts, USA.*

**D**r Kane, followed by Agents Patterson, Smith and Rodriguez carrying cases of sensitive equipment, approached the security doors. Two guards in military uniform stood sentry at the entrance.

Dr Marcus Kane removed the lanyard from around his neck and pressed it against a security panel. The sound of a magnetic lock releasing echoed down the narrow concrete tunnel of the personnel entrance to the secured underground facility deep inside Bare Mountain, Massachusetts.

Two underground bunkers resided in the mountain; the first, a former USAF base called 'The Notch', is now a library archive. The second bunker was intended as a secret, much larger extension of 'The Notch' until the US Air Force and the National Security Administration established a new joint operations initiative, G.A.R.D., taking command of the site, making it a separate facility.

Dr Marcus Kane had worked for the *'Genetic Anomaly Research Division'* or G.A.R.D for nearly 15 years. Formerly a combat rescue officer with the 212th Rescue Squadron of the US Air Force based in Alaska. He later attained a PhD in Genetics and worked on a research team mapping the human genome. His combination of skills made him a prime candidate as a research agent for G.A.R.D.

Dr Kane, followed by his men, went through the open door which led to another concrete tunnel, at the end of which was an elevator. Entering, he selected two floors from the panel, which revealed four levels to the facility.

"I want the data uploaded to the server right away. Once complete, run an analysis factoring for the Schumann Resonance," Dr Kane orders Agents Smith and Rodriguez, who nod and exit the elevator at sub-level 2.

Before the door could close, he jammed his foot in the gap,

"And get the samples to the lab, testing for microbes, contaminants and isotopes. Check for structural alterations; compression, recrystallisation and pH. Got it?"

"Yes, Sir." They replied.

The Dr and Agent Patterson exited at sub-level 3.

"Take care of the photography and run a spectral resolution analysis once team A have uploaded their data."

"Yes, Sir," Agent Patterson heads down the corridor the opposite direction to Dr Kane who is standing in front of a door marked 'General McAllister'. Without knocking, he enters.

The office is a blend of functionality and technology, designed to provide information with maximum efficiency. Dominating the centre of the room is a sleek, rectangular conference table.

Embedded in the table is a massive touch screen. At uniform intervals, there are tablet-sized touch screens. Eight high-backed leather chairs, each embossed with the G.A.R.D emblem; a double helix intertwined with the delta wing of the US Space Force, sit around the table.

The wall opposite to the door Dr Kane entered through is entirely composed of soundproof and electrochromic privacy glass, providing a panoramic view of the busy operations room beyond. The screens, seen through the window, display real-time satellite feeds.

At the far end of the office is a desk with four large computer screens mounted on articulated arms. On the wall behind the desk is a shelf adorned with models of spacecraft from popular science fiction. A single bonsai tree sits centre stage.

The general stands from behind his desk. A thin man, about 6 foot tall, wears a pristine white shirt with four stars on his epilates. His navy-coloured tie displays the G.A.R.D emblem.

"Dr Kane. Coffee?" He asks with a husky New York accent.

"Please. Sir, I didn't expect you to still be here."

The general moves to a barista station in the corner of his room. The aroma of coffee mingles with the faint ozone of electronic equipment.

"Last minute requests from President Bernstein. Take a seat. How are things with Carol? Have you worked out your differences yet?" The General requested. His concern, sincere and friendly.

"No, Sir. She has proceeded with filing divorce papers," Dr Kane replies, not showing any sign of emotion or remorse.

The General hands the Dr a coffee and sits at the table.

"That is a shame. The life we choose takes its toll on our relationships, but our duty is greater than our sacrifices. How was Montana?"

"Sir. The Exajoule energy emission left some trace signatures. I have sent the results for analysis, but the preliminary readings at site, indicate a frequency of 1.21 TeraHertz, this activated the latent energy from the discharge. We should have a better understanding in a few hours."

"And this matches London?"

"Yes, Sir. We have detailed results from 2014 and last month. I sent the report to the emissary, they confirmed our suspicions."

"And Japan?" The general asks.

"I despatched a surveillance team to monitor the girl. If she knows anything, we will discover what that is." Dr Kane takes a sip of his coffee.

"Good work Marcus. Any change regarding Newton?"

"No, Sir. The emissary is maintaining their belief he is with *The Creators*. But If I could speculate?"

"Your insights have not let you down yet, go ahead."

"Thank you, Sir. I believe he has returned."

The general put his coffee down and frowned.

"And you suspect this how?"

"One Exajoule, Sir. We have reviewed all data points since we first had contact with the Emissaries *Nexil* species. We have used H.E.L.I.X to analyse them. Let me show you what we know." The Dr pulls the tablet placed in front of him to a 33-degree angle. Unlocking with facial recognition. After a few taps, Dr Kane brings up an image on the large display inset to the table.

A Folder labelled H.E.L.I.X - '**Hylozoic Evolved Learning and Interactive Xeno-Intelligence**' is opened and a series of images with explanatory text displays.

"Sir, we don't believe the '*Nexil*' have the capability for one Exajoule, at least not in the manner displayed in Montana."

"What about the other species?" The General asks.

"Sir. We cannot be certain. However, from what we understand about *The Creators* they do."

"Dr Kane. So you believe Newton was with these *Creators* and has now returned?"

"Yes, Sir."

"Hmmm..." The General stands and walks to the window and looks over the control room beyond.

"This could have significant implications if you are correct. I will need to have a conference with the Generals and the Director, but only when your analysis is complete. Is General Harris still on board the Vanguard?"

"Just a moment, Sir." Dr Kane calls up a menu on the tablet and selects Space Force Operations, then United Space Fleet. A dozen spacecraft are displayed. He taps on the flagship, the USF Vanguard. Dr Kane then selects active crew members. The page displays a complement of 150 active personnel, with Colonel Wainwright in command and General Harris currently onboard.

"Yes, Sir. He is."

"Thank You, Dr Kane. We will have to relay the conference via Moonbase Alpha. Keep me apprised of the analysis. That is all."

Dr Kane quickly finishes his coffee and leaves the office. He walks down the corridor to a door labelled *Operations Centre* and enters. In front of him is a brief run of metal stairs which lead to the open-plan operations room visible from General McAllister's office.

"Where can I find Agent Rodriguez?" Dr Kane asks the nearest operator.

"Sir. He was here a moment ago. He may have returned to the spectral analysis lab."

Turning, Dr Kane walks towards a metal storage unit on the wall. Pressing his lanyard against a panel which unlocked a drawer. He retrieves an earpiece, placing it in his right ear. The drawer automatically closes.

"HELIX. Has the spectral analysis of the photos from Montana started?" His attention drawn to a screen at the front of the room which displays a computer-generated human avatar which speaks.

"Dr Kane. The data from alpha team has just finished being uploaded. It will take me several hours for a full level one analysis. However, I have some initial observations. Would you like me to present them to you?"

"Yes, In my office." The screen returns to an image of the Earth showing the position of several G.A.R.D satellites in orbit. Dr Kane enters a room to the side of the operations centre. The lights automatically activate. It is a small room, sparsely furnished, except for a simple desk equipped with a computer and four monitors on extending arms.

"HELIX, continue." He asks, taking a seat at the desk.

"Of course, Dr Kane. My initial observations are that the energy signature first detected by G.A.R.D HelixStar 2 was an intense energy pulse of one exajoule, and the dissipation rate, based on the readings from Montana, suggests an initial microwave frequency range of 44.3 gigahertz with minimal spectral spread over a narrow bandwidth. This overlaps with the frequency range of some radio transmissions.

I have commenced monitoring of online chatter for discussions about interference at 44.3 gigahertz. The peak frequency was in the order of 640 Terahertz in the visible spectrum. I also have to point out that since the damage in Montana was minimal, the one exajoule suggests that this was not a weapon.

The dispersal rate suggests that whatever was transmitted **is** the source of the energy."

"Are you suggesting that something came with the energy pulse or is the energy pulse?"

"Yes Dr, I suspect something with great energy arrived in Montana."

"My god. HELIX, let me know as soon as you have finished your analysis," Dr Kane walks over to his desk and pulls out a tumbler and a bottle of Single Malt Scotch Whisky.

With a large pour in his glass, he downed the lot. The liquid burned as it went down his throat, causing him to cough violently.

# CHAPTER 4 MEI

## SEPTEMBER 16 2021

*Bruges, Belgium.*

It was past 1 a.m. by the time the Newtons got to bed. Theo knew his parents would have problems sleeping, so with their permission, he connected with their minds, applying a sleep-inducing neurological process to activate adenosine production.

Theo, though, no longer required sleep. He needed to rest for regeneration. Sleep provided minor benefits to *Zirconine* and *Vitronine* in synthesising protein for repair and energy replenishment. At night, contemplation and meditation replaced his need to sleep, helping his mind focus and gain greater control of his abilities.

*7:10 a.m. - CEST / 6:10 a.m. - BST*

In the kitchen that morning, Theodore found Theo preparing breakfast.

"Sleep well?" He asked his dad.

"Probably the best sleep I have ever had."

Theodore looked well rested. His eyes had a sparkle and were noticeably less puffy.

Theo poured his dad a mug of coffee and handed it to him.

"I was thinking son, because you can sense my location. Can you not sense other people like us?"

"I can. Some are stronger than others." Theo replied.

"So can't you use that ability to find the order?"

Taking a sip of coffee, Theo thought for a moment,

"I can't work out who is part of the order and who isn't."

"I thought you said everyone like us was *the Order*?"

"Technically they are, but you didn't know about the order until I told you. I have to assume there will be others who do not know."

"Ah," Theodore exclaimed, "I had not considered that. You say that some are stronger than others. Any clue why?"

"I guess that those whom I can sense more strongly, have an active trait, but I can't be certain. Is Louise up?"

"She was asleep. Is breakfast going to be long?"

"It is almost ready. After we have eaten, I will call the number on the card."

After breakfast, the father and son were sitting in the living room preparing to make the call.

"I was wondering. Not that I want it. But can you enhance the traits of others like us?" Theodore asks.

"I can, between you and me. There are lots more that I can do than even the Aelioxar realise. It is almost as if.." Theo pauses and closes his eyes, his eyelids flickering, like he is carrying out a self-diagnostic reminiscent of an android on a popular sci-fi show. He continues, "As if they over-engineered me."

"Oh. Just imagine the possibilities," Theodore looked at his son wearing a look of pride. "What were you doing just then? With your eyes?"

"I receive so many sensory inputs, not just vision or sound. I can't explain it in a way that would make any sense. It is like I have a connection with everything everywhere all at once. Occasionally I get a gut feeling, which I focus on, it may need me to intervene, depending on what it is. Sometimes I fix things remotely."

"Like what? Explain it to me?"

"Just now, I was aware that a passenger plane had a faulty landing gear. I manipulated matter and extended the wheels enabling the plane to land safely. No one will be any wiser. The pilot will report the alert and it will be repaired. Does that make sense?"

"That is amazing, you can do that, fix a mechanical issue from so far? The sensory overload must be incredible. I don't get how you can filter everything out."

"As I say, its hard to describe. I am still getting use to filtering out the noise and homing in on where, in this case, the distress call was coming from," Theo shrugged, "I think it's time to make the call."

Theodore looked at his son, placing a hand on Theo's.

"Once you make the call son, there will be no going back. Are you ready to dive into the rabbit hole?"

"I am ready. But I still can't work out how I should reveal myself to the world? And do I need a superhero name?"

"Don't force it. I am sure there will be a time when it feels right. Let's find out what the order have to say first. As for a name, not a clue."

Theo picks up the phone and dials the number. After a couple of rings, it connects.

"Burgess, Hoyt and Mann Legal. How may I direct your call?"

"My name is Theo Newton, I.." The lady on the other end of the phone interrupts, "I will put you through now Theo." He glances at his dad, sending a thought to him. *'They were expecting me, it is Burgess, Hoyt and Mann'*

Theodore, eyes wide, looks at his son. *'Mr Chapshaw? No way. What the hell!'*

After a moment's pause, a man spoke.

"Hello, Theo. I trust you are on a burner phone? The line is secure at our end." The man spoke with a very English voice. His vowels were crisp and his consonants clear, very much like a newsreader on the BBC. With no regional accents and a controlled, even pitch.

36

"I am. Who am I speaking to?" Theo questions.

"My name is Herbert J. Montclair QC."

"I need to meet with the order."

Louise enters the room, draping her arms around Theodore's shoulders.

"We will convene on Sunday, 5.30 p.m. at Sawley Abbey. There is a secret tunnel under the building in the southeastern corner. The code to enter is the six digits of your birthday. We are all very much looking forward to seeing you Theo." The call disconnects.

"Where is Sawley Abbey?" Theodore asks as his mental connection with his son disconnects.

"I believe it is in Lancashire," He pauses momentarily, trying to recall if he knew more about the Abbey. "It's north of the town of Clitheroe. It's a 10th Century Abbey, just ruins now."

"Oh, is the Order? What a strange place to meet," Louise suggests.

"What do we do now?" Theodore asks. He didn't enjoy sitting around, waiting. He was becoming more impatient with age.

"You don't need to go. How long do you have left in Bruges?" Theo suggests, trying to ease his father's frustration.

"We have two more nights here. Remember, I am a member of *The Order* so maybe I should be there!"

"Of course, sorry Dad. Finish your stay. When you get home on Saturday, we can drive to Lancashire. Stay over somewhere."

"OK. Is that alright Louise?" Theodore turned to his wife, who was feeling left out. However much it upset her, she wouldn't let on.

"Yes. I don't need to go. We have been away from the charity for a week. I will catch up with work." Quickly scrambling for an excuse.

"If you are sure?" Theodore stretching to kiss his wife's cheek. "What are you plans until Sunday, Theo?"

"I have to get back to London. Meet with the Professor."

"About your PhD?" Louise asks.

"Yeah. He is an early starter so I can catch up with him. Then I want to see Mei Lin. She will be worried sick."

"Do you need money for the flight?" Theodore offers.

"Dad, did you forget? I don't need to.."

Rembering, Theodore interrupts. "Sorry son, this is taking some getting used too."

"What are you going to say to her?" Louise asks.

"I don't know. I want to be truthful with her. But right now, I think its best I keep my secret." Louise moves towards her stepson and takes his hands. "You need to be honest with her. But that doesn't mean she needs to know everything right away. Tell her you need time to process your thoughts, but that you will tell her when you are ready. She will appreciate that, it will strengthen your bond."

"Thank You." Theo embraces Louise, then his dad.

"I need to get going. Watch this."

Theo instantly changes from his regular clothes of jeans and hoodie to his super-suit. His parents looking on in amazement. The transition was so fast that they questioned what they thought they saw. Theo winks as he rises off the floor. With his back to the window, he floats through the closed pane and turning invisible as he went.

"My god. Did that just happen?" Theodore, shaking at what he had witnessed his son doing. "My Son is a goddamn superhero." Pausing for a moment, he continues. "No, he is a god."


Rather than fly back to London. Theo teleported. Since he knew the layout of the main campus at the University of Central London, he could emerge where he knew he wouldn't be seen.

*7:25 a.m. - BST / 8:25 a.m. - CEST*

*London, England.*

Stepping out of the 3rd-floor men's lavatories, he was now wearing jeans and a black hoodie with the words *'I'm a scientist. I have an OLOGY'* on the front.

He made his way down the corridor, stopping at the door of Professor James R. Lubbock. Knocking on the door, a hoarse voice answered. "Come on in."

Theo entered the room. The professor, who was sitting behind a battered wooden desk, looked up, and a happy but shocked expression stretched across his face, eyes beaming as if he was meeting an old friend that he hadn't seen in years.

"My good boy. Where have you been?"

"Sorry professor. Things got out of hand after Tokyo. I had to lay low."

"Indeed. Well, it is great to see you. And I must congratulate you on your magnificent performance in the Games," the professor extended his hand, shaking Theo's with a little too much enthusiasm.

"Please, take a seat. I trust you received my correspondence?"

"Yes, Professor."

"Please, Theo, do you not consider me your friend? Call me James," the Professor laughed. The other students nicknamed him Professor Claus, an apt name, not only because he was a large man with an equally large white beard, but also for his jolly laugh and pleasant disposition. He was very much the favourite of the Archaeology faculty staff.

"Of course, James. I apologise, sometimes there is a need for decorum." Theo responded with a look of embarrassment.

"I appreciate the respect you show me, but when it is just the two of us, you can dispense with such formalities. Right, no more dilly-dallying, let's get down to business," The Professor opened his filing cabinet, retrieved a folder labelled, 'Theo Newton' and returned to his seat.

"Now Theo. Have you had time to consider your chosen area of research?" He asked, peering over the bridge of his spectacles.

"I was considering climate change and human adaption."

"I see. That is quite a broad area. Do you have a specific area with which you wish to focus?"

"I was considering technological innovations."

"Young Theo, If I did not know you as I do, I would consider your ambitions reckless and ill-conceived. Can I assume you wish for interdisciplinary collaboration?" The professor asked as he wrote some notes in the folder as Theo responded.

"Yes, I would like to meet with Professor Jackson in Palaeoanthropology"

"And your methodologies?"

"Fieldwork mainly Hampstead Heath and Normandy, France. I will employ LIDAR and GIS."

"That is very specific. Do you have some insight that you wish to share?"

"Just observations and a hunch. I believe there is evidence that goes back further than the Mesolithic. If I go down to the black matt layer we may discover more than just pits, post holes and charred stones. I strongly believe we will discover evidence of how our ancestors could survive the ice age and the subsequent period of cooling of the Younger Dryas."

"And a flair for the dramatic and controversial. Theo, the peer review of your proposed paper may be received with contempt. You know many in our discipline are enshrined in a doctrine of unabiding tribalism.

They do not like anyone rocking their metaphorical boat. Fortunately for you, I am also a black sheep. I don't hold back the advancement of archaeology with such narrow-minded beliefs."

Theo let out a sigh and smiled, which made the dimple in his left cheek appear.

The professor continued. "I suspect you will apply the same level of dedication to this endeavour as you have proven with your recent performance in Tokyo. Have you considered a title for your paper?"

"Thanks, James" Theo paused and considered the question for a moment before responding.

"I don't have a specific title in mind at this time, but the working title could be *'Technological Responses to Climate Change: Paleoanthropological adaption'* or similar."

"That will do for now. Do you wish for me to meet with Professor Jackson or do you want to take the initiative?"

"Time is pressing James. I would be grateful if you could meet on my behalf. I have to fly out to Tokyo later."

"Tokyo? Well my boy, you certainly are keeping yourself busy." Letting out a belly laugh. "That is not a problem. I will contact you on Sunday. Best of luck, young man."

The pair stood at the door, discussing current affairs for a few more minutes before Theo had to excuse himself. Reminding Prof. Lubblock that he was pressed for time.

'I'm glad that's sorted. I expected more pushback. He's a sweet man. Would make an excellent Santa,' he thought, letting out a laugh.

His next task was to go to Japan. The time was 3:55 p.m. in Tokyo this gave him some much-needed thinking time as Mei Lin usually finished at her office at around 6 p.m. He didn't feel teleporting was the right call, it would use energy unnecessarily and he would arrive hours before Mei Lin would be out of work.

First on his mind was which route he would fly. He could take the most direct path, the 5,943 miles as the crow flies, taking him across Denmark, Sweden, Finland, Russia, and China close to its northern border with Mongolia, before reentering Russia north of Vladivostok and finally crossing the Sea of Japan.

Or he could fly the 10,200 miles via the USA and the Pacific Ocean. *'Hell I could even fly via the Moon if I wanted,'* he thought to himself. But he remembered flying home from Montana. He had already seen the Atlantic, although briefly. Deciding he wanted to have some fun while also testing himself on his abilities, but more specifically, challenge the response capabilities of Russia and China.

Theo made his way up the stairs to the tenth floor of the building, exiting onto the roof. The campus building was on the south bank of the River Thames. The view to the north, the iconic dome of St. Paul's Cathedral, catches the sunlight, revealing intricate details of the facade that only Theo could see from such a distance.

*7:56 a.m. BST / 3:56 p.m. JST*

He transitioned into his super-suit, then flipped the hood, morphing into a face mask. As he ascended skyward, he went invisible, adjusting his orientation to a north-easterly direction, accelerating to just below mach one while climbing to 60,000 feet.

In under 5 minutes, he was passing Colchester. Once over the North Sea, he sped up to mach four, forming a sonic dispersion bubble around him. At this speed, he would arrive in Tokyo in a little under 2 hours and the Russian capital in 25 minutes.

50 miles from Moscow, he slowed to mach two while climbing to 65,000 feet. He adjusted the size of the dispersion bubble while also making it visible to radar and the eye, making it appear like a flying saucer. It was time for some fun.

As he flew over the capital, he rapidly descended to 25,000 feet, slowing to mach one point five. Not long had passed before two Russian Su-57 stealth-capable jet fighters buzzed him. The pilots would need to use their radar and targeting systems to keep a visual on him. *'Game on'* he thought to himself.'

As the fighters came for a second pass, Theo accelerated to mach two and pitched into a dive for the ground. The jets followed. At 5,000 feet, Theo changed direction and flew directly between the two aircraft, then ascended to 60,000 feet and continue in an easterly direction.

A couple of minutes later, the jets were once again in pursuit. The pilots would not be certain what they were following, but would consider it hostile. *'Time for more fun,'* he thought.

Once he could sense that they had a heat signature lock on him, he made himself invisible to infrared. The lock was lost.

The pilots adjusted their targeting systems, acquiring a less precise radar lock. One fighter fires a missile. It drops from the underside of the craft before the rocket ignites, propelling the hypersonic missile towards Theo. He matches speed. "This thing is fast," he says out loud as he passes mach twelve.

The fighters are now too far behind. Theo stops, allowing the missile to explode. In that instance, he re-enables his stealth, absorbing the energy of the blast. As far as the pursuing aircraft were concerned, they had hit their target. But the only debris they would find would be parts of their missile.

'That was fun,' he considered, allowing his internal voice to have a laugh.

Theo continued to Japan at the same speed. Arriving a little sooner than he had planned. As he descended towards the Games museum and administrative building, he turned invisible. Landing next to a tree near the entrance. A quick scan revealed no one was looking. He reappeared in his usual clothing, but this time his hoody was sporting a sneezing character from a well-known Japanese animation.

*4:58 p.m. - JST / 8:58 a.m. - BST*

Theo entered the building and headed over to the coffee shop. "Amerikano o kudasai," Theo said in practiced Japanese. The server gave a brief bow before turning to prepare his Americano. He taps his phone onto the terminal to pay. Shortly after, he received his drink. "Arigatō" he gives his thanks and walks over to a seat near the lift.

The large flat-panel TV on the wall is playing highlights from the recent games. 'Oh crap, I hope they don't show me', realising that someone may make the connection. He bends down and retrieves his backpack, which he materialised to appear under the table. He pulls out his cap and facemask, putting them on. However, it was in vain. As a couple had already spotted him as they made their approach.

"Excuse me, but aren't you Theo Newton? The English gold medallist?" The man asks in a southern US accent.

"Don't you mind my husband, well are you?" The woman asking now.

"Yes, I am Theo Newton, pleased to meet you. Whereabouts in the USA are you from?"

"See I told you, Beth, we have ourselves here a superstar. We are from Louisiana. Could we trouble you for a selfie?" The man asks.

Theo finds himself in a predicament, while he didn't object to having a selfie, it posed a problem. Just over an hour ago, he was in London meeting with his professor. If the couple were to share the photo on social media and by some chance, his professor saw the post, how would he be able to explain how he could be in Japan several hours before he could physically have arrived using conventional methods?

"Sure. Why not," he replied.

The couple stand with Theo in the middle and the man extends his phone out, capturing a photo. After checking it, the couple are pleased with the image. Before they can make any further requests,

Theo excuses himself and heads to the lifts. Once in the lift, he creates a small electromagnetic field around the man's phone, causing the electronics in the device to fail.

*'I really did not want to do that. What choice did I have?'* He thought to himself as he pressed the button for floor 6.

The doors to the lift open on the sixth floor and Theo stands face-to-face with Mei Lin.

Seeing her friend unexpectedly, she shouts, "Theo!" Stepping out of the lift, she embraces him.

"Where did you go? The news reported that you went missing. I was worried for you." A tear rolled down her cheek.

"I am sorry, Mei Lin. Something happened to me. Something that I am still trying to come to terms with." Pausing, he took hold of her hands and looked into her eyes. "I am not ready to talk about it yet, but when I do, you will be the first to know."

"Just as long as you are ok, I missed you, Theo," wiping the tears from her eyes.

"I missed you too. Do you want to grab some dinner?"

"That would be nice, but why are you here?"

"I wanted to see you; I left Tokyo in a rush, I feel I owe you an apology." Theo's eyes were sparkling and a cheeky smile crossed his face.

"Don't apologise." She said, leaning in to kiss his cheek. "Is it ok if we go to my apartment first, to freshen up and change?" Mei Lin asks.

"Sure it is."

Theo and Mei Lin talked as they walked the short distance to Kokuritsu-kyōgijō Station. There, they caught the subway train to Asakusa Station in the Taitō City district of Tokyo. Mei Lin's home, which she shares with a couple of friends, was only a street away.

*6:07 p.m. - JST / 10:07 a.m. - BST*

Mei Lin arrived at her apartment and was shocked to discover that someone had forced her door open. Theo entered first, flicking a light switch revealed unknown intruders had ransacked her home. The property was in a state. Drawers had been pulled open, and the contents emptied onto the floor. Broken china and glass littered the kitchen. Her bedroom wasn't any better, the wardrobe had been emptied, and the bed was on its side with the mattress slashed.

Mei Lin collapsed onto the floor, sobbing.

"Who did this? Why did they do this to me?" She cried.

"Maybe it was a random crime? Perhaps whoever was responsible wasn't targeting you?" Theo bent down and picked Mei Lin off the floor. They stood embracing as she continued to cry. While he couldn't prove it, he suspected it had something to do with him.

"Burglary in Japan is so rare now," she said as she wiped her eyes. "This was a targeted attack on me," staring at Theo intently.

"How do you know? You seem so sure." Theo felt anger course through his being.

"I have been followed. Most days now for the past month. Not always the same person, I have counted three different men and two women, morning and night," she continued to sob.

"Why didn't you say something before? Grab some clothes, I don't want you to stay here," Theo trying to comfort her once more.

"Where are your roommates?" He asks.

"They are probably still at work."

"I think you should let them know what has happened here. Get your clothes together, at least for a few nights. I will try to get the front door shut securely and clean up a bit. Are you ok?"

Mei Lin nodded. Theo kissed her forehead and then headed to the entrance of the apartment. He pulled out his mobile phone and composed a message to his dad.

*'With Mei Lin in Tokyo. Her place has been broken into. She suspects someone is watching her. You and Louise need to lay low. Stay safe Dad. Love Theo'*

Theo looked at the door. It was made from plastic. The forced entry had warped the door and splintered the frame around the locking mechanism. He needed a few seconds to make some repairs so as not to be seen; he froze time. Standing with the door stile in front of him, he focused his vision.

His genetic enhancements had altered his meibomian glands, allowing him to secrete a focusing oil onto his pupil, together with optical amplification and his ability to manipulate matter, he could focus a concentrated beam of photons as if from his eyes onto any surface he looked at. Over a few seconds, he heated the door, making it malleable, then applied force through a combination of body strength and placing the door into a bubble of high-pressure air.

Finally, he heated the frame around the lock clasp in the doorjamb and moulded it back to its original shape. The door, while not perfect, would stay secure for the time being.

Unfreezing time, he went into the living room. Moving at incredible speed, he tidied. Finally, while in the kitchen, on his hands and knees, slowly brushing the broken glass and porcelain into a dustpan, Mei Lin entered.

"I've done as much as I can. Are you ready?" He asks.

"Yes. Thank you, Theo, how did you tidy so fast?"

"You are welcome," he said, avoiding answering the question by distracting her. "We need to get going. Did you contact your roommates?" Theo picked up Mei Lin's backpack and placed it on his shoulder.

"I will do that when we leave. I still can't believe this has happened. Where were you staying this evening?" she asks.

"Actually. I never planned where I was staying. I thought maybe it would be ok on your sofa. Can you go to your parents?"

"I wish we could. They live in Itoshima, it's in Kyushu, nearly 1200 km to the south. We won't be able to get there tonight."

"I suppose we had better find a hotel," Theo replied.

"There is a great Hotel in Sumida City. My roommate Emi works there, but it is expensive."

"Don't worry about the price. I have that covered."

*6:44 p.m. - JST / 10:44 a.m. - BST*

After a quick subway ride, the couple arrived at the luxury hotel next to the Tokyo Skytree in Sumida City.

Mei Lin went to find her friend and arrange accommodation for the evening. Theo excused himself to use the restroom. He suspected they had been followed. Once in the bathroom and invisible, he rapidly exited the building.

Standing outside the hotel was a man and a woman, speaking with an American accent.

"They went into the hotel. Go in and wait for the female to return, try and find out what their plans are. Do not approach either of them. I will contact base and check in. I'll meet you inside soon," the man instructed as he moved away to a less public spot. The woman entered the hotel, taking a seat in the foyer.

Theo stood in front of the man, who, unaware of his presence, made a call.

"This is Tokyo Yankee Seven, code Nine-Nine-Three-Alpha," the man waited for a response before continuing. "Request G-A-R-D, Bare Mountain, General McAllister." Once more, he waited.

*'Gard? Bare Mountain and General McAllister, I wonder if this has any connection to the confiscation of the video footage.'* Theo thought to himself.

"General McAllister. Agent Jackson reporting in. I confirm the sighting of Newton, he is with the girl. Our flush succeeded. They are in the Royal SkyTree Hotel. Agent Jones is close call recon. Request orders Sir," Agent Jackson turned to look through the window of the hotel. Agent Jones was still sitting near the reception desk. Mei Lin had not reappeared.

Theo felt his hands turn to fists. He was fighting his anger as it coursed through his veins. He stopped himself when he heard a voice respond over the call.

"Agent Jackson. Do not approach Newton, we have reason to suspect he isn't what he appears. However if you get the chance, fit a tracking device to them both and stand down. Helix will monitor them remotely."

"Sir, Yes Sir. Track them and stand down. Out."

The call disconnected. Theo had a chill run through him. Who was Gard? How did they know he was more than he appeared? Realising his plans had to change.

Theo reentered the building and returned to the restroom, then quickly exited. He couldn't sense where Mei Lin was. He closed his eyes, regulating his breathing as he concentrated on her. 'Bingo' he thought to himself as he homed in on her location. She was in the first-floor restroom directly above where he stood.

Looking up, he manipulates his vision and sees through the concrete and steel ceiling above Mei Lin had just exited the toilet with Emi and was heading for the lift. Theo ran to the stairwell. Once inside, he flew through the stairs to the first-floor doors and calmly walked out onto the landing. Mei Lin and Emi were waiting for the lift they had called.

"Mei Lin. We need to leave. We were followed." The girls let out a gasp. "I suspect by two of the people who have been tailing you." He continued.

Mei Lin shook. She held onto Emi, who began to cry.

"It is going to be OK. Emi, how do we get out of here without using the main entrance?"

"The staff entrance. It's in the basement next to the service facilities." Almost screaming out the answer, "what am I to do?" still sobbing and drawing attention to the group.

"You can come with us. I can keep you both safe, but we need to move. Is that OK?" The pair nodded.

"We can't use this lift or stairwell. Is there another?" Emi points down the corridor towards the restaurant.

"Thanks. Lead the way."

In the foyer, Agent Jackson was talking to a receptionist, while Agent Jones was wandering the open plan space, trying to spot their targets with no success.

"The receptionist doesn't have a booking for any of the names." He announced.

"I haven't seen them. They must still be in the hotel," Agent Jones suggests.

"We need to split up. You stay here and watch the entrance. I will go to the first floor. The housemate, she works as a waitress here?" Agent Jones nodded in reply.

The male agent headed for the stairs, while Agent Jones went back to the seat she had been sitting in. She angled her body, maximising her view of the lifts and the main entrance.

Agent Jackson exited the stairwell onto the first floor. Looking both ways, there was no sign of his targets. He hurriedly walked to the restaurant on entering a concierge approached him.

"Good evening Sir. Do you have a reservation?"

"No. I am not dining. I have a question. Do you know if Emi has finished her shift?"

"I am sorry Sir, I think you have missed her," Agent Jackson turns and races down the corridor away from the stairwell he came via. Frantically, he stared at every sign, looking for any indication of another exit. He pulled out his phone and dialled.

"I think they have left. Monitor the front, I am going down the service stairwell." He hung up the call and raced down the stairs, stopping at the ground floor. There were two doors, one of which returned him to the ground floor and the other had a keycard access panel leading to the basement.

He pulled out his wallet to reveal a white card with a USB lead, which he connected to his phone. After opening an app on his mobile, he placed the white card onto the access panel and waited. After 30 seconds, the panel light illuminated green and the magnetic lock to the door released.

Back in pursuit, he charged down the stairs to enter the basement's service corridor. The signage was now in Japanese. Looking both ways, he tried to determine which direction to follow. He let out a smirk as something clicked in his mind, and he headed down the corridor to the right.

In a few moments, he found himself next to the staff room and entrance. He pushed the exit bar on the door to find the staff car park and exit. His targets were nowhere to be seen.

"Bastard," he shouts as he punches the air.

*7:24 p.m. - JST / 11:24 a.m. - BST*

Theo and the two girls were now on a subway headed toward Tokyo Station. He discussed their next step. There, they would catch a Shinkansen to Kyoto, where Emi's parents lived. The bullet train would take them 2 hours and 10 minutes. For the rest of their subway journey, neither of the girls spoke; it was only when they had purchased their onward tickets they seemed more at ease.

"How did they find us?" Mei Lin asks.

"I guess they broke into your apartment, then stayed outside and watched. Waiting for us to leave. I suspect it is me they are after. So, I am going to bait them. I am sorry but I can't go with you to Kyoto." Theo looked affectionately at Mei Lin as he rested his hand on her cheek. "I will be OK. Once you are at Emi's house, don't message or call me. I suspect your phones are bugged. It is probably wise for you to turn them off before you board the Shinkansen and leave them off."

"I don't understand why you don't come with us. Are you sure you will be safe?" Mei Lin looking teary once more.

"Honest, I will be fine. There are things I will tell you. But now is not the time. Your train will leave soon."

Theo stepped forward to embrace Mei Lin, but the petite figure jumped, grabbing onto Theo as she wrapped her legs around him and they kissed.

Emi felt awkward and faked a cough. Mei Lin coyly released her embrace of Theo as she dropped back to the ground.

"Stay safe Theo. Please," she begs. "How will we contact each other?"

"I will find you in a couple of days. I have Emi's parent's address."

# CHAPTER 5 BAITED

## SEPTEMBER 16 2021

### *Tokyo, Japan.*

Once Theo had seen the girls safely away on their train, he found cover before teleporting to Tokyo Haneda Airport. He emerged from the male toilets and headed straight to the booking desk of Grand Pacific Airlines. There, he purchased a single ticket to Los Angeles. During the booking process, he ensured he looked at every camera. He wanted to be seen booking and then boarding the flight.

*11:04 p.m. JST / 3:04 p.m. BST*

After a couple of hours of waiting in the departure lounge, Theo noticed Agent Jackson with another male sitting close by.

'*Baited. Now for part two.*' Theo thought to himself.

The airport was not busy. Tempted as he was to play a game of hide and seek with the agents. He didn't want to cause a panic and so thought better of it.

He rose from his seat and walked towards the departure screen. His flight was now ready for boarding. He calmly turned and headed to his gate. With his back to the Agents, who followed twenty metres behind, Theo changed the image on his hoody to the movie poster from 'Catch Me if You Can' he purposefully turned around on the travelator and looked directly at the agents, ensuring that they could see the meaning on his top.

'If I cant play, I'll mock them.' He thought as he returned to face forward and walked to the end of the conveyor. Approaching the gate, boarding of the place had already started. Like the departure lounge, there were few passengers, perhaps over half full.

A little over five minutes later, he was in his aisle seat on board GPA7. With a flight time of about 10 hours, the Agents, who were now seated 3 rows behind him, would be pawns in his scheme.

While he sat in his seat, he could hear the pair behind whisper their plan. Once the pilot allowed them to move about the cabin, one of them would leave their seat and, when passing, inject him with a tranquilliser.

*'They don't know about my abilities. That is reassuring.'* He thought.

The flight departed shortly after 11:30 p.m. And then, after 25 minutes and at an altitude of 38,000 feet, the seatbelt lights were turned off. Theo made his preemptive move and headed for the toilets. Before he entered, a stewardess caught his eye.

"Excuse me," Theo approaching the air hostess, "Could you do me a favour? In about 5 minutes, would you take a couple of light beers to the two gentlemen sitting in seats 27H and 27J, tell them it is compliments of Theo Newton and better luck next time," he handed the lady a $20 note, then turned and entered the toilet locking the door behind himself.

Once again, he considered playing a game of cat and mouse. Perhaps turning invisible and staying long enough to watch them search the aircraft for him. But once again, his responsible nature got the better of him.

Theo switched to his super-suit and, using intangibility, passed through the wall of the aircraft into the outside air. He hesitated, wanting to stay and watch the chaos unfold, but he had other things on his mind, his parent's safety being his top priority.

Theo generated an anti-sonic-boom bubble and, while fully stealth-enabled, climbed to a geostationary orbit of 36,000 kilometres in less than a second. There he slowed to 11,100 km/hr to match the speed of the surrounding satellites. Methodically, he began searching the orbiting equipment.

He wasn't entirely sure what he was looking for, but suspected that he would know when he found it. Sure enough, after checking over one thousand satellites, he found a US Space Force craft baring the words G.A.R.D HelixStar 4. He looked inside the device using his enhanced visual perception, identifying its purpose and capability. The advanced photonic laser and high-yield ion missiles were enough of a clue as to some of its purpose.

*'Time to be decommissioned.'* Theo thought as he punched a hole through the power relay connecting the solar panels to the battery. Then he sent a pulse from his hand, which was projected out of the antenna towards the other HelixStar in orbit. The satellite went offline. Grabbed the craft, which was the size of a bus. He began pushing it at high speed towards the sun. After a few seconds, he released it, allowing its momentum to carry it the remaining distance to its inevitable destruction.

Satisfied his point was made, he flew towards London and home.

*12:04 a.m. - JST / 4:04 p.m. - BST*

On board flight GPA7, Agent Jackson looks down at his watch, then at Agent Carter. "He has been in there over five minutes,"

"Maybe he is taking a large dump?" Carter replies.

"Still, I don't like it. I will…" Before he could continue, Agent Jackson is interrupted by a flight attendant bringing two beers for the pair. "These are compliments of Theo Newton. He sends his regards and wishes you better luck for next time," Agent Carter looks at the hostess and then the beers.

"He sends us light beer!" He exclaimed.

As he goes to take a sip of the bottle, it is knocked out of his hand, falling to the floor, which causes the liquid to effervesce. The beer, spraying adjacent passengers, much to their annoyance.

"Fool. He has played us." Agent Jackson states as he rushes to his feet, pushing past the hostess, who falls to the aisle floor, banging her head against an armrest. He hurriedly reaches the toilet door and bangs on it with his fist. "NEWTON come on out."

His shouting draws attention from the rest of the passengers. Several of who get nervous. Questions are muttered and several men prepare themselves to intervene.

"Agent Carter, bring the flight attendant." Agent Carter rises from his seat, grabs the woman from under her arms, and pulls her to her feet. A small trickle of blood runs down her face from a cut to her forehead. Screams and gasps can be heard from the panicking passengers. The tension in the cabin rachets up.

"Let her go." One passenger shouts and he rises to his feet.

"You are hurting me." The hostess protesting at what was occurring.

"Stop complaining, we are Agents of the US Government."

Agent Jackson looks at the woman, then at the locked door.

"Open it," the hostess looks confused, "OPEN IT," banging his fist against the door again.

Cautiously, the woman lifts the sign on the door to reveal a sliding lock. She moves it to the side, changing the display to read 'Vacant'. Agent Carter pulls the woman back as Agent Jackson pushes the door open, revealing an empty lavatory.

"How the hell," Agent Jackson exclaimed. "Is there another way out of this toilet?" Entering the small room, he checks the ceiling and feels around the walls for any sign of a hatch.

"No." The stewardess responds.

"Did we miss him leave?" Agent Carter suggests.

"No. At least I am certain I didn't, my eyes were fixed on the door the whole time," He stopped and looked at the hostess dead in the eye. "That was until you brought us those drinks. He could have quickly exited. Newton has to be on board. He can't escape."

*Bare Mountain, Massachusetts.*

"Get the commander." The technical sergeant shouts as he stares at his display in disbelief.

Within moments, Dr Kane approached.

"What's the situation, Technical Sergeant?" Glancing down at the screen in front of the operator.

"Sir, it's HelixStar Four. It's offline," he was panicking as he struggled to get his words out. "…it's…"

"It's what?" Dr Kane pushed the operator away from his station as he leaned over to look at the display. "That's impossible. Carry out a system diagnostic. Reboot the satellite if you need to." he moved away, allowing the operator to regain control.

Dr Kane turned his focus to the large screens at the front of the room. His attention was now on a projection of the satellites orbiting Earth. HelixStar Four was no longer shown as in geosynchronous orbit.

"Sir, it's out of range. Our estimation is it's travelling at over twenty two million miles per hour and should reach the sun in a little over four hours."

"How the hell is that even possible? None of our craft can go at that speed. I need answers. **NOW.**" Dr Kane slams his arm across the desk in front of him, launching an open can of soft drink towards the front of the room. Turns and returns to his office, slamming his door closed.

"Helix. What information do you have about HelixStar Four? Why did you not raise an alarm?"

"Dr Kane, If I may. My systems are still showing HelixStar Four in orbit. Adjusting to backup pathways. Correction. There is

57

currently a cascade failure of systems occurring in all seven HelixStar satellites."

"**WHAT?**" Dr Kane races out of his office and into the command centre. All the operators are standing, mouths open, staring at the large screens in front of them. The entire display wall, a checkerboard of red alert warnings. The words critical failure flashed at seven locations in Earth's orbit.

"CAN SOMEONE PLEASE EXPLAIN TO ME WHAT THE FUCK IS GOING ON HERE?" Dr Kane walks over to the closest person, a young female operator, grabbing her by the throat. "**WELL?**" Turning white, a tear wells up in the corner of her eye. Dr Kane violently pushes her to the floor. "FUCK. I NEED ANSWERS. NOW. Helix, where is Agent Rodriguez?"

"Agent Rodriguez is currently on sub-level four, detention cell seventeen."

"When I get back, I want answers, anyone unable to cooperate will have to explain themself to General McAllister."

Dr Kane storms out of the control centre and walks along the corridor to the elevator, cursing as he goes.

Agent Rodriguez was exiting the cell when Dr Kane entered the detention wing.

"Dr Kane, Sir. Team A has just informed me the analysis of the data is complete. I was about to begin spectral resolution analysis." The agent could tell his superior was in one of his famous moods as he continued, "I have repeated my attempts to extract more about Newton from the woman, but she is not cooperating." Glancing back to the closed steel door.

"We don't have time for her now. Follow me." The pair exited the detention wing and made their way through a long, inclined corridor.

"We have a situation with the HelixStar Network. The entire system has sustained a critical failure. Number four is no longer on the grid. I suspect it and Montana has something to do with

Newton. We need the results. We are already hours behind schedule. The General, unlike me, is being remarkably patient."

"Sir, did you say off the grid?"

"YES," he replied, his voice raised.

"How is that even possible? Was it impacted? Sent off course?"

"I don't know. It is, for now, still transmitting." For a moment, he stops walking.

"Sir?" Agent Rodriquez noticing the sudden hesitation.

"If the shits upstairs do their job correctly, they will analyse the information collected by the Helix Lunar array. The moon is in the waxing gibbous phase, visible from Japan. Since HelixStar 4 was in geostationary orbit over Japan when it went off the grid, logic dictates that the array will hold some answers."

"Sir. What are your orders?" The agent asks.

"Can you to oversee the spectral resolution with the lab team. I also want you to take the lead on the investigation into the failure of HelixStar. I will contact our Agents in Japan."

"Yes, Sir."

"Oh, and I am having suspicions about H.E.L.I.X's loyalty. Let me know if anything unexplained occurs."

"Sir, Such as?"

"Anything. You will know it when it happens. I never have trusted the Nexil."

Dr Kane left Agent Rodriguez at the lab entrance and made his way back to sub-level two. He entered a communications room and took an earpiece out of a drawer.

"Helix, give me an update on Operation Sun's Origin."

"Dr Kane. The last contact from Agent Carter was that he and Agent Jackson had boarded Grand Pacific Airlines flight number GPA7 bound for LA. They were following the primary target."

"What is the status of the flight?" Kane asks.

"It departed Tokyo at 11:32 a.m. Atlantic Standard Time. It is 57 minutes into its flight. I have additional information regarding its journey."

"Continue."

"Dr Kane. It was reported 35 minutes after departure, that an incident occurred on board. The Air Marshall has arrested two men for causing a disturbance. A member of the aircrew was injured during the unrest. From the information I have retrieved from the Transport Security Administration servers, both of our operatives are the men who have been detained."

"Fucking Fuckers can't do a simple job. What about Newton?"

"Theo Newton is still believed to be on board the aircraft."

"Helix. Remove the files from the TSA servers. Contact the Air Marshall, identify yourself as a ranking official for the Department of Homeland Security and have our men released. I want eyes on Newton. Redirect the flight to LA airforce base if you need to. What is the update on the girl?"

"Dr Kane. Agent Jones reports that they have not found the girl. I am currently running facial recognition from all sources, she was not with Newton at Haneda Airport."

"OK. Find out where the girl went. Once you have a location, deploy Agents Webber and Nash to intercept. Recall Agent Jones. She has failed once too often."


*11:32 a.m. - EDT / 4:32 p.m. - BST*


Dr Kane stood outside General McAllister's office, sweat beading on his temples. He felt uncomfortable, almost wanting to throw up. Admitting that your team screwed up, failing their assigned objective, was never easy.

Nervously, he knocked on the door. The General had told to him early in his career with G.A.R.D that if he was to bring bad news to knock, otherwise he was welcome to go straight in.

"YES," came the reply from the room.

Dr Kane entered, not knowing where to look. The General intimidated him, but only when he was bringing bad news. He never could understand why he felt so afraid. McAllister was very personable in everyday situations, but he did not tolerate failure. Dr Kane felt that his behaviour was why he had to act nasty around his subordinates, blaming the General as a reflection of his management style.

"Marcus Kane. Please take a seat. Do I need a stronger drink than coffee to cope with the news you bring me?"

"That may help, sir." The general stood and pulled a bottle of barrel-strength bourbon from beneath his barrister station, plucking two shot glasses from the same shelf. He placed them down on the table in front of Dr Kane, pouring a single shot.

"You can have one, once I have decided if the news you bring me warrants it. Carry on, Major General." The General only ever used Dr Kane's military rank when he was considering a reprimand. It was a warning to Marcus to choose his words wisely and maybe consider not to reveal details that could later be resolved. The General loved playing little mind games.

"Sir. The HelixStar system is offline. A cascade failure has resulted in number four going off the grid. It has been lost, Sir…" He paused, considering his next option "I have concerns about H.E.L.I.X, it failed to detect the issue. It was only when it switched to its redundant systems that it confirmed the situation. Sir, I will ask again, how much can we trust the Nexil?"

"That is indeed alarming. H.E.L.I.X is just one of many advancements that we would not have if it weren't for the Nexil. I do not think they have any alternate motivations that they have not already revealed to us. Contact USF Lincoln, they are the closest. Have their engineering team look if a remote system reboot doesn't work. As for number four. Hmmm."

Dr Kane interrupts "Sorry, Sir. I have my team analysing data from the Helix Lunar Array, if there is any external influence, we will find it there."

"Good work Marcus" The General poured a shot of Bourbon into the second glass. "Good health" he continued, raising the drink.

# CHAPTER 6 TROJAN

## SEPTEMBER 17 2021

### *Dunthorpe, London.*

Theo arrived home late afternoon on the 16th of September. Changing, he then went for a run. He did not need to train for fitness anymore, but it was an activity he enjoyed and wanted so much to continue having a normal life. So he had decided that went he would train, he would push as hard or as easy as he did before his powers were fully awoken.

Running allowed him to think about everything that had happened within the last year. It gave him clarity of thought. He considered his identity. He didn't want to hide being Theo Newton superstar. The people of Dunthorpe knew where he lived, seeing him around the town. He didn't want to raise any suspicions about him, so when stopped several times on his run, he was courteous and when asked about his disappearance, explained needing some time away from the media. He welcomed selfies and the occasional autograph.

Back at the house, he ordered a takeaway and binge-watched the TV shows he missed during his time at *The Games* and while with the Aelioxar. Going up to his bedroom at 12:30 a.m. to meditated.

*1:02 a.m. - BST / 5:02 p.m. - PDT (Pacific Daylight Time)*

Shortly after 1 a.m., Theo's heightened awareness alerted him of an emergency unfolding. He could sense panic at LAX air traffic control. Something had happened to Flight GPA7.

In a blink, he had teleported himself to 4,000 feet above the Pacific Ocean and near the Californian coast. Beneath him, the burning fuselage of the Grand Pacific Airline flight, plummeting to the water. Diving, he scanned the craft for signs of life, but could not detect any. The scorched wreck displayed a telltale sign: a missile had hit the plane. *'Who would do such a thing?'* He thought, as he considered, with his great powers, could he have stopped it from happening?

There was nothing more he felt he could do. While he wanted to move the wreckage to land, doing so would reveal himself to the world, *'I'm not ready for that yet.'* his mind was torn; on the one hand, he could assist with the recovery operation of the debris and bodies, but then on the other, would he be blamed?

Theo shot up through the atmosphere, stopping beyond geostationary orbit. He observed the universe, the *'Extherix'*, as the Aelioxar knew it. The majesty of the constellations in all their splendour, visible with his enhanced vision.

As Theo took what lay before him, he contemplated, with all of his abilities, he was still insignificant amongst the vast universe. He knew he still had much to learn. He had made mistakes in the last couple of days. Was he ultimately to blame for what happened to flight GPA7?

*'Had I chosen a different option than getting that flight, would everyone still be alive? Is it on me?'* Tears beading in the corner of his eyes, his head hung low, reflective.

As he looked up, glaring at the moon, his fist clenched

*'NO! Whoever these people are who are after me, Whatever Gard may be, I am certain they are behind all of this. They will answer for their crimes.'*

But as he turned to look back at Earth, he noticed a craft heading towards the planet's night side. His enhanced vision made out the craft in great detail. It was at least half a kilometre long and as tall as wide, at least one hundred metres. The markings identified it as a United Space Fleet craft, the USF Lincoln. With three images beneath the name; Space Force, USAF and the flag of the United States of America.

*'This was what the Baruch was suggesting when she said*

**'You are much more advanced than your leaders would let you believe.'** Theo thought while floating in the vacuum of space, continuing to stare at the craft, his eyes wide and mouth open.

*'But why are we being told, man will return to the moon and then Mars? We have that ability now! What are they hiding? And why is it military and not NASA?'* His childhood curiosity had the better of him. He needed to know more.

Becoming invisible to detection, he flew to the craft, taking in every detail. On the port and starboard sides, there were several recessed doors identified with a hazard death symbol and labelled as ordnance. Seeing through the door as if it were glass, he counted dozens of the same high-yield ion missiles he had observed on the HelixStar satellite.

On the underside, more hatches marked as laser weapons beyond.

*'More, advanced photonic lasers,'* he thought. At the rear of the craft is an ion propulsion system.

*'This engine isn't enough to manoeuvre,'* reaching out as he touched the craft. He could feel the imperfections in the alloy body, the vibrations of the vessel. He concentrated, capturing every aspect of the ship at the sub-atomic level. Suddenly he pushed away, feeling a presence onboard with malevolent intentions.

*'Shit, they are here,'* Baruch had warned Theo that there were species who had desires for Earth, and that some had already arrived. But what he felt on board the USF Lincoln was akin to something from a nightmare.

Not knowing a great deal about these other species, only a basic outline. Unsure if he could identify one it if he looked it in the eye.

He would need to tread carefully. His appointment with *The Order* couldn't come soon enough.

For the next several hours, he observed the ship carry out maintenance work on several satellites, including the HelixStar network. Slowly but methodically bringing them online. The electromagnetic pulse he proliferated through the system was low power, not intended to permanently damage the network. The analysis carried out by the engineers of the USF Lincoln would reveal the cause, a calling card that would have them scurrying to work out what the source could have been.

It was when the ship sent out a low frequency harmonic variance signal, through a hyper-tube between entangled points in space, that Theo's intrigue peaked. He sensed discrete changes to the electromagnetic field onboard the ship. They employed the Casimir effect for faster-than-light communication, by using quantum vacuum fluctuations.

Multiple locations, both within and outside of the solar system had received the signal. However, he was aware of it being received by the moon that demanded closer examination.

Travelling the 384,400 km distance to lunar orbit in 1.2 seconds, that of the speed of light had a minor drain on his energy levels. He could feel his body getting stronger.

Circling Earth's first satellite, he took in the amazing landscape, the spectacular craters and the bluish tint of the Sea of Tranquillity contrasting against the bright off-white almost brown-grey of the rest of the moon.

He passed over an artificial structure, devastated by millennia of impacts from space debris. From what remained, he guessed it was the Aelioxar observation base they had built for their close observer protocol.

Very close to the ruins, he observed the landing sites for the Apollo missions, the lunar rovers and landing modules, discarded as moon litter.

Theo completed a full orbit. Other than 'alien' reconnaissance probes and crashed craft, there were no other structures visible.

'*Of course, you idiot.*' Theo realised that the logical place for any lunar base would be on the moon's southern pole. The craters providing a perfect balance between sunlight for energy generation and shade for keeping cool from the sun's radiation.

The base, camouflaged to match the craters where it was built, was massive and easily supported tens of thousands of people. Tunnels buried beneath the surface linked the various structures in each of the body's southern impact sites.

At intervals along the upper ridge of each crater were missile batteries and photonic lasers. The concentration of weapons increased near an enormous structure that he identified as a hangar.

The scale of the technology on display was mind-bending.

'*But why all the weaponry?*' Theo could only conclude that the scale of deception on the people of Earth was unimaginable and very troubling. The Aelioxar had alluded to this.

Theo moved away from the Moon and focused on the darkness of space.

'*Mars. There has to be something on Mars,*' Thinking that would be his next destination, however, it was the 'Mars Solar Conjuntion', the planet was out of sight, hidden on the other side of the sun, almost 378 million kilometres distant.

'Theo, think,' kicking himself for not being smart enough, he could reach Mars in a little over 21 minutes travelling at the speed of light. He would pass very close to the sun, boosting his energy levels, but energy use wasn't his concern at this time. Baruch had warned him about being away from Earth for too long. Mars being in solar conjunction may limit his awareness of his home world.

'*Jupiter,*' he thought, 'Why not?' At 750 million kilometres distant, it would take around 44 minutes at the speed of light, but that time would pass in an instant for him because of the laws of relativity in physics. But being special, he could bend the rules.

In an instant, he was in orbit around the largest planet in the solar system. He knew it would be an incredible experience, but he wasn't prepared for the reality.

*'My God. It's beautiful. Nothing could prepare me for how big this thing is!'* Mesmerised and in awe, he didn't register the bus-sized piece of ice and rock hurtling on a collision course with him.

Travelling at 21,000 kilometres an hour, he only noticed the asteroid at the last moment, instinctively reacting with intangibility, he passed through the body, as it continued its journey, eventually impacting with the Jovian atmosphere, emitting a two-second flash of light as it was obliterated.

*'Shit! How close was that?'* He grimaced, his arms tensing and fists clenched *'Theo, get a grip, you have learnt anything, have you? Stop being so careless.'*

The asteroid could never of harmed him. It had a reason for impacting with the planet and he would not have prevented its fate. The issue was twofold; He needed to be more aware of his surroundings and, secondly; he had to be mindful of causality.

Deciding to abandon the scout mission around the planet, he teleported directly to his bedroom, where he thought about the events of the day and what he could learn from his mistakes.

## 1:05 a.m. - BST / 8:05 p.m. - EDT

### Massachusetts, USA.

The phone couldn't have rung at a more inconvenient moment. Dr Kane stepped out of the shower and picked up his mobile from next to the sink.

"Marcus Kane," he announced to the unknown number,

"Sir, It's Agent...," the sound of running water made the voice on the other end of the line difficult to hear.

"Just a moment," turning off the tap, he returned to the call. "Sorry. Say again."

"Dr Kane, It's Agent Patterson. We've received information that flight GPA7 is down. It splashed into the Pacific, about 200 miles from the Californian coast. All lives presumed lost."

"Any indication as to the cause?" Dr Kane placed the handset on the countertop. Tapping speaker, he dried himself. His concerns from earlier in the day no longer troubled him.

"Sir, our ATC interception with the pilot leads us to believe a missile hit them. We have notified General McAllister."

"Thanks, Agent Patterson. What does tracking say about the origin of the missile?"

"Sir, early indications suggest it was friendly."

Marcus Kane picked up his phone. Disabling the loudspeaker, he put the device to his ear.

"Just say that again?"

"Sir, we believe it was ours. Friendly, Sir."

"Shit. Have Helix run a source projection analysis. Have it check all launch authorisations. And Agent Patterson, cross-check Helix's log files for activity for the past half an hour."

The agent, unsure of the last order, "Sir?"

"You heard me, Agent Patterson. Do it." Dr Kane ended the call, his hands shaking. Dropping the phone, he crouched down and sat with his back to the door. "What have you done Helix," whispering to himself.


2:35 a.m. - BST / 9:35 p.m. - EDT

Bare Mountain, Massachusetts.

General McAllister, sitting at his desk, his eyes fixed on the bottom left of the four screens mounted to his desk. He adjusted his reading glasses and leaned in closer to the screen, his brow furrowing as he read through the analysis report.

The harmonic frequency analysis detailed the energy signature detected and then surveyed a couple of days ago. The anomaly had piqued the interest of the entire scientific staff at G.A.R.D.

As he read through the findings and recommendations, a sense of unease registered in his gut. Having to re-read the last paragraphs of the report.

> *'The analysis confirms an entity of immense power has traversed the QUANTUM CORRIDOR. The energy signature is unlike anything previously recorded, suggesting a potential threat of unprecedented magnitude.*
>
> *It is recommended that security levels be elevated immediately and that all known targets be secured for interrogation and containment. This threat presents a real and present danger to the security of the United States of America and the Nexil Concordat.'*

McAllister leaned back in his chair. The quantum corridor was only theoretical, although, with the technological advancements shared by the Nexil, a breakthrough was imminent.

He had no more time to consider the report. Clicking on an alert to join a video-conference, the four screens changed to display eleven individuals. He flicked a switch under his desk, activating a magnetic lock on his door, as the view to the command centre beyond the windows darkened.

"Good, we are here. General Harris has sent his apologies," the grey-haired man announced. David D. Bernstein 81, was a large build, wearing a tailored suit which appeared at least a size too small. As a former President of the United States, he served in office between 2004 and 2005, sworn in following the assassinations of his predecessor, the vice president and the Speaker of the House. As *President pro tempore*, he was 3rd in the line of succession.

A powerful figure in politics and a technology tycoon, he made it clear he had no desire ever to be *President of the USA*. It was a position thrust upon him by circumstance. In the aftermath of the assassinations, he implemented a major reform of the security services and increased cooperation between agencies.

However, many high-ranking officials at the time saw no substantial change and cited additional national security risks because of the increased cooperation. Bernstein pushed ahead with the reform, creating a new black budget shadow organisation with command oversight of all US security and military services.

Bernstein became the self-appointed director of the most powerful organisation on earth. The *'**Strategic and Advanced Federation of Enforcement**'* - ***S.A.F.E.*** comprised twelve individuals, all senior personnel at the highest levels of unelected government in the USA and UK. They had the power and influence to dictate world affairs.

"David, you are looking very well," Dr Harriet Schwimmer exclaimed.

"Harriet, it's all thanks to your wonder drug, Vitrastatis."

"Don't thank me, Sir; thank the Emissary. The advancements the Nexil have shared with us have had a transformative effect on healthcare. SynthNova Pharmaceutical continue to be number one in the industry." A wry smile creeps across her face.

"We continue to serve the people of Earth, so long as you continue to keep the concordat." The Emissary responded in a monotone voice, lacking emotion or emphasis on the words they spoke.

"Without the Nexil and your representation, we would not be close to achieving a type two civilisation," Bernstein replied. "I think it is time we brought this meeting to order. How are we proceeding with the recent events in Montana?".

"Sir, to recap. On the 15th of this month, a one exajoule energy signature was detected by G.A.R.D HelixStar Four. The location was Chouteau County in Montana. I deployed Dr Marcus Kane to survey the site. The results confirm that the energy came through a quantum corridor, the source as yet unknown." General McAllister coughed to clear his throat before continuing, "An entity came through the corridor. From our analysis and evaluation assisted by H.E.L.I.X, the entity is the cause of the energy readings."

Gasps could be heard from several of the conference members.

"How does this tie in with Newton? If the briefing report sent to me earlier is correct, the disappearance of Newton shares the same spectral frequency as Montana." The question came from David M. MacTavish, former British Prime Minister and major shareholder in *British Atlantic Defence, Munitions, Aeronautics and Naval*.

"If our suspicions are proven correct, Newton is the entity," McAllister replied.

"Where is he now?" Bernstein asks.

"At just after 5 p.m. Pacific daylight time, flight GPA7 headed for LAX, sent out a mayday. It splashed into the Pacific approximately 200 miles from the Californian coast. Newton and two of our agents were on board. The latest report is all lives lost," McAllister answered.

"Recovery?" Bernstein requests.

"I am liaising with the Admiral," McAllister replies.

"Now that the US Coast Guard is under the jurisdiction of the Navy, I have deployed a response team and we will be at the debris site soon. Full recovery and containment will follow," Admiral Bernard Gibson of the US Navy answers.

"Sir, I have more information to provide, I said all lives lost, however, that may not be strictly true," McAllister adds. "Not long after GPA7 was lost. We received alerts that HelixStar Four was off the grid. Something sent the craft out of orbit. Soon after, the entire HelixStar network had a cascade failure. The USF Lincoln is currently correcting the situation."

"Is there a connection with Newton?" Bernstein, looking increasingly uncomfortable, asks.

"While you were speaking. I consulted the Nexil High Council. We believe Theo Newton to be a dangerous creature, corrupted by the creators and under their command. You must make it your priority to destroy him before he intervenes in all that we have established with the concordat." The Emissary did not wait for a response to his statement, disconnecting from the conference and maintaining the weight of fear and influence the Nexil had over the committee.

"The Emissary has spoken. Generals and Admiral, place our military on full readiness. David, use your influence and have the Prime Minister briefed; perhaps depict Newton as a spy, whatever it takes. To you my friends in the security agencies," Bernstein was now addressing Dr Andrew Goldman, former director of the CIA, James R. Schwartz, former Director of the FBI and Barry L. Mason, the former director of the NSA, all now members of H.O.U.S.E, the *Homeland Operations Unit, Surveillance and Espionage*, the highest level of authority and clearance in matters of national security, the public face of the secretive S.A.F.E, hidden from public scrutiny and even the current President of the USA.

"I need up-to-date surveillance on Newton. If he did indeed escape from GPA7, I need to know how, what abilities he possesses, with whom he has been in recent contact, bring in his nearest and dearest and have them interrogated. And to you **ALL**, what happened to GPA7?"

Each of the officials nodded and confirmed their acceptance of the orders from their one true president before disconnecting from the conference.

David D. Berstein remained on the call with Dr Schwimmer of SynthNova Pharmaceutical, Dr Lesley Simons, the wealthiest person alive, as a Venture Capitalist and owner of multiple technology companies, she was considered a tyrant by her competitors, and finally Dr Simon Brandon the former administrator of NASA, now the foremost expert on implementing Nexil technology on Earth.

"Now the Jarheads and Safehouse have left, let us discuss how Operation Synapse is progressing," Bernstein said with a mischievous look.

# CHAPTER 7 THE ORDER

## SEPTEMBER 18 2021

*6:23 a.m. BST - (British Summer Time)*

*7:23 a.m. CEST - (Central Europe Summer Time)*

*Bruges, Belgium.*

Theodore was certain they were being followed. Exiting their holiday rental in Bruges, a couple across the street caught his attention. As he and Louise walked to their car, the couple appeared to follow.

On leaving the car park, he observed them sitting in a parked vehicle near to the exit. Then, to confirm, Theodores suspicions, the car turned around and followed them. It was only after running through a red traffic light that he eventually evaded the pursuers.

The Newtons were to board a Eurostar back to London, however, Louise suggested driving north into the Netherlands and booking the overnight ferry to Newcastle. It would put them in the North of England and closer to the meeting with 'The Order' and if they succeeded, could avoid being followed.

Pulling into a service station outside of Bruges, Theodore had the idea to switch his number plate with another car of the same model. Fortunately, his Volvo XC90 appeared to be quite common, so the switch was performed without being observed and they continued to head north to Amsterdam, hoping they could secure a last-minute ferry crossing.

Theodore had considered that they may need to abandon the car before boarding the ferry. Assuming their pursuers were government agents, they would have access to number plate recognition cameras and once the switched car was identified, the decoy would be up and their stolen plate tracked. He considered that using their passports would reveal their plans and when used, they would be traced once more, but that could not be helped. He needed to delay that happening for as long as possible.

Close to Amsterdam, Theodore had another cunning plan. After driving around for a while, he found what he was looking for. A Volvo dealership. Parking around the corner, he removed the stolen plates from his car. So as not to be seen, carefully entered the car park filled with customer's cars until he found a few XC90s. Once again, switching the plates around, leaving with a new set of number plates.

"Let them try and sort out that mess," he laughed as he drove onward to the port.

Louise doubted his plan's success, so begged Theodore to let his son help. Theo would sense his father needed help and could be there in an instant. However, he didn't want to involve Theo. He wanted to allow his son to keep his secret for as long as possible.

"You are a stubborn but protective fool," Louise told her husband, crossing her arms. "What now?" She continued.

"We will go into the booking office and see if there is space for the car," Theodore said matter-of-factly. "If there is, we'll book ourselves onboard."

"How will this work? As soon as we book in with our passports, assuming it was the government who were following us, wouldn't they just meet us at the port in Newcastle?"

"Deflection my dear. Once we have our passage booked, paid with cash, I may add. I am going to book us on a couple of flights. One from Amsterdam Schiphol to whichever London airport it goes to and another from Brussels to London. They will have to spread their resources to monitor each location."

"What if they have local police waiting for us in Newcastle?"

"That is a good point. I will have to think on that one, deal with whatever is presented to us if it happens. Do you have any suggestions?"

"Yes. Theo!"

The ferry departed the Felison Terminal at 5:30 p.m. CEST, taking just under 17 hours to cross the North Sea, arriving at the North Shields-Newcastle Terminal on the River Tyne shortly before 9 a.m. on Sunday, 19th September.

To his surprise, the booking process was easier than expected. Border patrol was experiencing some computer issues, and their passports couldn't be scanned; unusually, they were waved through without additional checks. The crossing was relatively trouble-free, except for a couple of hours of rough sea making the journey less than pleasant.

During disembarking, Louise thought a group of suspicious-looking men in a Range Rover were paying particular attention to her and Theodore, but she realised they weren't paying them any further attention as they left the port and headed toward the A19.

"No police. No agents. Not even a customs inspection. That was too easy," Theodore said, as he stopped the car at a small retail park near the port.

"What are you stopping for?" Louise asked.

"The sign said there was a coffee shop. If you could grab us a couple of drinks and snacks for the road while I see if there is a mobile phone store. I don't want to use the burner phone, but I need to contact Theo and let him know of our change of plans."

"Can't you do you connection thing?. And won't his phone be monitored?" She asked, her speech quicker and more high pitched that normal.

"Yes, I am certain it will. But I have an idea," Theodore announced with a wink and a smile, "And darling," he continued. "Try to relax, it will be ok." Leaning over to kiss her cheek.

"Do I even want to know?" The couple parted as Louise entered the coffee shop. Opposite to which, and to Theodore's surprise, was a small, independent mobile phone store.

After the brief excursion, the couple were back in the car.

"I bribed the owner, traded like for like, same handset, new sim card. He accepted cash for the new phone because I was giving him the old one for free. He figured he was getting a great deal"

"Sounds like he did. I got you a large Americano and a pain-au-chocolate. So what is your grand idea for contacting Theo?" She asks, her eyes narrow and eyebrows raised.

"Woah! What's with the look? You not trust me?" He asks, letting out a laugh. His wife could only smirk in response.

"I'm going to use T9 - Just like Derotev. I will key in the entire message in numbers. But I was thinking. If I add additional numbers in front and behind each word to indicate the order of the sentence. So the first word will be prefixed and suffixed with one, the second word two, the third a three, and so on. But then scramble the order so the first word becomes the fifth and the tenth word the second and so on."

"Do you think he will figure that out? It sounds awfully convoluted?" Louise continued, "would it not be easier to send a few words in plain English that would bring him here, I don't know maybe "Theo Help Dad." Louise was staring at her husband, her eyes pleading with him.

"You are probably right. Let's do it your way" Theodore powered on the phone. After a brief activation with the network, he keyed in the message and then sent it.

In less than two seconds, Theo was sitting in the backseat of the car.

"Hi, Dad, Mam. What we doing near Newcastle?"

"Bloody hell Theo. Are you trying to give me a heart attack?"

"Sorry Dad, but, you messaged me!" Theo said, laughing.

"Hmm. Ok." Theodore twisted his body in the driver's seat so he could look back at his son. "We are certain we were being followed when we were leaving Bruges. But lost them. We covered our tracks as best we could and figured IF we were being followed, we needed to avoid London. So we took the overnight ferry and here we are. We're driving on to meet with 'The Order'. If that is ok?"

"Why didn't you contact me? The second you even suspected you were being followed, I could have been there and sorted it."

"I told your Dad. You know how stubborn he can be," Louise exclaimed.

"Thanks for your support, Louise." Theodore glared at his wife before continuing. "I am sorry son. But I didn't want to unduly involve you. I am still your Father."

"Still Dad. Next time call me." Theo leant forward and kissed his dad's head.

Theodore powered off the mobile and dropped it in a waste bin before starting the engine and beginning the journey to Lancashire.

Theo explained the events of the previous couple of days. The biggest concern he shared was with his failings, the errors he felt he had made, his ill-thought cockiness and rash decisions. Theodore did all he could to convince his son he was still learning and, as with everything in life, it takes practice and experience. That includes learning from mistakes. No one in human history had ever been a superhuman, so there was no training manual for how to be one.

With seven hours to make the trip to Sawley Abbey, Theodore insisted it would be wise to stay off main roads and avoid licence plate recognition cameras where possible, even though the foreign plates they were using were possibly still safe.

After unavoidably having to use the A19 South, then the A690 via Houghton le Spring, they used minor roads via Sherburn to join the A688. It was at Barnard Castle that Theodore switched places with Louise because of tired eyes.

Louise wanted to take the A66, but Theodore insisted they cut through the Yorkshire Dales National Park. A longer and slower route, it was more picturesque as they took in the beautiful scenery, passing through the villages of Buckden, Starbotton and Kettlewell, choosing to stop for some food in Grassington.

The journey while pleasant was tiring. Theodore slept a short while in the back of the car, while Theo was a passenger up front. Arriving at the village of Sawley a little before 5 p.m.

"Maybe we should find somewhere to stay tonight," Louise suggested.

Looking in his wallet, Theodore pulled out £45 in notes, and Louise had another £20 to add.

"I don't think £65 is enough for a room for us all, and I really don't want to use our bank cards if they can be traced," Theodore declared.

"I have an idea. Dad, give me one of your cards and let me have your pin," Theo requested.

He did as requested, without question. Theo was gone only 30 seconds, returning with £300 in notes.

"If you are being tracked, then as far as your pursuers are concerned, you have just made a cash withdrawal from a machine in Ventnor on the Isle of Wight," Theo declared with a broad smile.

"That is brilliant thinking son. Now let's see if there is any room at the Inn."

5:28 p.m. - BST / 1:28 p.m. - EDT<br>Sawley, Lancashire

The father and son exited the Spread Eagle Inn, accommodation secured for the night. Theo was wearing his black hoodie, which featured the movie posted to the final 'Lord of the Rings' film. They turned right towards the Abbey which lay a short distance across the road. Arriving at the main entrance, they found the gates locked. The wall surrounding the site was a little over a metre high and proved to be no obstacle for Theodore, who quickly scrambled over. Theo and his dad crossed the field diagonally to the corner where a small wooden building stood.

Looking around, they saw no one. It was unnervingly quiet.

"Maybe everyone is already inside waiting for us," Theo suggested.

"Did you not use any of your powers to determine that?"

"I thought about that, but I want to keep as much of this a mystery until it's revealed, let it develop as naturally as possible. I can only go through this once, I want to make the most of it. If that makes any sense," Theo replied to his dad.

"I completely understand. Enter the code on the lock and let's get this party started." Theodore placed his arm over his son's shoulder.

Theo entered the code 261200 into the lock, letting out a laugh. "I have just realised my birth date, as I've entered it, is technically the day after the traditional date for the birth of Christ. Go Figure!"

"You have only just noticed that? I thought you were supposed to be smart?" His dad exclaimed while ruffling his son's hair.

Pulling open the wooden door, the space automatically illuminated to reveal a storage area for ground maintenance equipment; ride-on lawnmowers, petrol trimmers, wheelbarrows, spades and many tools and chemicals. On the floor, there was an open trapdoor with a sheet of artificial grass folded to the side.

Light was glowing from the hole in the floor. Approaching, they could see spiral stone steps leading down into the earth. Theo led the way. A few steps later, a sign on the wall instructed them to close the trap behind them. Theodore grabbed the handle of the door and pulled it down, hearing the artificial turf flap back over with a thump.

The staircase spiralled down for what seemed several flights until it stopped at a dimly lit tunnel illuminated only by a series of flame torches guiding the way. The passage had a smell of damp earth, reminiscent of petrichor from the first rain after a hot and dry summer. There was a warm draft coming from the tunnel and the gentle whistle of rushing air echoed in the confined space, only adding to the suspense.

"What do you see?" Theodore asked his son.

"There is a door about 50 metres down the tunnel. I can hear voices, perhaps 30 distinct people of varying accents."

Reaching the door, it appeared to be oak, iron bands rusted and pitted, crisscrossing the wood. Inscriptions were engraved into the bands, however, were badly corroded. It had a large, ornate handle, shaped like two intertwined S's, one being the mirror of the other.

Theo could make out intricate details on the handle, symbols similar to those he observed on Genetrix. He reached out and grabbed the handle, expecting some reaction, but it felt like a cold metal shape in his hand. Turning it, the latch released, and the door pushed open.

The voices from within the room stopped as warm air whooshed down the tunnel as it filled with light.

Stepping through the doorway, the pair enter a vast vaulted cellar. The ceiling arches high above, supported by thick stone columns. Modern spotlights illuminate the space, revealing rows of medieval pews. The smell of the damp, poorly hidden by burning incense. A large lit fireplace at the back of the cellar provides warmth. Near the fire, an imposing altar stands, carved from a single block of Aswan granite, engraved with the same symbols as those on the door handle.

The smoke from the fire rose to a chamber where it met airflow that carried it up to join several chimneys, each one exiting from properties in the village.

Next to the altar was a throne, carved from what to Theo, appeared to be a meteorite. He had suspicions about its origins, raising questions he was certain he already knew the answers to.

Over 200 people packed the pews, filling the cellar.

As Theo stepped forward, everyone knelt at their seat and bowed their heads.

A voice shouts "Our lord has arrived".

"NO" Theo shouts. "None of that. I am not your Lord."

"My Lord, but you are," the man replies as he approaches Theo and his father. "Let me introduce myself, I am Herbert J. Montclair, we spoke on the phone the other day. I am your servant. We are all your servants."

Everyone in the room suddenly stands, hundreds of pairs of eyes all focused on Theo.

He continues, "I am, how should I put this, I am the secretary of *The Order of the Etheric Veil*. Come let me introduce you to your disciples."

Theo glares at the man, his body tenses, "I told you I am not your Lord. I am not your king or your leader. And I am most certainly not the second coming. Or anything else you may think that I am." Aware of how frustrated and tense he was becoming, he tried to relax. Theodore grabbed his arm and giving him a sharp look of disapproval.

"As you wish. But come." Herbert raised his arm, directing down the aisle towards the altar. Everyone in the room sat, except for the first two pews where eleven people were still standing.

"This is the undercroft of Sawley Abbey. It was built before the Abbey, by several hundred years in fact. The order have kept it secret since it's construction. So it does not feature in any writings or documents. It simply does not exist. There are several such sites across the world. Many are more elaborate than this one. Their function was originally as sanctuaries for the ancient bloodlines, members of the order, during periods of unrest. But in recent history, their purpose has changed. Many remain unused, hidden from the world. But now you are here, I should imagine they once again have a use." Herbert J. Montclair was in his mid-50s, bald, tall and lean. His voice was deep and powerful. He spoke with authority and assurance. Theo could read him and was comforted that he felt he was a good and honest man.

As they approached the altar, Herbert indicated to Theo to sit on the throne.

"It looks like it is carved from a meteorite," Theo said

"You are quite correct." A different voice spoke. Turning to look at the person, Theo could see it was from a woman aged in her mid-30s.

"I am Juliet Lovell. I am an astronomer and astrophysicist. The meteor we believe to be a fragment of Earth. We suspect it was debris that fell back to Earth after the collision with Theia. That collision we believe formed our moon. We also believe it is the oldest Earth meteor to have been found, around 4.5 billion years old."

"Amazing. I think I prefer to stand," Theo replied.

"Do you mind if I sit there?" Theodore requests.

His request causes a commotion among those members of the order who were standing as if his taking of the seat was a breach of some law.

"Go ahead, Dad." The discussion stops as they glance at Theo and bow their heads. This action angers him further.

"Ok. Enough already. I acknowledge maybe you consider me to be some divine being, but I am just Theo. So please if you could stop. We are all equals here."

"So what are we doing here?" Theodore asks.

"Let me introduce your Acolytes," Herbert looks at Theo for confirmation that he approves of the term. Theo nods reluctantly in response. Motioning to Theo to follow, he walks to the last person in the front row before continuing.

"May I present, George Godfrey, he is the accountant. A senior official at the Federal Reserve. If there is money moving anywhere, he knows about it, he has connections to every major financial institution. Much of what he does for us is hidden from his employers. While he is a senior member of the order, he does not possess any active traits. He manages your wealth fund."

"Pleased to meet you, Theo. The portfolio at your disposal is..." Herbert interrupts, "All in good time George."

Theo shakes his hand and thanks him.

"Aren't you Sir Malcolm McKenzie MP?" Theo asked the next man in line. A tall, thin, but well-groomed individual, with receding grey hair.

"Very good Theo, I am the very same," He replies

"Weren't you Defence Secretary a few years back?" Theo asks.

"Indeed I was. I am your representative in the government. I have tactical insights and contacts at your disposal."

"May I introduce Clementine Le Fleur, She is the current President of the European Council in the European Union."

"Enchanté Monsieur Theo." Theo bends and kisses her hand.

"This is Sir Alastair Vincent Mountbatten, The Chief of the General Staff, he is the head of the British Army."

"Please to meet you, Alastair. I take it you can keep me informed of any immediate threats to Earth?" Theo asks.

"Yes, Sir. I am privy to the highest clearance level of National Security and beg your pardon Malcolm, but even above yours when you were DefSec."

"Here we have Dr Isabella Fortuna. She is a leading authority on Infectious Disease Epidemiology," Herbert said.

"I look forward to outlining the concerns I have about some experiments being carried out by research laboratories regarding gain-of-function. And beg your pardon Alastair, but engineered viruses pose more of a risk to humanity than the military." She looks dead-eyed at the military leader, who rolls his eyes as he lets out a snort of derision.

"Now then, can't we get along like friends? After all, we are all on the same side, aren't we?" Herbert pleads.

"Isabella. Can I ask? Was Covid-19 an example?" Theo questions.

"Actually, that was one of the discussion points I wanted to raise with you. In answer to your question. Yes, I believe it was."

"Thanks. So many times I have heard that question asked and it was always considered a controversial one." He continues, moving on to the next person in line. "Professor Lubbock, you are a member of the Order?"

"Yes Theo, I am indeed. Great to see you again my boy. I said I would speak to you again on Sunday. Well, here I am." Theo enthusiastically shook his professor's hand.

"Now Theo, I have the pleasure of introducing to you General Ivan Gorbachev. The General was one of the most senior officials in the Soviet space program, then later in Roscosmos. He has an unparalleled understanding of the existential threat facing Earth from non-terrestrial things."

"Comrade Theo, can I say, this is honour to be here to serve. I point out, you will not see any American from NASA or US Department of Defence here to help you," Ivan was almost shouting with his booming voice.

"Thank you, Ivan. I look forward to some long conversations."

"Now then Theo, here I present to you possibly your most unexpected advisor, Dr James R Llewelyn-Jones, former Pentecostal Bishop, now a teacher of Theology and Pentecostal Studies." Herbert took the hand of his Caribbean friend and vigorously shook it.

"Theo, I know what you are probably thinking…"

Theo interrupted, "Sorry for interrupting James, but I understand Pentecostalism is a deeply spiritual religion, with beliefs in prophecy, healing and miracles. I am sure you have studied the link between acts displayed by those who carry the ancient bloodline and experiences of god through the Holy Spirit. From a theological perspective, the acts that some members of the order can perform could appear as god given or as a sign of god. I understand that and look forward to your counsel."

"Thank you. They were not wrong about you, for you are wise," the former bishop replied.

"Next we have Lillian Barnstaple. We have to thank Lillian for helping to finance our little endeavour. You may not have heard of her, she keeps her private life separate from her business life where she operates under a pseudonym. She likes to cloak her business affairs under layers of shell companies, much to the annoyance of Mr Godfrey I should imagine. She won't mind me telling you she is a billionaire tycoon with interests in technology, pharmaceuticals, agriculture, chemicals, aerospace and automotive. Am I forgetting anything, Lillian?"

"I am very pleased to meet you, Theo. Herbert, you forgot diamonds, rare metals, retail, fashion, conservation, philanthropy and many more."

"For that, I must apologise. Theo, watch her carefully, before you know it, she could buy you in one of her hostile takeovers," Hebert laughed at himself, as Lillian joined him.

"Ah, I do amuse myself," he continued. "Finally and I'm not sure how to introduce this gentleman. We have Eric Jameson. Would you be so kind as to let Theo know what you bring to the order?"

"Sure. I bring disorder to the order. I am a reporter, I focus mainly on conspiracy topics. I am a numbers guy, I love analysing data, discovering patterns and uncovering the lies they conceal. I am also a computer programmer."

"Now then Eric, don't be modest," Herbert requested.

"I am a hacker, actually the correct term is a cracker. My public persona is a hacker. A corporate customer let's say, will hire my services, I will examine their systems or software and find security flaws. I advise them on how to fix their issues. But then I am also a cracker. I illegally access systems and networks, find information, you know, dig around, find evidence here and there, then expose them. Of course, some information that I find is on behalf of the order."

"Aren't you concerned you will be caught and arrested?" Theo asks.

"When you have the contacts that we have, such things are trivial, Sir Mckenzie when he was Defence Secretary, ensured that Eric here was enrolled into the British Secret Service, he now has the protection of an enduring form of diplomatic immunity," Herbert added. Eric winked and popped a piece of chewing gum in his mouth, offering Theo a piece.

"Thank You, but no thanks. Who is everyone else?" Theo looks at the rows of pews lining the undercroft.

"They are all members of the order. Many have a specific role in between their day-to-day lives. Others are employed by the order to carry out important duties. Most of the people you see here today live in the British Isles, others have travelled here specifically to see you. However, time is pressing and we need to discuss the affairs of the day. Except for the twelve, who are your acolytes," He pauses and thinks for a moment before continuing. "Sorry, I am not too comfortable with that term. Instead, I shall call them your cabinet. The twelve will stay but everyone else is free to leave."

Turning to the audience, he thanks them for coming.

The noise of shuffling feet and conversation echoed around the cellar. In a very orderly, almost rehearsed process, the members of the order walked to four different points on two sides of the undercroft. There the walls seem to transform from solid stone to a panel of blue light. People one by one walked through the blue surface, vanishing.

"You have Aelioxar technology?" Theo asks.

"You didn't think they would leave us with nothing, did you?" The response came from his Professor who was now standing next to Theo.

"How do they work?" Theodore asks as he approached and examined the closest doorway.

"They are spacial gateways or portholes so to speak. They are folded points in spacetime. To be honest we have never truly understood the science behind them." Juliet Lovell answered.

"Come now, let us go to your cabinet room and begin with the proceedings," Herbert requested.

# CHAPTER 8 TWELVE

## SEPTEMBER 19 2021

*6:30 p.m. BST - (British Summer Time)*

*1:30 p.m. EDT - (Eastern Daylight Time)*

*Sawley, England.*

Once the undercroft was empty, but for the twelve, Theo and his father. The group walked over to another blue panel next to the altar. Passing through, Theo entered a modern conference room. The space was round, glazed on all walls except for the wall from which they entered. It reminded him of the room he spent his time in on Genetrix-7X.

In the centre of the room was a large round table with fifteen seats. On the floor and in the space between the table was a large coat of arms. It featured a shield inscribed with the same letter S and mirrored S as had appeared in the undercroft. Theo could make out that it was a primitive double helix, but with the way the light reflected off the paint, it also appeared as an infinity symbol. Below the shield was a motto in Latin: it read;

*'Ordo Velaminis Aetherici'*

Loosely translated as Order of the Etheric Veil.

The Order's secretary ushered Theo to the head of the table. His father sat to his left, and Herbert to his right. The remaining members of the order took their seats.

"Who sits there?" Theo asked, pointing to the single empty chair directly opposite himself.

"That seat is reserved for any members of the order who are invited to sit on this cabinet or perhaps a citizen of Aeliox. But since this is the first official cabinet meeting of the order, that decision lies with you," Sir Michael McKenzie answered.

"A couple of points, that I am sure Theo will have raised himself. First, you have had meetings before? And second, the way the order appears to operate, I may be wrong, so I apologise now, but it appears as if you are all Government Ministers, those back there who have just left are civil servants and Theo is the President. Tell me I am wrong?" Theodore asked, looking at Theo, who responded with a glance, confirming his father's suspicions.

"As the secretary, I feel I should answer this. No disrespect Mr Newton, but you are not an official member of this cabinet, as such you do not have a voice here. We have allowed you to stay as this is the first sitting, as such we have not brought our business to order, but you may be asked to leave. Secondly, yes, you are correct, we alluded to the fact earlier, but all members of the order are your staff or as you put it 'Civil Service', they will do your bidding. And finally, you are more than our President…"

Theo stood while making eye contact with Herbert. "Come on Dad, let's go. I don't think these clowns have listened."

"Wait, Son. I think I understand." Theodore opened his mind, allowing Theo to hear his thoughts.

*The Order is your Government, like it or not. You need to give them explicit orders. Whether you want to be their president, Mosiah, king or god or not, that is what they expect, so give them limits and provide them with a name you want to be referred to as. I think you need them at least for now, OK, Son?'*

Theo nodded at his dad, then turned and looked each person directly in the eye. "From this moment forward you will refer to me in person as Theo. Outside of this room, I am to be known as 'The One'. I am not your president or your god, nor am I your king. I work for you, for 'The Order' and for humanity, as much as you work for me. We are all equals, we have the same rights and entitlements. You are not my cabinet, you are my 'Order of Counsel' and if anything I am your chairman. You will guide, inform and advise me on all matters of concern, threat or importance to the security of this planet, humanity, the Aelioxar and the 'Galactic Council of Peace'. My Father is the 13th member of this 'Order of Counsel', he will be my voice when I am not here. I make this ruling not because he is my father, but because we have a telepathic link. As of now, my mind is open to my father to alert me when I am needed. I trust his decisions and this is my ruling."

One by one, the members of *the Order* confirm their agreement by stating 'Yes Theo'.

"Thank you. What is the first item of business?" he authoritatively and confidently asks.

"If I may read you a list of pressing items for your attention?" Herbert nervously asked. Theo nodded in response.

"Miss Fortuna has evidence confirming COVID-19 was indeed a genetically engineered virus and was deliberately released into the population. Second, some instances of the vaccine have been deliberately adjusted to cause cardiac failure in specific demographics or cause long-term health concerns resulting in early mortality. The most troubling aspect of our research shows that there appears to be nanotechnology within the vaccine." Theo glanced at Isabella Fortuna. She looked back, her face pale and eyes wide, showing fear glistening from the formation of tears. Her lips pressed to a thin line, trembling slightly as she tried to maintain composure. She spoke barely above a whisper with a soft quiver, "Yes, that is correct".

"Was it Wuhan? Who was involved?" Theodore asks.

Isabella responds, her voice less shaky, as she wipes a tear from her eye. "Yes, we believe it to be a yet unidentified organisation, our primary suspects are the USA, India or China."

"I will visit Wuhan and see what I can determine. Do we know what the nanotechnology does?" questions Theo.

"We are at an early stage in our investigation, but we suspect the nano devices are remote neuro stimulator." Ms Fortuna answered.

"That sounds ominous, nano tech, got it. What is next?" Theo asks.

It was Sir Malcolm McKenzie who answered, "We are aware from our Aeliox contacts that there are several other non-terrestrial species on Earth. There is one specific race, we are not sure of their name, but we have decoded communications that suggest they call themselves the '*Nexil*'. They are a particularly tricky race to pin down. We have never seen them, nor do we have any photos.

What our research suggests is they have been visiting Earth since the 1960s when we first went to the moon. Then in the 1980s they made contact with the Americans. We received information from an operative from inside the US intelligence community that they later signed a treaty with the USA. If they have, the US Government has released no details nor have they informed anyone of the fact.

We have one name that keeps occurring, GARD. We cannot be certain what it means, but we suspect it relates to the Nexil. We also believe GARD is holding Dr Katherine Williams..." Theodore gasped and looked at Theo in shock.

"Do you know where she is being held? When did they take her?" He asked.

"She never returned home after she met with you, Mr Newton. She has been missing for eight days now. We suspect she is being held somewhere in the US, but we don't know where exactly."

Theo placed his hand on his father's shoulder.

"I will find her. Is she one of us? Is she a member of The Order?"

"She is." The former defence secretary confirmed.

"I will find her. About GARD. I have some information to share."

Theo briefed his advisors on his experience in Japan, the events that transpired on Grand Pacific Flight 7, its subsequent crash and the HelixStar satellites.

"This information confirms other intelligence we gathered," General Ivan Gorbachev added in response.

"In the 1980s following a speech made by the then President of the United States, members of the executive committee of 'The NSA', 'The CIA', and 'The FBI' secretly met. They discussed the need for a new organisation which would be unsanctioned and therefore a non-executive, black budget department. This new organisation would recruit the best talent from within their agencies. It would have backdoor access to all the intelligence data and capabilities of their agencies.

We suspect they agreed. They then approached and collaborated with high-ranking leaders in the US Air Force.

We believe this new agency went live in 2004. The public know them as H.O.U.S.E 'Homeland Operations Unit, Surveillance and Espionage'. They have operational oversight of the entire US security service they also have command of the Space Force. We do not have any evidence to suggest they have an advanced space fleet. It is disturbing to think that slipped us by.

However, we have evidence to suggest that there is a higher level of operation, which is covert and without executive oversight. We believe it to be known as S.A.F.E. It operates with the same high-ranking officials as run US security agencies, allowing them to work in the shadows. Because of the highly compartmentalised structure of the Secret Service in the USA, the left hand never truly knows what the right hand is doing. Information sharing is limited, concealed by 'need to know' or 'eyes only' clearance levels.

Perhaps GARD is under the operational control of SAFE? What we can assume is that they know about The Order, they know about you Theo and that we are their target," Sir Alastair Vincent Mountbatten joining the discussion revealed.

"Do you have any concerns that they know that any of you are part of The Order?" Theo asked.

"The longer they hold Katherine, the greater that chance becomes," Clementine nervously suggests.

"Is there anything else?" Theo requests

"For the moment, No. The rest can wait," Herbert said.

"Ok. I have an idea of what I need to do. Thanks." Theo looked at his dad with a confident gaze.

"Can I ask?" Theodore sees his opportunity to ask a burning question. "What significance does Sawley Abbey have, I mean, of all the locations, why did you choose to meet here?"

"Ah, the Abbey." Dr Lesley Simons answers. "Right now, you aren't in Sawley. You are actually in London, this room being in one of my buildings."

"We chose the site of the Abbey because we are only a few miles from Pendle Hill," Professor Lubbock adds.

"I don't understand the significance of Pendle Hill?" Theodore glanced at his son with a confused look.

The Professor continues, "Pendle Hill is the site of bronze-age burials. But that is not the reason. In the 17th century, it was the location of the infamous Pendle Witches. Many of the accused lived around this area, they were tried for being witches. 9 women and two men were executed by hanging.

While accused of being witches, their crimes were for being traditional healers, using herbal medicines, talismans and charms, leaving them open for accusations of sorcery. They were, of course, members of The Order. They had particularly active healing or telepathic traits. They took their secret to the grave, making the ultimate sacrifice to keep our secret. We honour them by choosing Sawley Abbey."

"You learn something every day. I had never heard of the Pendle Witches. Thanks for answering." Theodore acknowledging the Professor and the Dr

"I have a question. While I was on Genetrix, Baruch mentioned time travel. She said that I could travel into the future, but travel into the past while possible, would mean I could only be an observer and not interact with or change an event. But it was never clarified how I could time travel. I do have a theory, but wanted to hear your thoughts?" Theo asked eagerly.

"Time travel? Really son?" Theodore looked at him as if he was saying something ridiculous.

"I think this question could be answered by Juliet or Ivan, perhaps even Eric has an insight?" Herbert responded.

"Thank you, Herbert," Juliet replied. "Time travel is completely theoretical. We are not aware of the Aelioxars' understanding of any hypothesis or if they have indeed successfully managed to travel in time. But several factors need to be taken into account when considering time travel. Firstly, ignore everything you have ever seen in science fiction, particularly in the movies. Dr Who, however, has it partially correct. Take the T.A.R.D.I.S - Time and Relative Dimensions In Space. We consider time to be linear, that is, it flows from the past into the present and the future. That is the linear view of time.

However, time is more flexible and can be influenced by factors such as gravity and velocity. Time can bend and stretch, so it is not strictly linear.

Quantum theory, specifically I suppose, quantum entanglement allows for no time to pass. For the benefit of those in the room not versed in entanglement. We can take a particle, let's say, an electron here on Earth. We can 'in theory' entangle it with another electron anywhere in the universe in an instant, that is, there is no delay in time in the entanglement occurring.

We do not fully understand the mechanism that allows for the communication of entangled particles, however; it implies that the communication process is not limited by time.

Next, we have space. We consider space to be the distance between things, in atoms, molecules, the air we breathe, between me and Theo, between the earth and the sun, and so on. We consider out there, for space to be a vast three-dimensional continuum with relative positions and directions. However, we know there is a 4th dimension known as time. The combination of the three dimensions of space with time is spacetime.

What we know is that massive objects can cause spacetime to curve. This curvature affects the motion of objects and the flow of time, leading to a phenomenon known as gravitational time dilation, where time passes more slowly in stronger gravitational fields.

Finally, while we believe faster-than-light travel is impossible, there are theoretical particles that we believe can travel faster than light. However, a spacecraft could not achieve such speeds because, as a craft gets faster and so, its mass increases. Therefore, at light speed, it would have an infinite mass, but would also require an infinite amount of energy to achieve those speeds.

So travelling back in time would require levels of energy that we simply cannot create. It may also require negative energy and a wormhole. We cannot do that either.

I know I wandered a bit off course, but time travel requires a level of understanding of spacetime, gravity and quantum physics that we do not yet have.

We do not have the technology to test any hypothesis we may have. What were your thoughts, Theo?"

"I can generate a quantum bubble; I can propel myself at orders of magnitude greater than the speed of light. I can manipulate matter and energy, entangle particles and control my mass, even generating a gravitational field.

What I have observed while in space is that massive objects, such as our sun, leave a gravitational echo in their wake, a slight tear that is unperceivable, but it is there. It is like a ribbon cutting through spacetime, a temporal rift, so to speak.

My thoughts are this. If I quantum entangle myself with an object known to exist now and in the past, I can use it as a homing beacon so that I can find Earth. I generate a spacetime bubble and so make myself have no mass, a process that Baruch shared known as a 'Quantum Mass Descaling'.

Using four pulsars or quasars as a location fix, I travel at light speed, passing into the tear in spacetime caused by the sun's gravity wake travelling back to a point in history."

"Can you do that son? Why do you need a positional fix?"

"The Earth is constantly moving around the sun, which is moving around the Milky Way, which in turn is moving through the universe. The Earth is never in the same place. If you wanted to time travel back just one week to this room and didn't factor in the position of Earth in space, you would end up floating in outer space, millions of miles from where we were a week ago." Ivan added.

"If I maintain light speed using the quasar fix for a baring in time and an exact distance in the temporal rift, exiting at the precise moment, I should find myself back in time. Of course, I will likely find myself within the sun, but that is nothing I can't handle. I can then return to a past Earth."

"That is incredible; the hypothesis appears sound. However, suppose this works and you are at a point in the past. How do you intend to return to the present? There will be no temporal rift from the sun as it will not yet have created one. The will be no path back to now," Juliet questions.

"Light speed. I will travel at light speed, perhaps around the sun for, and this sounds awkward, a fixed 'time', again locking on to the pulsars as a navigational point in space."

"But aren't the pulsars also moving relative to everything else? The variables will be enormous when calculating the math for both trips," Eric adds.

"They are, I have already studied the data we have on four different pulsars and quasars and am confident that I have the equations correct."

"Why do you need to lock onto the pulsars for your return trip? If you are orbiting the sun, surely that is your navigational fix?" Theodore questions, uneasy at his son's proposal.

"You are forgetting, the pulsar fix is so I know when I have to stop travelling at light speed. The fix on the stellar objects and their relative positions tells me when I am in time and not where I am in space.

Think of them as four arms on a clock, when they are all at pre-calculated positions, assisted by varying magnitudes of brightness, will tell me when in time I am."

"This is incredible. It is groundbreaking in fact. And you think this will work? Can you not just will yourself into a different time?" Ivan asks, amazed, wide-eyed with a manic expression.

"That is what I want to confirm. Since I have never time travelled, I have no point of reference for how it feels. How the *extherix* changes and how the etheric surge adjusts to changes in the flow of matter and energy. I will pay close attention to varying quantum states, to the sub-atomic and forces at play. I have abilities that I do not yet know how to use or even understand. Baruch instructed me to be very careful, to be mindful and so I tread with caution while I am still learning to be me."

"Son, you aren't actually considering time travel, are you?" Theodore reaches out and holds his son's arm.

"Yes, I am. And I am ready to attempt it now." Theo responded with a look of self-confidence.

"When in time do you propose to go?" Herbert asks.

Theo doesn't answer. Instead, he stands, placing an arm on his father's shoulder, and whispers, "I'll be back right away."

In a blink of an eye, he vanishes.

# CHAPTER 9
# BACK TO THE CRADLE

## DECEMBER 26 2000

*5:30 a.m. GMT - Greenwich Mean Time*

*London, England.*

The trip back in time went exactly as Theo had calculated. However, he did not consider how much energy he would expend. There was a reason Baruch told him he had the power of a star that had now become clear to him. Baruch told Theo everything he needed to know without telling him how or why it was important.

Being in such proximity to the sun, Theo's body was recharging. He could feel his fatigue wane and knew he would need to rest before going back to the future.

He could see the pale blue marble over 90 million miles away. Ironically, he didn't have the time to fly towards Earth and, while he was still feeling tired; he knew he had enough energy to teleport.

He materialised in a Darling Memorial Hospital parents' room. Except for the furnishings and the dripping boiler, the room was empty and quiet. Beyond the confines of the room, the sound of electronic beeps and alarms could be heard. He knew he didn't have too much time; he was feeling too drained to slow time.

Glancing around the room, he noticed the clock on the wall, *'That will do,'* He thought to himself as he reached up and pulled the clock from the wall. He looked at the face and chuckled. Reading that the brand was *'Agamemnon',* he changed the image on his hoody to the poster from 'Time Bandits' then proceeded to take the battery out of the clock and adjusted the hands to show 5:42 a.m.

After placing the clock back on the wall, he went over to the sofa and sat. He cast his mind back to the conversation with Baruch about time travel. Something she had told him didn't add up.

Hearing a male voice in the distance say 'thank you' stopped his train of thought. He recognised the voice, although the person he could hear was younger than the one he knew.

Theo put his hood over his head and lay with his back to the room, pulling the blanket that had been left behind up and over his body. The door to the room opened, and someone entered. He knew who this person was; they were all too familiar, but they were in distress.

Theo wanted to sit up and embrace the man, but he knew he couldn't. The little change he had made to the clock would have to be enough for the moment. He would talk about this moment when he saw him again in his future.

The man briefly sat at the table and flicked through the pile of magazines before standing and staring at the clock. Theo heard him mutter "Strange coincidence". Theo fidgeted briefly, as to show he was being disturbed, but the man stayed in the room. For fifteen minutes, the man stared out of the window. Theo was overwhelmed with the thoughts of grief, the internal battle the man was having about how he could continue after losing his Izzy.

Theo had to battle his will power, he was desperate to embrace his father, to reassure him everything would be ok. But he knew he couldn't.

A nurse entered. Seeing someone lying on the sofa, she asked the man to join her in the corridor. Theo was left alone in the room; he was crying from the pain his father was experiencing. It was overwhelming. He knew his dad loved his mother, but the emotion he felt was greater than he was prepared for.

Theo sat up and considered what being here, in this time and place, meant, not just to him but to his father. Should he visit himself as a newborn? The idea it would create a temporal paradox was nonsense. Neither version of himself would pass out or unravel the fabric of spacetime. What he actually wanted was to see his mother.

Theo stood and became invisible. He walked through the closed door of the parents' room and down the corridor, instinctively stopping at a ward bay with six intensive care cots.

He approached the cot with 'Baby Newton' written on a whiteboard. Looking down at his tiny self, he had a strange sensation. The child was establishing a telepathic link with him. There were no words, no meaningful communication, just emotion; he could sense the baby wanted to share memories of his time in his mother's uterus, of muffled conversations between his parents. Those memories were there already in adult Theo; he just needed to recall them.

Standing looking down at himself, he recalled the last memory he had of his parents together. The love they shared was tangible. It was infectious. A piece of Theo that had been missing seemed to finally fall into place. He had never experienced true love or even loss, but in the most unexpected of places, he was granted the most extraordinary gift.

"Thank you, young Theo," he whispered as he turned and left the bay. Exiting the ward, he made his way to the nearest stairwell. Signage pointed to the morgue being in the hospital's basement.

He stopped at the door to the area where his mother was being kept. Feeling uneasy, he knew this was something he needed to do. Passing through the door and along a short corridor, and entered the cadaver room.

The sight of his mother's lifeless body on the metal table sent a shiver down his spine, but even in death, he could see how beautiful she was. He took a deep breath, focusing his mind on the faint electrochemical energy still lingering in her brain, undetectable by medical technology. Reaching out, he slowly re-energised her neural pathways, just enough to connect with her thoughts.

'Isabella,' he called out in his thoughts.

'Isabella,' he called again.

'Who is this? Where am I? Why is it dark?' a voice called back.

'Isabella. You are in hospital,' Theo replied.

'I died, didn't I? Is this heaven?'

'You did mam, I am sorry, this isn't heaven,' Theo answered back in his thoughts, a tear rolling down his cheek.

'You called me Mam!, is Theodore here, where is here?' She was confused, trying but failing to see, to hear. Everything was empty, except for the voice in her head.

'I am your son, Theo. You died before I was born. Dad isn't with me, I am sorry. This will be the only time we can talk. Dad loves you so very, very much, and he misses you. But I need to tell you something.'

'My darling Theo, you don't need to tell me, I know. I know it all,' Isabella responded gently with a peaceful, serene voice in Theo's mind.

'I know what your destiny was, what it meant for me...' Isabella was struggling to stay with the connection 'They told me, but I never told your dad, please do not tell him'

Theo didn't expect the revelation. Baruch never informed him of his mother's knowledge. Tears continued down his cheeks.

'Who told you?'

'Dr Williams, then, them. I am so tired Theo.'

'You sacrificed yourself for me!. You never told Dad? I wish I knew you, wish there was something I could do.' Theo could sense his mother's synaptic pathways were shutting down. He knew she didn't have long left.

'Don't worry about me; I will always be with you. How is your father? Has he moved on?'

'He still misses you, he did an amazing job raising me, but he is at peace with himself now, more so since he found out what my destiny was.'

'I am pleased. Your destiny has been realised. Are you as powerful as I was promised you would be?' Isabella was struggling, the final energy in her neurons waned.

'I have the power of a star; I can manipulate matter, be anywhere in the blink of an eye, even time travel. They call me The One. But Earth does not know about me yet.'

'I am tired Theo. You should know that I am so very proud of you, my son. They told me you need to believe in yourself and that almost nothing is impossible. Take care of your father for me. My boy..' The connection was lost. The fleeting activity in Isabella's brain was over. Theo stood holding his mother's hand, his eyes red from crying. He was thankful that he had spoken with his mam, discovering more about her part in his destiny. He was more at peace than he could remember. The gift he had received from his late mother was the closure he needed.

His time in the year 2000 was over. However, there was the small matter of returning to 2021 to overcome. He was still too tired to make another temporal excursion. With that in mind, he exited the hospital and took to the skies, ascending quickly to the Earth's thermosphere.

There was one more question that needed clarification. He held his position for a minute, facing the sun, soaking in all the energy he could before circling Earth, identifying every item in orbit.

Counting significantly fewer satellites; there were 769 in 2001 versus 4,760 in 2021. None were marked G.A.R.D., confirming part of what the Order had told him earlier.

Theo departed Earth's orbit and made his way to the moon. The derelict alien base passed below. To his surprise, in one of the moon's polar craters, the same base he observed in his own time. The defensive fortifications were not as numerous, but nonetheless, a worrying revelation.

*'If this is not G.A.R.D Then who? The Nexil Or something else?'* He thought to himself. He was eager to look, however he was hesitant. Aware that what the Aelioxar had told him about time travel was not true, that being the case, what other facts have they distorted? He did not know the capabilities of the Nexil, if indeed this base was them, but he couldn't risk contaminating the timeline. His desire to learn more would have to wait until he returned to 2021.

He closed his eyes as he focused on the Etheric surge building within him. The surrounding space shimmered with blue energy as he felt the quantum bubble forming, a precise yet powerful construct allowing him to tunnel through the spacetime interlock. With a deep breath, he released the surge. In an instant, he was no longer near the moon.

Everything blurred around him as the fabric of space bent and twisted as he travelled through the quantum tunnel. Within moments, he emerged into the orbit of Mars.

Theo circled the red planet; his enhanced vision scanned the surface below. As he approached the northern pole, he spotted a massive crater shrouded in shadow. Within the crater, he saw it—a sprawling base.

His heart raced as he took in the sight.

*'Is this Alien activity? It predates S.A.F.E and G.A.R.D.'*

He enabled full stealth as he flew into the crater. He observed craft departing what appeared to be a hangar, all classic disc-shaped flying objects. His suspicions were confirmed. He followed one of the craft closely. There were no thrusters, no obvious engine, or means of propulsion.

Focusing his vision, he looked through the composite metal-polymer skin of the vessel. He concentrated on the material, the atomic structure and the chemical bonds. The metal was an alloy of titanium, aluminium and an unknown heavy metal with a nucleus of 130 protons and 200 neutrons. The polymer was a form of carbon and silicon, layered similar to graphene, in a hexagonal lattice. Each layer was alternately bonded to the alloy, creating a strong yet flexible material.

Looking deeper into the vessel, the lower section housed multi-directional gravitation generators powered by the mysterious element 115. Above in the flight control deck, two aliens were piloting the craft. Humanoid in appearance, they matched the classic grey alien with large hairless heads disproportionate to their body. Large almond-shaped black eyes, lacking ears or nose. A slender, frail-looking body with long limbs and a small torso.

The sight of the aliens stopped Theo in his pursuit of the vessel, over 70 years of purported UFO visitations, and here they were. He watched as they sped off toward Earth. But something else was on his mind. His interest in the craft was, for the moment, less important. He was now focused on piecing together the deception that was revealing itself. He took one last look towards the alien base. Were they the Nexil?

If they were, when did they begin cooperating with US security services? What were their motives? Technologically, they appeared less advanced than the Aelioxar. Were they a threat to Earth? But then, was Baruch telling the truth, was she being deceptive, he was already aware that she was holding back information and being selective with the facts.

It was time to return to the future, but Theo still felt too drained for another temporal excursion.

'Why didn't I think of this before, you plonker, I can sense space and time,' he thought, giving himself a telling-off. 'I don't need to follow the sun's gravity well; I can time travel by the power of the Etheric Surge and thought alone. It's less energy-sapping.'

To ensure he had energy reserves, he made his way closer to the sun, soaking up its radiation. Then, when he felt sufficiently charged, he concentrated on the place, the meeting with the Order and the time, the moment he left on the 18th of September, 2021. The surge built. A blue glow engulfed him before a brilliant flash of blinding light, and then he was back, standing in front of his seat. His father was to his left, and the members of the order sat around the table.

"You were gone for a second son," Theodore exclaimed. "Did it work?'

"Yes, Dad. Oh did it work!" Looking at his father with an adrenaline-filled rush as if he had just stepped off a rollercoaster. But his excited expression didn't last. He turned and looked at each of the Order in turn, a stern look of distrust.

"You need to tell me everything you know about the Aelioxar," Theo demanded.

Sir Malcolm McKenzie was the first to look Theo in the eye and respond, "Where does one start?" The former defence secretary asked, his voice shaking.

"From the beginning. When were we first aware of the Aelioxar? And I don't mean pre-history. In modern times, when were we aware of them? When did we first meet with them?"

"The Aelioxar contacted the Russians. It was the 12th of April 1961. Following the Soviet Union successfully sending Yuri Gagarin into space, they received a transmission shortly after, the words 'Внеземный. Познакомьтесь С Нами. 51 16 14 N 45 59 50 E' Translated it meant 'Extraterrestrial. Meet us' followed by the coordinates close to where Yuri landed near Engels in the Saratov region. The bizarre fact about this communication is that it was sent before Gagarin returned to Earth. They knew where he was going to land," Sir Malcolm explained.

"Then what happened?" Theodore asked.

"If you don't mind?" General Gorbachev asked. Sir Malcolm waved his hand, conceding the floor to his colleague.

"This before my time and much kept secret by KGB. However, you do not get become General and an expert in Cosmos without becoming aware such things. Since we had a landing radius for Yuri, and he landed in radius, we already close enough to arrive at coordinates in time for landing.

Soon after, they came. Arriving in a large cylindrical craft, similar to the body of aircraft, perhaps the size of 737. Called themselves 'The Creators'; explained who they were and involvement in human history and evolution of life in the universe.

They not a threat, very peaceful, but concerned with humanity. They explained Earth was on the brink of annihilation, not only from ourselves but from forces in the cosmos.

They would not share technology with us, only their warnings. Said we were not alone; that there were others from distant worlds, some already here, and that Americans knew. They were already cooperating with a species."

"This is similar to what Baruch was telling me. Did they mention anything about Time Travel? When did the Order first meet with them?" Theo asked.

"We have carried the secret of our ancient blood and the creators with us over the millennia. We have scrolls that have records of the Aelioxar, but they are too fragile to read. In modern times, they next contacted our most senior member back in 1997. They told us to prepare for the arrival of you, Theo. But they did not tell us about time travel. Why do you ask?" Herbert responded.

"Baruch told me quite clearly. Future time travel was possible. However, travelling back in time, I would be an observer and could not interact with objects or people. This is not true. I can only conclude that they lied, they did not know, or I am more powerful than they predicted."

"You interacted with people?" Juliet asked excitedly.

"Dad. What can you remember doing after you met me for the first time in the hospital?"

"Erm. I asked to see your mam. But the nurse had to find out if it was ok. Why?" Theodore answered, puzzled by the question.

"Can you remember where you were, where you waited?"

"It was a long time ago. Let me think," Theodore leant back in the chair and raised his hands to his face for a moment before returning to the table and resting on his elbows. "The nurse took me to the parent room. Such a depressing environment. There I waited for about 15 minutes. It could have been longer, the clock on the wall wasn't working."

"What else do you remember about the room?" Theo probed his father to remember all he could.

"I remember there was a chipped mug, or maybe it had a handle missing. There were no other cups. A dripping kettle. A stack of magazines. A pen taped to the table. Uncomfortable chairs. A large sofa, there was someone asleep. Why?"

"I went back to the day I was born. I visited myself as a baby. But before that, I was in the room. Dad, I was that person on the sofa. I wanted to talk to you, but I knew I couldn't risk it affecting the timeline."

There was a collective gasp from the room. Theodore stood and embraced his son.

"Did you see your mam? Can you not save her?" Tears were rolling down Theodore's face.

"I went to the morgue, there was nothing I could do, Dad, I am so very sorry." A tear rolled down his cheek.

"But you can go back to before she dies and heal here. Do it. Please." Theodore dropped to his knees, the emotion of his loss on display, reliving his grief.

"I am sorry, Dad, really I am, there is nothing I can do. I can't save her. Doing so could have implications we can not predict."

Juliet stood and walked around the table to where Theodore knelt. She bent down beside and held him.

"He is right. We don't know what would happen to the timeline, to any of us, especially to Theo." She said.

Theodore looked up at his son, his eyes pained with the resurfaced emotion. "I am sorry, son. Forgive me. I didn't expect to still feel this way after so many years."

Theo pulled his dad to his feet and embraced him, whispering, "I won't stop looking for a way to bring her back, even if I give up my powers trying. I promise." He kissed his dad's cheek and asked for him to sit down.

The Order took a brief recess to freshen up before reconvening.

"Did you learn anything else while you were in the past?" Professor Lubbock enquired.

"I discovered the Luna base on the southern pole is there, but with fewer armaments. There is a non-human base on Mars. I followed one of the saucer craft. Examined its composition and its means of propulsion. The beings piloting it are like classic grey aliens. Does that mean anything to any of you?"

"Classic greys are believed to have been those in the Roswell, New Mexico crash of 1947. Our data on the subject is limited; the Americans don't care to admit, less share this information with even their closest allies. However, we don't believe them to be the Nexil. We suspect that the Americans have made technological advances because of recovered Grey saucers." Alistair answered.

"So, for my understanding, If I have been following correctly. There are the Greys from the 1947 Roswell crash. Then, the Aelioxar introduced themselves following Gagarin going into space in 1961 but then in 1997 returned and activated the Order. In the 1960s, the Nexil contacted the USA, who, in the 1980s, signed a treaty with them. So when does The Predator turn up?" Theodore asks, looking amused.

"Your summary is correct, from what we know. Perhaps the Nexil are the Predator? But then they may also be Vulcans to

111

suggest another fictional alien race." Eric continues, "I have extensively cracked American security services systems. I have no tangible evidence; it's more of a gut feeling, but I feel like whenever I am behind their firewall, they know I am there and are feeding me information they want me to see. It is like there is an adaptive archive of information controlled by an intelligence. Like, I get to a dataset and enter, but the information that I thought was there changes to something else on entering, however, that data is interesting enough for me to want to look."

"You are almost describing quantum information. What I mean is, with quantum data, the act of observing the information results in the data being destroyed or changed, hiding the actual information," Isabella responds "An example is the double slit experiment with photons, that is, light, the experiment changes when it is observed, photons sometimes act like a wave other times like a particle. I have seen similar results in the pathogenesis of viruses."

"What do we suppose Eric's observations suggest?" Herbert asks.

"An advanced Artificial Intelligence." Sir Malcolm McKenzie replies.

"Theo, do you have the ability to interface with computer systems?" Eric asks.

"I haven't tried," Theo responded. Thinking about it, he continued, "I can visualise everything around me at the sub-atomic level. Control the flow of particles, fields and waves. I could give it a go. However, isn't it just binary instructions with billions to trillions of floating-point operations per second? I know I can see the real-time operation of the transistors in a processor, but reading what that activity means, converting it from zeros and ones to something I understand, I think that is beyond me." Theo shrugged.

"I agree. I think it would be beyond you to understand trillions of on-and-off signals and then translate the operations in real-time," Eric replied with a sly smirk.

"Eric, if you believe I have an ego to bruise or a point to prove, you are mistaken. I recognise there are things I cannot do, but there are also things I have yet to discover I can do. Without sounding clichéd, I am on a journey of self-discovery," a serious-looking Theo replied.

Turning to Malcolm, he continued, "While I was speaking, I attempted to unlock the phone in your pocket. As it has a touch screen, there are no physical buttons to press. I tried to manipulate the facial recognition system by generating a photonic matrix upon the optical chip, but that didn't work. I then manipulated the resistive touch screen. I could determine what your passcode was based on the density and distribution of oil from your fingers. In short, I unlocked your phone and took a photo. However, I was not able to interface directly with the CPU or memory. I can keep up with the speed of the screen refresh, meaning I can input an instruction before the screen has fully loaded. So, I have to concede; I cannot interface with a computer"

"We may have a device in one of my technology concerns that would give you a cybernetic implant. You could feed the binary instructions into the implant in real-time. It would then do the translation of binary signals to code and, with the interface, give a construct of what the computer was doing," Lillian suggested.

"Thanks for the idea, but no. It would present more issues, making the problem insurmountable." Responded Theo, he continued, "I think we are getting off track here. Does anyone else have anything to add to the proceedings? Before we adjourn?"

One by one, the order of counsel shakes their heads. Herbert J. Montclair bangs the table. "Let's conclude this meeting. I will briefly summarise our next steps".

The meeting continued with a summary discussion for another hour. It was decided what Theo's next steps were to be. Reluctantly, Theodore agreed he and Louise were to hide out in a safe house until Theo had established what exactly they were up against.

# CHAPTER 10 H.E.L.I.X

## SEPTEMBER 18 2021

*6:23 a.m. BST - (British Summer Time)*

*7:23 a.m. CEST - (Central Europe Summer Time)*

*Bruges, Belgium.*

Finally, after a long and monotonous period of observation, communication came over the radio, announcing movement from the apartment and instructions to get into position.

Agents Dubois and Durand hurried onto the street and waited. A few moments later, a couple exited their rental accommodation. The agents followed, staying on the other side of the street, matching stride for stride until reaching their vehicle. The couple they were tailing entered the multi-storey car park.

"Get in," Agent Dubois ordered her male colleague, "You drive." Climbing into the passenger seat, she reached to her head, pressing a button on the earpiece, "Tom reporting in, Jerry is heading to their automobile, preparing to catch the mouse's tail."

A Volvo appeared at the exit of the car park and stopped. It wasn't clear what they were waiting for; it was still early morning, and the traffic on the stretch of road was very light.

"What are they doing?" Agent Durand questions. Suddenly, the Volvo turns and crosses the street, passing the parked agents and heading in the opposite direction. The driver stares directly at Agent Durand. With a smirk and a wink, he accelerates away.

"Quickly do a U-Turn" Dubois orders. The car violently shoots forward, tyres squealing as the handbrake is applied, spinning the car 180 degrees. Again, the car lurches as it accelerates in the direction of the escaping Volvo.

Agent Durand struggled to catch the Volvo, which was an equal match for the German hatchback they had been supplied. The quiet streets of Bruges provided few hindrances to the fleeing car.

"Tom, requesting drone assistance, Jerry is proving a difficult mouse to trap," Agent Dubois looked nervous. "Can't this thing go any faster?" She continued, barking at her colleague.

"I am doing the best I can. We are approaching a busy intersection; they have nowhere to run," He responds.

The Volvo was perhaps 50 metres ahead of them as it weaved its way through what traffic there was on the one-way street. Beyond them was the medieval *Gate of Ghent*, followed by the traffic-light-controlled intersection of Gentpoorstraat and Buiten.

"We have them, when we get close, move in and block them on their right." Agent Dubois orders.

The Volvo, approaching stationary traffic, slammed on its brakes, narrowly ploughing into the car in front. But before the pursuing agents could block the car to its right, the Volvo moved off, mounting the small traffic island, then sped up toward the narrow cobbled walkway, which was usually busy with cyclists and pedestrians.

Agent Durand floored the chase car, attempting to keep up but was blocked by a driver ahead who saw the Volvo illegally pass and the pursuing car trying the same thing.

Using the gap to the right-hand side of the queuing traffic, the chased car quickly advanced through a red light, making a sharp ninety-degree turn, narrowly avoiding a cyclist.

Agent Dubois, seething, climbed out of the car. Drawing her gun, she advanced on the car ahead. Pointing her weapon at the driver "MOVE YOUR CAR," she screamed "NOW." Discharging a round into a one-way signpost close by.

But it was too late. The car they were pursuing was too far ahead, with no hope of catching. She climbed back into her vehicle and ferociously pounded the dash with the butt of her gun.

"You are getting the blame for this fuck up! I am not taking another reprimand for your incompetence." Screaming at her colleague.

Agent Durand tried to give chase down the parallel street of Gentpoorvest, but their view was blocked by trees and progress by traffic. Still angry, she again contacted base.

"This is Tom. How are we with drone support?" The response agitated her further.

"I guess we don't have drone support?" Durand muttered.

### 7:41 a.m. CEST / 1:41 a.m EDT

H.E.L.I.X opened a communications channel to the Bruges agents. Using its sophisticated neural vocal processor, it imitates a human operator.

"G.A.R.D command, orders for Tom to head to Gare du Calais-Frethun immediately, Jerry has a booking on LeShuttle."

H.E.L.I.X then accesses protected systems in the vast network of the modern world. Beginning with automated number plate recognition systems across Belgium and Northern France.

Surveillance cameras dotting the picturesque streets of Bruges fall under its control, every frame now analysed by its insidious gaze. Military tracking systems are co-opted by Helix; its superior software brushed aside their encrypted defences generating new access codes.

Satellites orbiting Earth are re-targeted, their sensors focused on Northern Europe with pinpoint precision. Override control statements are issued to each operating department stating the authority of the United States Department of Homeland Operations Unit, Surveillance and Espionage. With each connection established, Helix's influence grows, encompassing the entire region like an omnipotent spectre. The AI's aim is clear: to locate the Volvo or the fleeing couple. Data flows seamlessly from disparate sources, converging into Helix's vast neural network, where patterns are analysed and probabilities calculated with a capability dwarfing the combined power of all the world's supercomputers.

But Helix runs and reruns, a reoccurring probability that the fleeing couple are not boarding LeShuttle but are instead making alternate arrangements. Further connections are established, this time with all booking networks and passenger manifests.

Over a period of a few hours and terabytes of data later, multiple bookings are flagged, but the AI dismisses them as deflection. Calculations suggest their true plan has not yet been revealed.

Helix applies a 24-hour lockout on the couple's bank cards; their attempted use would halt their progress and reveal their location.

The LeShuttle booking came and went with no sign of the fleeing Newtons. Agents Dubois and Durand looked at each other and shrugged. Before they could report in, Helix, portraying a superior, instructs Agent Durand to go directly to Ostend-Bruge Flanders International Airport. Without question, she accepts the order, instructing her colleague to drive there are quickly as possible.

*11:11 a.m. CEST / 5:11 a.m EDT*

*Earth Orbit*

"Colonel Patterson, Sorry to disturb you, Sir, We are receiving orders from Fleet Command, they are instructing us to move into a stationary orbit above Western Europe, top priority, Echo Delta, Sir."

"On my way." The commanding officer replied.

118

Colonel Patterson entered the bridge. A mid-50s female, she had been in command of the USF Lincoln for nearly a year. In that time, command orders were usually very mundane, from repairing or deploying satellites or probes to scouting the solar system. Other than drills, for which they were always warned in advance, she had never seen an Echo Delta command.

The communications officer looked at their commanding officer, awaiting a response.

"Let me see that." Colonel Patterson requests, looking down at the display in front of the communications officer.

*FLEET COMMAND ORDERS TO USF LINCOLN*
*AUTH_CODE: ZULU-CHARLIE-ECHO-4592-BRAVO*
*LOCATION: WESTERN-EUROPE, BELGIUM*
*HAWKEYE: 51.07611° N, 2.70375° E*
*OBJECT: AUTO-IDENT:LIMA-FOXTROT-99-ALPHA-8457-09*
*COMMAND: ORBIT_STATIONARY_50KM*
*WEAPONS_READY: ECHO-DELTA-773 PULSE_1SEC_25_PWR*
*ENGAGE: CONFIRM_CHARLIE-OSCAR*

"Helm set a course for Western Europe, stationary orbit 50KM. Co-ordinates are set to your nav." The Colonel orders.

"Aye, Captain. Co-ordinate set. Beginning orbital thrust."

"Weapons, activate the photonic laser, bay 3, weapons to ready," Colonel Patterson orders. "Comm, double check the auth code and verify engage command."

"Sir, the orders are confirmed." The Comm officer confirms.

"It seems we have a bug to burn. Helm, make sure we have atmospheric stabilisers engaged, we don't want to rock the boat and melt some innocent passers-by," chuckling to herself "Time to target?"

"Sir, we will be in position in 9 seconds. Tracking target, they will be in the Hawkeye window in 60 seconds." The weapons officer confirms.

"Excellent. This should go someway toward securing our status in the fleet as the most efficient ship. I am proud of you all."

"Sir, visual is coming online." A bridge officer announces.

Attention of the bridge crew is on a display screen with a high-resolution video feed of E40 road outside of Veurne. Cars are seen moving along the road, overlaid with a thermal image.

"Weapons ready. Set targeting and firing sequence to automatic." The colonel orders.

On the screen it display's a red circle around a vehicle as it moved in from the left side of the image. The camera tracks the car as it passes others on the road at high speed. It was when the car occupied an area of the road with little traffic around that a blinding flash, lasting a second, engulfed the object before it was seen crashing off the side of the road in an inferno.

"Target destroyed, Sir." The weapons officer confirmed.

"Stand down weapons. Helm, take us up and resume the previous orders. Well done all." The Colonel exited the bridge to her private command room.

"Helix open a secure line to Agent Patterson." Colonel Patterson orders.

"Connecting."

"This is Agent Patterson." The voice on the line responded.

"Hey Son, Are you at Bare?"

"Hi Mom, I am. Why?"

"We have just executed orders to fire on an automobile in Belgium. Do you have any intel about who they were?"

"Just a second," Agent Patterson said as he climbed out of bed and pulled open his laptop. His biometric details granted him access to the system. "I see nothing on executive orders. Do you know what the target ident was?"

"It was ALPHA-8457-09".

An icy shiver permeated down Agent Patterson as he read the details of the ident code.

"Mom, That was Lucy and Agent Durand." He screams in disbelief. His heart races and confusion clouds his judgement.

"What?" she replies, her jaw tense and eyes widening.

"Why was an execution order given on our people? Mom, is Lucy dead?" Agent Patterson's eyes welled. "I was going to propose to her when I saw her next. What have you done?" There is a momentary pause. His eyes were red and face frozen as he collapses to his knees he screams "WHAT HAVE YOU DONE?"

"Son. I.. I.."

"I have to go."

"Wait, Craig, Please." The plea was too late, the call had disconnected. "Helix, get Agent Patterson back."

"I am sorry, Sir. There appears to be a communications issue. The line cannot be reconnected at this time. Please try again later."

"Helix. Get command on the line."

"I am sorry, Sir. The communications issue is affecting all external contacts."

"Helix, run a ship-wide level one diagnostic. Order Colonel K Patterson, Zebra-99-Kilo-Papa. Initiate."

"Authentication code accepted. Ship-wide level one diagnostic will commence in 10 seconds. I will be offline during the diagnostic."

The Colonel accessed her computer terminal and called up event logs for the last hour.

"Lieutenant Colonel Sharp, report to my executive office." Colonel Patterson paced back and forth in her office. Located next to the bridge, it gave her the privacy her role demanded for confidential and high clearance matters while also being able to access the bridge quickly.

121

The first officer, Lieutenant Colonel Sharp, entered. A tall man, aged in his late 20s, with short dark hair and a well-groomed beard and moustache. He wore the standard uniform of the United Space Fleet, a combat-ready black and dark grey jumpsuit with the US flag on the left shoulder and the US space fleet insignia on the left chest. Three silver concentric circles designate his rank around the collar, which at the zip continue vertically down the jumpsuit to meet a horizontal line midpoint of the torso. The three circles are also repeated on the cuffs of each arm.

"Will. Take a seat." Colonel Patterson orders her first officer,

"Did anything strike you as unusual about the execution order we carried out?" She stands with her back to her second-in-command, trying to compose herself and hide her tears.

"The authentication and engage codes checked out; we verified and double-checked. The power level was measured and appropriate to our altitude and the composition of the target. It is not our duty to question our orders. So nothing appears unusual. It was by the book, Sir." Lt. Col. Sharp shifted in his seat, trying to get comfortable in the short chair for a man of his height.

"What I am about to tell you is confidential and off the record; it will not go in either of our official logs. Is that acceptable, Will?"

"Kathleen, It is."

She turned and looked directly at her first officer. Her eyes red were red, a single tear rolling down her cheek.

"Kathleen?" Will said in shock. His commander presented a polar disposition to her usual steely resolve.

"Will. I contacted Craig. I asked him to run a check on the target ident. We targeted two Gard agents. One of them was Agent Lucy Dubois." She stood rigid, tense, with her arms crossed across her body, almost as if she was trying to protect herself.

"Isn't that Craig's girlfriend? It must be a mistake?"

"It is no mistake; I ran the ident check myself. I wanted to find out who gave the authorisation, but the Auth code isn't resolving to the authorisation log."

"That's not possible!" Will interrupted, looking at his superior like she had made a mistake.

"Please, check for yourself." She replied.

Will stood, walked around the desk, and accessed the commander's computer using his biometric authorisation. After a minute of checking the communication logs and cross-referencing, the command authorisation log for firing the laser to the authorisation log from space fleet, no authorisation ident code match could be found.

"Kathleen, you know what this means?" Turning to look at his superior, he said, "It will appear as if we fired on a target without authorisation. There isn't even a command log entry with your authorisation. Which would infer that you are not in full command of the Lincoln."

"Will, it's more worrying than that. Someone is playing us, making out that we are responsible. I have tried to contact command, but the communication relay is offline. I have ordered a level-one ship-wide diagnostic."

"Level One? Is that not an overreaction?" Questioning his commander's judgment.

"It is the only way that I could legitimately take Helix offline. I spotted a strategic opportunity and used my executive powers."

"You think Helix is behind this?"

"I would be negligent in my duty as Captain of this vessel not to rule out potential areas of compromise. Helix compromises this ship and organisation." The Colonel stood and walked over to the command display. "We have another 10 minutes before Helix is back online. It's not just Helix that I don't trust. I think there is something else behind this. I have had my suspicions for a while."

"Colonel. You are my superior, so I will act upon your orders. However, I will question nothing that comes from Fleet Command. I will still follow the rule of rank. Anything you ask me that is contrary to command orders I will note in my official log. Is that clear, Sir?"

"You want to protect yourself and remain a loyal military man; I respect that. Find out what you can about the authorisation we received. Establish what Agent Dubois and Durand were doing in Belgium. Speak to Marcus Kane if you need too or General Macallister if you have no other route of enquiry. Don't trust anyone, and weigh what you say. That is all. Dismissed."

"Sir."

## 11:15 a.m. CEST / 5:15 a.m. EDT

### Space Force Command Centre - Ghost Shift

"I think we need to wake the commander." Technical Sergeant Harris shouts as she rises to her feet. The Space Fleet operation room was on night shift. With only two operators on duty, most of the key operations being monitored and controlled by an AI they knew only as H.E.L.I.X.

"Another Exajoule alert, Tina?" Technical Sergeant Bruce laughed as he walked over to his colleague.

"Laugh all you want, but I have registered weapons fire from orbit. Can you bring up the HelixStar network and triangulate the source?"

"I can't. HelixStar is still offline. The maintenance work is scheduled until eighteen hundred hours. I'll try CommSat and ESA." TS Bruce replied.

"The Chinese, are you mad?" TS Harris chided.

"Not a problem. When the commander gets here, I will let you explain. I'm going for a coffee." TS Bruce motioned for the exit door of the control room.

"Okay, Okay. Just do it. Please," TS Harris begged, grabbing her colleague's sleeve.

He returned to his station and pulled up a satellite override procedure. After a few moments of a graphic bouncing back and forth representing the satellite connection, a confirmation notification appeared.

"I am in. Bringing online CommSat, I also have ESA assets at my disposal. I am establishing an encrypted comm link, routing the signal via a Russian satellite. Good luck trying to identify the source, dear comrades. Uploading a triangulation algorithm."

"How long will it take?" TS Harris asks.

"Any second. Parsing the data packets. Decrypting. Hang on. This can't be right," TS Bruce gulped and, with a scared expression, turned to his colleague, "Call the commander. It was the Lincoln."

Reaching for her handset, TS Harris felt hesitant and pulled her arm back. "Are you sure that's wise? Maybe we should forget we ever saw anything. Your access can't be traced."

"What has you spooked? It was your idea." Rising to his feet and placing his hands behind his head, he asked, "Are you saying we should just sit on this?"

"Yes. Space fleet activity, especially weapons hot events, are above our clearance level."

"OK, I'll call." TS Bruce grabs his handset, puts it to his ear, and presses a speed dial button on the console. "The line is dead. Check yours."

TS Harris picks up her handset, confirming it is also dead.

Suddenly, the power to the control room shuts off, plunging the pair into darkness.

"I think we should leave." TS Harris suggests.

"For the first time, I think you are right." He replies.

The pair head to the exit, only to find the door is locked.

"This isn't right. In a power cut, the magnetic locks should release. We are trapped."

Unaware that the air in the room was being replaced by carbon dioxide, diverted from the fire suppression system and pumped in via the ventilation system. Within minutes, they would be dead on the floor.

*11:15 a.m. CEST / 5:15 a.m. EDT*

*Bare Mountain, Massachusetts*

"Sir, I think our systems have just experienced a glitch." The operator announces.

Agent Rodriguez was into the last hours of the night shift in the Bare Mountain Control Centre. It had been an uneventful night, except it hadn't been. He was unaware that the surveillance of the Newtons in Belgium had led to abject failure.

His last intel was that they were being followed by the two agents, Agent Dubois herself had informed directly him. He didn't want any drama, anything that would mean he would have to explain himself to Dr Kane.

Approaching the station operator, he glances toward their display, not noticing anything unusual. "What's up?"

"Sir. I received an energy notification. But only for a moment. I cannot confirm the intensity or exact source, but it was there." The operator explained nervously.

"Run a station diagnostic and check the event logs," Agent Rodriguez orders.

"Sir. If I may, I had a similar glitch." Another operator announces.

"Has anyone else had any glitches or noticed anything unusual?" The agent shouting across the control room.

126

Six operators staffed the control room, with Agent Rodriguez, the acting commander, during the night shift. Each operator reported back confirmation of a minor glitch. Describing either an alert notification or a dataset changing. Diagnostics yielded no system issues and the event logs were unchanged.

"I'll note it as a ghost in the machine and report it to Dr Kane when he gets here. Helix, report. What is the latest from Tom and Jerry?" The Agent made his way to the office.

"Tom has eyes on Jerry. They have reported that they are queued and ready to board the LeShuttle for Great Britain. I have mobilised Agents Webber and Nash to intercept on arrival." Helix replies.

"Compile a briefing for Dr Kane's arrival. That will be all for now." Agent Rodriguez removed his earpiece and placed it down. He sat back in the chair, placed his feet on the desk, and stretched before putting his hands behind his head. Within a few moments, he was asleep.

*12:30 p.m. BST / 7:30 a.m. EDT*

Dr Kane swiped the legs away from his desk, causing his colleague to wake and instinctively draw his sidearm.

"Good morning, sleepy head. Did I wake you up?" Dr Kane asks sarcastically.

"Sir. No, Sir. What time is it? I mean. Sorry." Agent Rodriguez stood, offering the chair to his superior.

"What is the situation in Belgium?" He asks, choosing to stand.

"I had Helix compile a report." He paused.

Dr Kane crossed his arms and raised his eyebrows. "Sir, I can see that may not be the best approach. Agents Dubois and Durand followed the Newtons to the LeShuttle, where they were observed boarding. Agents Webber and Nash, who were recalled from Japan, were instructed to intercept the pair once they arrived in the U.K. Dr Kane, we also experienced a minor systems glitch on all operators' terminals at approximately 05:15."

"What kind of glitch?" Dr Kane asked as he looked to the control centre.

"They report their monitoring systems temporarily displaying different datasets and or a temporary notification. Sir."

"Did you have Helix run a diagnostic?" Dr Kane looked sternly at the Agent.

"No, Sir. After our prior conversation, I thought it wise not to intervene in such matters involving our digital friend."

"Good. Have you heard from Webber and Nash?"

Agent Rodriguez hesitates, realising his dereliction of duty, picks up and positions his earpiece. "Helix, give me an update on Tom and Jerry. On speakers."

"Good morning, Dr Kane. LeShuttle departed at 11:32 a.m. Central European Summer Time, arriving in Folkestone at 12:07 p.m. British Summer Time. However, Agents Webber and Nash reported Jerry was not on board. I have been unable to contact Agents Dubois and Durand. On another note, I regret to inform you that an electrical safeguard alert was triggered in Space Force Operations overnight. The fire suppression system was activated. Unfortunately, Technical Sergeants Harris and Bruce succumbed to hypoxia."

"Fuck! This is not the start I need today. Has General Harris been informed of the death of his daughter?" Dr Kane turned, briefly looked at Agent Rodriguez and then back to the operations room. "Why is everyone so fucking incompetent?."

"Sir. General Harris has not been informed yet. There is still a communications outage with the space fleet. Did you want me to contact the General when comms are re-established?" Helix answers.

"No. It is probably best coming from General McAllister. I require you to run a comprehensive reference analysis of all feeds coming from France and Belgium, including biometric recognition algorithms, employing pattern-matching protocols. Flag all anomalies. Then cross-reference and verify them through the integrated intelligence network and Interpol. Let's leverage the geospatial intelligence to identify potential egress routes. Notify me the minute you locate them. And get Dubois and Durand back. That's an order, Helix."

"Very good. Sir."

Dr Kane and Agent Rodriguez leave the office and exit the control room.

"If you don't mind me saying, Sir. That was some word salad; what did any of it mean?"

Without warning, Dr Kane pulls Agent Rodriguez's sidearm, pinning him to the wall with his arm crossing his neck and pointing the gun at his head.

"Let's get this straight, I do not tolerate fuck ups. Last night was one fuck up after another. And I hold you accountable. That was a dereliction of duty soldier. If I ever find you asleep on the job again, I won't wake you; I'll pump lead into your brain, that's if you even have one. Understood?"

"Yes.Sir."

"Good. Quietly. Find out what Helix is up to. None of this makes any sense. Try to shut it out of the systems while you access them, and check the logs on the WORM server. Make a copy of anything interesting from the past week,"

Dr Kane waits for the Agent to leave before he collapses to the floor. His heart raced; he could feel the throbbing pulse in his temples. With each second, short gasping breaths escaped his lips as he struggled to maintain composure. The corridor spun as a wave of nausea overcame him. Unable to focus on any fixed point, he leaned over and vomited.

He portrayed himself as a tough military scientist, but the stress of his marriage breakup and difficult career was too much. He felt alone, caught in a fight, and did not know which way to turn or who to trust.

It took a couple of minutes to compose himself. He returned to his feet and then cleaned himself up. It was time to face up to the General.

Marcus Kane stood at the door of his superior's office. He had gone over in his mind many times how the conversation would play out. Step one was to enter, not to knock, just to enter. That would put him on the front foot and catch the General off guard.

He entered, expecting to be welcomed, but the room was empty. He pulled out his phone and accessed the general's shared diary; there were scheduled conference calls, but nothing that would explain why the always punctual director of G.A.R.D was absent.

Dr Kane felt a wave of relief, thankful he could postpone the conversation. He left the office and alerted Agents Smith, Patterson, and Rodriguez to meet him in the briefing suite at 08:30.

He had time to carry out another conversation he had been putting off. Exiting the elevator at sub-level 4, he proceeded straight to detention cell 17.

"Dr Kane. I thought I recognised your foul stench."

"Cute. You know who I am?" Dr Kane responded with a sneer.

"Your men, not that clever, like most jarheads," sneering back, she continues, "I suppose you haven't come to your senses and decided to release me, have you?"

"Dr Williams. I want to make you an offer. Tell me all you know about Theo Newton; then I will tell you what I have planned."

"You aren't that good at this, are you? Do you need to study some more on interrogation techniques before coming back?"

"Again, cute. Your mocking is just wasting time," he advances over to her, raising his arm, motioning for her neck "YOUR TIME." She cowers into the corner as he continues, "I apologise, please take a seat, we are both intelligent people, we should respect each other."

Slowly but nervously, Dr Williams returns to her feet and sits at the table.

"Thank you. Let me start again. An introduction, perhaps. I am Dr Marcus Kane; I have the military rank of Major General. I work for the US Government agency known as G.A.R.D., that is, the Genetic Anomaly Research Department. We are a subdivision of a unified department of surveillance, espionage, military and space. Everything that protects the United States, her people, interests and security.

Sometime ago, we became aware that humans were not the only intelligent life in the Universe. I won't bore you with the details, but we have some serious concerns. We studied the alien phenomena, even recovering some extragalactic spacecraft and their occupants. We studied them. Uncovering their plans and objectives. G.A.R.D was established to study them further."

"Thank you for the disclosure, but what does this have to do with me?" Dr Williams asks, yawning into her sleeve.

"We know you have close connections to the Newtons, we have been following you for some time; we know about Herbert J. Montclair and George Godfrey, and others."

Dr Williams looks directly at Dr Kane, not able to hide her fear and concern. He now had her attention.

"Godfrey is interesting. I could have him brought in, or you know what, I could have him arrested, tried and convicted of Treason. Do you know what the maximum sentence is for Treason?" He paused for dramatic effect. "Do you feel like talking now?" Pausing again. Staring intently at her, "If it helps with the persuasion, you should know the entire Judiciary of the United States is under our control."

"Okay," she shouts, "What do you want to know?" A tear rolled down her cheek; she couldn't protect the secret anymore. Her oath to *The Order* now replaced by her faith in Theo Newton.

"Where did Theo Newton go? What were the energy surges we detected? How does Newton connect to the creators?"

"Ok. Where do I start?" Tipping her head slightly to the right and the floor, she considers her words, "Theo Newton is *The One*. He is the return of Our Lord, our Saviour. The creators are the ancient gods. They brought life to our planet and created the human race. They seeded life all over the universe. But they have returned to us, for we have sinned; we have all sinned. Theo is going to rebalance our ways. Correct our mistakes and show the meaning of true love to those who have forsaken god." Her eyes were red, but her expression appeared convincing, her tone and body language displayed passion, and it was as if she was radiating peace and love.

Dr Kane felt compelled to believe her. Something about this woman was believable. It didn't take him long to compartmentalise her response and apply a rational scientific approach.

"Hang on. Do you expect me to believe that your little outfit is a bunch of religious crackpots? That Theo Newton is the Messiah?"

"All you have to believe is what you feel." She motions her arms across the table and points at his heart. "In your heart. In time, you will believe, when you witness the incredible gifts *The One* will bring to the world. You need to be open to him and believe in him. He will only give one chance to believe in him. Everyone only has one chance."

"And if I choose not to believe?"

She looks at Dr Kane directly in the eye and whispers, "The Rapture."

"Thank you. For now, you are staying here. I need to corroborate your story."

Dr Kane left the cell and went to the briefing suite, where Agents Smith and Patterson were already waiting.

"Sir. I need to speak with you in private." Agent Patterson, with a raised voice, announces on seeing Dr Kane enter.

"Not now. It will have to wait. Agent Rodriguez will be with us soon." Dr Kane responds.

"BUT SIR." Agent Patterson insisting.

"SIT DOWN SOLDIER." Dr Kane orders as he uses a tablet on the conference table, activating confidential mode. The sound of running motors confirms that the air ducts to the room are sealed. A small pump can be heard from a corner of the room, confirming that the independent tanks are circulating air. The omnidirectional microphones and conference cameras are disabled.

"Gentlemen, I require you to turn off your mobile devices and place them in the Faraday box." The agents comply.

The room is now isolated from any data breach. Marcus Kane spends the next few minutes discussing what Dr Williams revealed.

Not long into the briefing, Agent Rodriguez enters, sees the Faraday box on the table, and instinctively powers off his phone and places it inside.

"Thank you. I was discussing the conversation I had with Dr Williams. I will catch you up later. What I am about to confer with you all is to remain confidential and is not to be discussed with anyone not present here. No records, logs or encrypted communication is to be made regarding any aspect of this conversation, not even with a superior. You do not talk about this subject outside of this room unless you need to discuss it with me. In this case, you need to ensure absolute secrecy and take the same precautions. The code word is *cracker*. An example of how you could use the word would be, Sir, I heard a cracker earlier, in which case I will reply, 'I haven't the time' or 'not now.' However you feel comfortable, but ensure you don't use the word in the same context each time. At an appropriate time we will discuss your *cracker* moment. Understood?"

The agents respond, "Sir."

"Very good. I have a concern that Helix is not playing for our team. There have been several events now that make little sense." Smith, leaning forward, incredulous, "What events, sir?"

Marcus Kane sighs deeply. "This morning, there was an electrical fire detected at Space Force Operations. We lost two of the team after the fire suppression system was initiated. TS Harris was one of them."

There was a collective 'Shit' from Smith and Patterson.

"Investigations have confirmed that it was one of our missiles that took down flight GPA7, which resulted in the loss of Agents Carter and Jackson. We could not establish authorisation for the launch."

"You think it was Helix?" Agent Patterson asks with anger in his tone..

"Then, somehow, Agents Dubois and Durand drop off the scope; we haven't heard from them since. The last report we had was that they had eyes on Newton Senior and his wife boarding the train back to Great Britain. But they didn't disembark at the other end. Then we have mysterious communications blackouts, not only with our agents but throughout Space Force operations. So to answer your question, yes, I think it is Helix."

"Hangon, Sir, you said that Agent Durand and Dubois dropped of the scope; Do you not know they are dead?" Agent Patterson thumped the table and stood.

"What? Where did you hear that?" Dr Kane asks.

"My mam, sorry Colonel Patterson contacted me earlier. She had a command order; Hawkeye was Belguim. Tina was one of the targets. I thought you or the General gave the order?"

"Sir, with all respect, do you not think that there could be someone else, maybe in S.A.F.E., giving out orders without involving us?" Agent Smith suggests.

"I have considered that. But to what end? Why compartmentalise us? We aren't the CIA or NSA; we are above them. Agent Rodriguez, did you discover anything this morning?"

"Yes. Sir." He replied.

"Go on."

"Sir. I examined the logs. Everything checks out. There are entries with the correct time index stamps. The metadata also checks out. I ran a tamper algorithm; every single checksum confirmed the integrity of the logs. It was too perfect. When you confirm log entries for a period, let's say, a year ago, there will be minor irregularities in the data, a piece of code that is slightly corrupted or has an index code out of step with the timestamp. These errors occur in minor systems with no operational significance. The cyclic redundancy checks, while almost 100% accurate, do occasionally show a fine degree of error. This was a deliberate safeguard we installed into the system when Helix was brought online. But when we check the logs against the WORM server, we see log entries that do not exist in the primary servers."

"I am confused. If Helix is carrying out actions, is it not smart enough not to record those unsanctioned actions?" Patterson asks.

"When the Nexil offered us Helix, we took some preemptive safeguards, similar to Asimov's 'Three Laws of Robotics'; however, where the first law states a Robot may not injure a human or allow a human to come to harm, we couldn't operate with such restrictions. So we introduced our own laws. We incorporated them into firmware, so to speak; it's called the 'Guardian Protocol'. Helix is not aware, but every log entry is first written into the WORM server, then replicated to the main logs. The WORM server is critical to Helix's learning model."

"Gotcha. That's clever." Patterson responds.

135

"Do the logs confirm my suspicions?" Dr Kane asks.

"Yes, Sir. Regarding the missile, it was launched by the Lincoln, the logs of the launch were removed, and the missile inventory was adjusted to balance the books."

"Shit, this is bad. Helix is an existential threat. Rodriguez, quietly download the entire source code for Helix. Patterson, I am sorry for your loss. You will need to contact Colonel Patterson. I don't know how you can do it without our digital nemesis knowing, but do it. Smith, with me, I need to speak to the General. I have some concerns about him; something he said once is troubling me. Dismissed."

Unbeknownst to Dr Kane and his agents, hidden sensors within the room silently transmit every word back to Helix. The AI, now fully aware of the Major General's concerns.

# CHAPTER 11 THE NEXIL

## SEPTEMBER 18 2021

*2:30 p.m. BST - (British Summer Time)*

*9:30 a.m. EDT - (Eastern Daylight Time)*

*Moonbase Alpha, The Moon.*

The craft didn't bear any of the markings of other vessels in the United Space Fleet; its design was, in fact, completely different. As it descended, allowing for an unobstructed view of the undercarriage, it was obvious that it was completely void of any identification markings.

The outer hull was smooth, with no obvious panels, no rivets or seams. There were no landing lights, or for that matter, any lights on the vessel. It was absent of windows or any obvious means of propulsion. Its shape was an ellipse, although its height was half that of its width, more reminiscent of a sleek computer mouse. The hull didn't seem to stay one colour. It was slowly and continuously changing with a pearlescent sheen.

As General MacAllister stood on the hanger deck of Moonbase Alpha, he couldn't help feeling apprehensive. He had only met with the Emissary in a video conference and had never knowingly met a Nexil in person; however, integrated into human society they had become.

He found the Emissary to be cold, calculating, and ruthless. Lacking all the qualities that make humans human. And yet they appeared to be integrating well into the population. The rise of mental health and diagnosis of spectrum disorders masked their presence.

As the craft appeared to touchdown, a series of lights pulsed out of four points on its underside, holding it in position without physically landing on the deck. The lights pulsed with a steady stream of illuminated rings. The General approached one of the pulsing lights to have a closer look but found a force pushing him back; it wasn't any turbulence or air pressure that he was familiar with.

The General turned with a confused look on his face.

"Gravitational stabilisers. The Nexil utilise a technology that can warp space; it manipulates quantum fields sufficiently that its able to generate anti-gravity. Calibrated to have its centre of mass sufficiently so to be in equilibrium with its environment." Dr Simon Brandon announces, holding out a hand to greet MacAllister.

"They have shared this tech with us?" The General questions, unsure and still in awe of what he witnessed.

"Yes, my friend. Throughout our technology." He answered with a chuckle in his reply.

"And have you met our friends?" The General asks.

"Yes, frequently. Ah, watch this." Dr Brandon points to the craft.

A section of the hull turned opaque, then a door appeared as if the hull dissolved away, which was followed by a ramp appearing from the dissolved hull. A figure appeared at the entrance to the craft. Humanoid in appearance, standing 6 feet. From the distance the General was, he would have assumed they were human. But as they descended the ramp, he could see the facial features were less defined, as if they were human but had undergone several cosmetic procedures.

"Emissary. Welcome back to Moonbase Alpha. I trust you had a pleasant journey. May I present General MacAllister, with whom you are already acquainted." Dr Brandon bowed slightly as he put his arm towards the General.

"General MacAllister," The Emissary spoke, monotone, "if we could proceed with the arrangements."

138

"Of course, everyone is waiting. This way."

Two armed servicemen led the way from the hangar and into a service corridor. The walls are covered with polished metal panels that appear to glow as they are approached. The floor has an iridescence, which, with each step, responds with waves of light rippling out of the foot strike akin to a pebble skimming across calm water.

The service corridor exits onto a concourse. A bustling hub of mixed activities. Automated forklifts silently carry equipment and supplies, personnel hurried to and fro, conversations overlapping with the backdrop hum of the many fans pumping and purifying the air throughout the base.

From the vantage point of the concourse, the many levels of the base could be seen, each providing specific operational roles and services, all hidden from view to an outsider by the crater walls. Over ninety percent of the base was constructed from excavating into the lunar crust.

The delegation crossed the concourse and entered a corridor. The walls, floors and ceilings are one gigantic panoramic display showcasing video of Earth's varied landscapes: forests, mountains, oceans and urban city scapes.

Midway down the passage, a panel in the display switches from video to a doorway, then like the Nexil craft dissolves away to reveal the conference suite beyond.

The remaining members of SAFE, except David D. Bernstein, were waiting. They rose from their seats around the table. The three arrivals took their positions; the Emissary, taking the head position opposite a large display, sat. Only then did the remaining members of the committee sit.

The display flickered to reveal Bernstein on a video link.

"Welcome, everyone; I apologise for not being in attendance myself, but I have an appointment with the president. May I thank the Emissary for joining you all on this auspicious occasion." Mr Bernstein was upbeat, unlike the prior conference.

"The Nexil appreciate your magnanimous didactic reflection." The Emissary announced.

"Thank you. May we begin. General MacAllister. An update, please." Mr Bernstein requests.

"I am afraid the news isn't good. Since we last met, we have not moved forward with discovering where Theo Newton is. We unfortunately failed to successfully apprehend his parents. How they evaded capture, I will be honest, we are still trying to understand. Dr Kane will come through; I need more time."

The Emissary stands and walks to his left, stopping behind where General MacAllister sits. Remaining still, the general is frozen in place by some force acting upon him. The Nexil places his hand on the right cheek of the G.A.R.D chief. Tiny, needle-like tentacles emerge from the alien's hand and wrap their way around the head of the motionless man before piercing his skin and penetrating his brain.

The tentacles throb and pulse as they feast on the brain of the now-deceased general. A moment later, the Emissary steps back as it removes its grip. Without his muscles engaged, the body of the dead man slumps to the side. A shift in the weight distribution causes the chair to roll back suddenly on the smooth floor. The motion of the chair and the body's limp state leads to an inevitable loss of balance, and the corpse flops out of the chair onto the floor.

There is silence as the audience watch the events unfold. The Emissary returns to its seat as two cloaked Nexil enter the room, followed by a human male wearing a military uniform and holding the rank of general.

The Nexil place a device on the deceased's body before they and the corpse vanish.

"We all know the consequences of failure. General MacAllister knew better than anyone. General Harris, please take the vacant seat and welcome to G.A.R.D. I trust you will succeed where your predecessor failed." Mr Bernstein announced with no remorse.

"You have my unswerving commitment and dedication. The death of my daughter this morning strengthens my resolve to ensure a lasting cooperation between ourselves and the Nexil. To the concordat." General Harris announces without a flicker of emotion.

"Your continued service and loyalty are commendable. With your leadership and expertise, I expect we will quickly get back on track and move on to the next stage of our hegemony," Bernstein continued. "We are progressing well, with only minor setbacks. However, we need to get a handle on this issue with Newton. Can anyone provide any updates?" He looked around the conference table, staring at each person in turn. A real-time video feed tracked his eye movement, displaying what he was looking at. No one answered his question.

"Very well. General Harris, apart from the objectives you have agreed to in your role, this is now your primary responsibility." The General nodded in acceptance.

Bernstein continued, "Following on from the untimely departure of General Glen MacAllister, we need to recruit from within our ranks; after all, we now number one less General." Snorting a self-satisfying laugh, "Consult among yourselves after this meeting who you feel embodies all that we believe. Suitable candidates will be indoctrinated and sit the test."

"What about Dr Kane?" asks former Prime Minister MacTavish.

"Marcus Kane, while proving useful in some regards, doesn't share in all our objectives. Psychological profiling by Helix suggests that soon, he may become a liability. I feel Nexilination is in his future." Bernstein replied. "Let's move on," He continued. "We have some exciting projects I hope to share with you in the coming days; one we have code-named Operation Synapse is entering its final stages, while I cannot share with you all the details at this time, it will be the fundamental change that all of you, my friends, have hoped for, it will bring to fruition all our hopes of the Concordat. I would like to thank Dr Simons, Dr Swimmer and Dr Brandon for their dedication in seeing this project through."

The trio each graciously bowed their heads.

"The Nexil are satisfied with this outcome. We had doubts that Humans would be capable of such licentious acts, but you have served the terms of the Concordat well. As a gift to you, we will further share our technology, the Celestial Collector Array; this device will provide you with limitless clean energy. However, you will need to prepare for section epsilon of the Concordat. A fleet of Nexil has been despatched in readiness for this next stage." The Emissary announced.

"Your generosity honours us and we will begin section Epsilon immediately." Bernstein replied. "I spoke with the Nexil high council myself before this meeting. They have assured me that humanity's place amongst the stars will be welcomed. The Celestial Collector Array will catapult our species towards achieving a level two civilisation. It won't just be high schools and airports that are named after us."

In unison, everyone but the Emissary stood, clapping and cheering. Several members echoed shouts of 'Congratulations Mr President'.

"Thank you, thank you, now settle," Bernstein requested "Mr MacTavish, you and I had better inform our Governments and then the UN. What a time to be alive."

*21st August 2021*


*At a little over 4 light years distant from Earth, Proxima Centauri B was the jumping point for the Nexil fleet. While not capable of light speed, they could cross light years of space in a month, which would take humans decades.*

142

The Nexil's fleet begins, ship by ship, to break the orbit of Proxima Centauri B. The sleek, flattened ellipse-shaped craft, had the same design as the one the Emissary arrived at Moonbase Alpha in, but with one significant difference: while the Emissary's ship was a four-person scout vessel, the fleet could carry millions of Nexil in their city-sized ships.

Numbering in the thousands, they glinted in the light of Proxima Centauri. Each vessel equipped with all Nexil technology. Orbiting the star are thousands of celestial collector arrays. Each made from a framework of photon focusing sheets. The intense rays are collected at a single point, where a series of apertures controls the flow of the intense energy through an artificially created wormhole linking to the engine bay of a ship in the fleet.

On the bridge of the lead ship, Nexil commanders methodically oversee final preparations. Their eyes, lacking emotion, flicker across holographic displays showing their projected trajectory to Earth, fuel and power levels of the photon tunnel drive, and the activation status of the Alcubierre drives.

"Initiate phase one," a Nexil officer commands in their guttural voice.

In synchronised unison, the vessels accelerate. The ion thrusters flare with a brilliant blue light, propelling them toward a target velocity of 29.36% of the speed of light. The acceleration of phase one would take fifteen days; only then would they have enough relativistic mass to commence phase two.

Several of the Nexil craft fail to ignite their engines. Without warning and unable to redirect the flow of energy, they spectacularly explode, sending debris in all directions. Several more are destroyed during acceleration as their forward defence grid develop relay failures, allowing varying-sized pieces of interstellar detritus to punch holes through the sanctuary of the habitat.

5th September 2021

*As the fleet reaches critical speed, the Alcubierre drives engage, warping space-time around each vessel. A shimmering distortion envelops each ship. They vanish from sight, propelled through the fabric of space in an instant.*

*As if to materialise from nowhere, the fleet, one by one, emerged close to the dwarf planet Pluto within the Sol system. The distant sun, too far away to cast even a faint glow on their sleek hulls, as they begin their approach.*

*The commanders issue new orders, and phase three begins. The ships adjust their heading, swinging around Pluto, aiming directly for Saturn. The massive planet obscures Earth's view of the approaching armada.*

*Once close enough to Saturn, they employ gravitational assist to reduce their speed before repeating the procedure around Jupiter.*

*Their powerful engines reversing thrust for the rest of the journey. In a carefully orchestrated manoeuvre, the fleet slows from almost a third of light speed, taking a little under 15 days to achieve a stable velocity, aligning for the final leg of the journey toward Earth. The Nexil would arrive sooner than expected.*

# CHAPTER 12 UNCOVER

## SEPTEMBER 19 2021

*12:30 p.m. BST - (British Summer Time)*

*07:30 a.m. EDT - (Eastern Daylight Time)*

*Bare Mountain, Massachusetts.*


**"**How can't you reach General MacAllister?" Dr Kane shouted back at the increasingly incapable AI. Pulling out his earpiece, he flung it onto his desk.

He sought answers. The unknown location of his superior only heightened his stress levels in attempting to find any member of the Newton family.

Entering the General's office, an unexpected visitor greeted him. Sitting behind MacAllister's desk was General Harris.

"Sir, I apologise. I hadn't been informed you were on site. Are you here for an inspection?"

"At ease, Dr Kane. No, nothing so formal. How are you keeping Marcus? You well?" The General was looking his new deputy straight in the eye with a manic and rather unsettling expression.

"I am well, Sir. Are you alright? Do you need me to get you anything?" He momentarily pauses, expecting a response. "I am so sorry for your loss. I heard about Tina."

"Cut the chat, Major General. Surprised?" He paused for a moment. As Dr Kane was about to speak, he continued, "I thought you'd be used to surprises by now, given your track record."

Dr Kane, still standing, shifts uncomfortably, sensing the underlying tension. *'What is his problem?'* He thought, trying to scramble some cohesive sentence together.

"Yes, well…erm. I was just about to inform the General on the progress of the latest objective. We have some promising results that.."

Cutting him off mid-sentence, the General raises his voice, "Save it. I'm well aware of the promising results. And I'm also aware of the failures. My predecessor paid the price for them, didn't he?" The General still staring Dr Kane dead in the eye.

His face pales as he realises the General knows more than he expected.

"General, I assure you, we're doing everything possible to find Newton. The circumstances were beyond our control."

"Circumstances. Funny how that word keeps coming up. My daughter, a technical sergeant, died under mysterious circumstances. Now I'm here, and I'll be watching every move you make, every decision. There will be no more failures. Do I make myself clear?" General Harris said with a veiled threat.

Dr Kane swallows hard, nodding. "Crystal clear, General. We will not disappoint. Sir, may I ask where General MacAllister is?"

"See that you don't. The consequences are… severe. Dismissed."

The General's icy stare seems to penetrate Dr Kane even after he turns towards the door.

"And Dr Kane, Glen MacAllister is dead. His cause of death, incompetence." Dr Kane's face drains of blood. He turns, briefly glancing back at his new commander, who was still glaring, but ever so slowly, a smile forms.

'Who is this man? He isn't the General I remember,' Dr Kane thinks as he closes the door behind him and leans against the cold concrete wall of the underground base. 'Has the loss of his daughter had a profound impact on him? Does he blame me somehow? What does he know that I don't?'

Returning to his office, he picks up the earpiece from his desk and inserts it. "Helix, an announcement to all senior staff, compulsory conference in 5 minutes, attendance in briefing suite Charlie."

"Certainly, Dr Kane. The General has put a do not disturb instruction in place; he will not be in attendance."

Removing the earpiece, he drops it back on his desk and heads to the meeting.

Upon arrival, several agents, senior researchers, and technical staff were already present. He kept his head low, avoiding eye contact and conversation with anyone. He made his way to the front of the room and to the lectern. There, he signed into the computer and called up analytical and statistical probability studies of Theo Newton's behaviour.

While more people entered, filling up the 50-capacity room, he studied the most recent tactical information provided by H.E.L.I.X.

Finally, he looked up. Bare Mountain's most senior staff across all disciplines almost filled five rows of ten seats, from contractors and scientists to military and security agency staff.

Pinning a wireless microphone to his shirt, he spoke.

"Thank you all for being here. I will be blunt. If you don't feel comfortable right now, that feeling is only going to get worse; you may even lose control and defecate and or vomit. If this sounds like you, I suggest you get up and leave, which I will take as you handing in your resignation. If you stay and you defecate and or vomit, I will take that as you not having the guts to do your job, and you will be let go. So make your choice now. We do not have time, nor is this the environment to mollycoddle and talk about feelings.

We are a United States Government department; you are the elite **FROM** the elite. Wokeness, duvet days, headaches, everyone is a winner mentality will not cut it here. Do you understand?"

Those from the military, in unison, respond 'Sir, Yes, Sir' while the civilian employees turn to one another, concerned and scared, displaying looks of shock. But no one stands.

Dr Kane scans the room, targeting specific faces from the Scientific and engineering faculties. After several seconds of silence, he continues.

"Thank you. Firstly, we have a new commander. General Harris, whom many of you will have met on his inspection tours. He replaced General MacAllister, who was executed for failure to do his job to the standards expected of him. Let this be a warning to all of you, myself included, as his deputy."

Gasps and screams came from the body of personnel. One individual continued screaming uncontrollably. Dr Kane looked at Agent Rodriguez, who nodded, stood and walked around the now-silent audience, except for the continued screams from the person in question.

The screaming only stopped when Rodriguez took hold of their arm from under their armpit, motioning for them to stand. Complying, he walked them towards the door, but before reaching the exit, the agent pulled out his pistol, despatching a bullet into their head.

"Oh and screaming. I forgot to mention that. My bad." Dr Kane added.

The audience remained silent; several individuals did their best to hold their composure. The only visible response to the trauma that they had witnessed was their tears.

"ANYONE ELSE?" Dr Kane shouts, once again glancing around the room, targeting specific individuals.

After a moment, he composes himself as he continues, "I have to admit, hearing of the late General's death hit me hard. But I dusted myself off and returned to my duties. General Harris's daughter died yesterday morning, yet here he is today in a new post. Is he moping around? Is he dwelling on the death of his only child? Is he pondering why? NO! HE IS AT WORK CARRYING OUT HIS PATRIOTIC DUTY." Dr Kane was red in the face; his mouth was foaming, his posture tense, his fingers gripped the lectern's sharp metal edges. Blood pooled and then dripped down the sides.

"Let us move on. We have many mission objectives here at G.A.R.D. Our primary goal, as you will all know, is to discover creatures. Things that do not fit. To identify anomalous varieties of all manner of living things. To capture them so that they can be studied. Establish how they came to be, what makes them different, where they came from, can we benefit from them, are they a threat. You get the picture. Of course you do, you do it day in and day out. And of course, sometimes, as you have seen, the gentle approach doesn't always yield the efficient results we demand. And so we are also a strategic defence and surveillance operation. We come across an unknown 'thing' and identify it as being a real and credible risk to the security of our great country. But despite our invitations to a tea party and a chat, it declines. So we do our thing."

Several Agents shout 'Huah' in response and clap.

Dr Kane, chest pumps and salutes in response, then continues.

"I am a scientist and soldier, so I understand both sides of this mission statement. However, something is evading us. Something that does not fit. I am talking about Theo Newton."

Gasps and uncertain murmurs come from the audience.

"Yes. You may be quite right to wonder. Some of you may not be familiar with the name. Some of you will know who he is. So, let me clarify. Theo Newton, for the most part, appears to be a very talented British athlete, son of a Jamaican and daughter of a.." He momentarily pauses, choosing his words carefully, "how should I put this? A person not of colour.

He had a tough start to life, but this did not delay his development. In fact, what to a lot of children would be a hindrance, he thrived. He has intelligence beyond his years, surpassing every milestone. At a young age, he was taller than he should be. Physically more capable than he should be.

Only a couple of months ago, he obliterated not one, not two, not even three athletic world records. No, he went so far beyond that he broke five world records. Now, in itself, that isn't necessarily an unusual thing. It is the manner and the events in which he did it. One of them makes him the fastest man ever. Additionally, he achieved world record reaction times TWICE.

Plug this information into our systems and it spits out a question about who this man is. But this is not the complete story. Roll back several years. We detect an energy signature on Hampstead Heath in London. We investigate and discover some interesting readings. Then, roll forward to last month. Again, another energy reading is detected in London, England. And finally, only a few days ago, we got a doozy: over an exajoule energy reading is investigated.

So we investigate. We..." Dr Kane raises his finger to his lips and makes a 'Shhhhhhh' sound as he winks. "Chat to some folk, god bless their souls. Good upstanding, well not so good or upstanding as it turns out, but American folk. And guess what links these events?" Dr Kane stops and points his finger at a twenty-something-year-old male wearing a laboratory coat, sitting in the front row, "You? What do you think links all of the events?"

"Sir, Theo Newton?" The young scientist nervously answers.

"Ding-Ding-Ding-Ding. We have a winner. THEO NEWTON. Alas, young Theo eludes us. We have details of 'him' or someone who looks like him in Montana just days ago. And then he shows up in Tokyo, Japan. But once again, he evades us. He has been seen in London. He was even on board flight GPA7, which mysteriously crashed. We don't take credit for that one. We lost two of our family in the accident.

So, where is Theo Newton? His father appears to have his son's talents, in so much as he is evading our capture, his current whereabouts are unknown. He was last reported boarding 'Le

Shuttle' in France. But soon after we lose another two members of our family.

I am positive Newton did not perish in the airline crash. We need to find him and any member of his family.

So this is what we are going to do. Tech guys, I am talking to you now. Write an app. Members of the public are going to assist us by uploading and sharing information, videos, photos, and anything they may have about where the Newtons have been seen.

We are going to start a public campaign utilising police and security services globally; the media will be our conduit, and to incentivise the public, we will provide a reward. The Newtons are now the most wanted people on Earth. They will not be able to go anywhere; they cannot remain hidden forever.

You have until lunchtime to compile and test the app. Scientists, I need you to re-analyse each energy encounter. Find any patterns, distortions, anomalies, or whatever we could have missed. You need to rerun the numbers.

Agents, stay here, everyone else is dismissed. DO NOT FAIL."

The speaker gives way to a buzz of chatter, chairs scraping across the floor, and the shuffling of feet as personnel quickly try to exit the room while also avoiding standing in the pool of blood that had collected near the door.

The six agents who had remained moved to the front row.

"Thank you for staying behind. I need you to pair up.

Rodriquez and Atkinson, I want you to take the lead on disseminating the information to our agents in the field.

Patterson and Barnes, you are to co-ordinate with our home-based assets and our partners in the UK, Europe and Japan. Get the word out about Newton, make him the most wanted.

Smith and Harrison, I need for you to go to the archive, see if you can find anything that could connect Newton. Any species, any technology, anytime in history. Since H.E.L.I.X cannot access the archive, you will need to do it the old-fashioned way.

This instruction goes to all of you. Do not use Helix for anything that could show our hand. Get creative if you have to. This means lo-tech or no-tech. Think of H.E.L.I.X as a double agent. Contacting overseas using your mobile or email is acceptable, but be careful. Got it?"

*5:30 p.m. BST / 12:30 p.m. EDT*

Leaning back in his chair, hands on his head, Marcus Kane waited for what felt like an eternity.

He was working in a laboratory on sub-level two. Several other technicians were in the room carrying out their duties, trying their best to ignore him, even to make eye contact. The events of the morning were still fresh in their mind. His reputation as a volatile leader could not have been more clear.

Wanting to review the data collected from the Montana field himself. His distrust of H.E.L.I.X led him to suspect that it could have manipulated the recordings, altered the images, and falsified the analysis.

Thankfully, the original data drives had not been erased. The protocol ensured so much. The corruption failsafe during upload meant that the H.E.L.I.X system could not implement a delete of the original data. It was one of a few standard operating procedures that only a human could carry out.

To further eliminate his AI nemesis from interfering, Dr Kane used an older supercomputer to carry out the analysis. There was no Wi-Fi, Bluetooth or Ethernet connections. It was a completely disconnected system. If H.E.L.I.X wanted to stop him, it could cut the power to the room, revealing its intentions. Without realising it, Dr Kane was now playing a game of chess with the artificial intelligence.

As he waited for the computational analysis to complete, he was relieved to be interrupted by Agent Patterson.

"Sir, a couple of updates for you. Firstly, we have issued a wanted profile for Newton across Federal and local police nationwide. The Metropolitan Police will be will distribute throughout Great Britain and Interpol in Europe. Secondly, we have a positive ident for Newton. We tracked a cash withdrawal at an ATM on the Isle of Wight from an account in the name of Theodore Newton, his father."

Dr Kane launched himself out of his chair, thrusting it backward and crashing into a laboratory technician.

"Excellent, have you analysed the CCTV footage?" he asks excitedly.

"Better than that, Sir. We cracked the bank's system at the ATM video feed, it was Theo Newton. I have begun facial recognition of all points of entry and exit to the island. Unfortunately, because of the urgency, I have resorted to using our friend."

"WAIT!" Kane hesitated, his temples began to spasm, and his eyelids twitched. Vigorously, he rubbed his face, his attempt to stop the involuntary actions. Agent Patterson watching, as his superior tried to process the news.

*'What is up with his face?'* Patterson thought *'Is he loosing it?'*

"Newton is alive?" Kane asks, giving up on stopping his tic.

"Yes, Sir."

"This supports our understanding that he is the entity we believe arrived in Montana," thrusting his fist into the air as if celebrating his team scoring a touchdown,

"Well done Agent Patterson, you were right to use all available tools. Update the Metropolitan Police, inform MI5 and MI6, I never know which is which. We need to activate all our assets. Drone and orbital surveillance." Dr Kane was foaming at the mouth and visibly flushed with excitement.

"Sir, I already have."

"Excellent." Dr Kane motioned towards his colleague, who, concerned, took a step back, only to be uncharacteristically and unexpectedly embraced by his superior. "Let's get to control."

Draping his arm across his subordinate's shoulder, he shouted an order at the closest technician to monitor the supercomputer and inform him when the results were ready.

The control room was buzzing with activity. The speech given by Dr Kane that morning appeared to have resonated with the personnel. One technical sergeant, observing his superiors entering, stood and shouted, "Major General in the control room." then saluted.

"As you were, Technical Sergeant Michaels," Agent Patterson saluted back, turning to Dr Kane, "The personnel have been impressive this morning."

Before the pair had made it to the office, a shout came from across the control room.

"Sir, we have had several ident matches." An operator frantically waved his arms, tying to be spotted amongst the busy control room.

Several positive facial recognition matches placed Theodore and Louise Newton boarding the overnight Amsterdam ferry, then disembarking at the Newcastle terminal. This then led to video footage of the pair departing in a vehicle that matched the one they were last seen using, however, the vehicle registration plate did not match.

After making adjustments to the automatic number plate recognition search, positive matches were immediate. They tracked the vehicle heading from north-east England in a generally southern direction before changing direction and heading west. Then a series of video frame were identified, that questioned the footage from the Isle of Wight.

"How can Theo Newton be in the car a couple of hours before being seen on the Isle of Wight?" Agent Patterson asked.

"That is an excellent point. One that conventional understanding can not answer," Turning, he ruffles the hair of the Technical Sergeant, "Brilliant work TS Allan".

In his office, Dr Kane reluctantly calls into service H.E.L.I.X to perform a detailed analysis of the new data.

The sentient artificial intelligence operated on a qutrits, a ternary quantum computing system. A theoretical advancement of quantum computers, that was, until the Nexil gifted it to S.A.F.E.

H.E.L.I.X was one of a kind on earth. It could perform a calculation in under a second, that would take a standard quantum computer 200 seconds and a regular supercomputer 10,000 years. No one understood the operating system's code. Even the many agencies and best specialists that were integrated into the shadow government of S.A.F.E.

It was a polyglot of the digital world. H.E.L.I.X could translate instructions into any language a programmer could understand, computer or human. Providing the ability to decipher, encrypt, decrypt, translate anything presented to it.

Within seconds, the extensive results were displayed.

"Helix, can you please narrate your findings." Dr Kane asks.

"Of course Dr Kane. Facial recognition identifies a 99.9% match for the individual in Yorkshire, England and Ventnor, Isle of Wight. Facial mapping suggests with a 99.9% probability that both individuals are Theo Newton. However, either could be a doppelganger; either a genetic clone or surgically altered individual.

However, including footage from Japan and London, this probability increases to a 100% match for Theo Newton and the likelihood of a clone drops to 40%.

This therefore discounts camouflage or holography systems being employed to give false evidence."

"H.E.L.I.X, can you please explain to me how he can have been in these disparate places within a short time frame and save me the long answer." Dr Kane interrupted without his usual anger.

"I am sorry Marcus, certainly. Teleportation, time manipulation or quantum tunnelling. But I also have a fourth possibility, which combines all these suggestions, Superhuman abilities."

Agent Patterson's jaw dropped, looking directly at his superior, who was equally confused.

"Say that again?" Dr Kane asks.

"Which bit are you referring?" The AI replies.

"The bit about you thinking Theo Newton has Superhuman abilities?"

"Of course. The only explanation for our observations is that Theo Newton has Superhuman abilities. He was observed onboard flight GPA7 which was destroyed, however he survived. Then he is witnessed in London not long after the crash. Followed by being in two distant places within hours of each other. While technology could have assisted him, I have not found evidence for the detection of any known quantum fields in proximity to these locations. My conclusion remains the only plausible one."

"Superhuman?" Turning to Agent Patterson, "Any thoughts how we can take down a Superhuman? Did you take supervillain 101 in military school?" Agent Patterson couldn't speak, just replying with a brief head shake, "Me neither."

"I have scheduled an immediate briefing with General Harris in the strategy room. Recommend we initiate full lockdown state Q1." Helix announces unexpectedly.

Dr Kane looks at the still bemused Agent and motions with a slight nod towards the door.

Once in the corridor beyond the control room, the pair stop, certain they were away from the ever-eavesdropping H.E.L.I.X

"I think our guest in the cell block wasn't lying when she said he was the second coming. But I suspect she also missed out a few details. We need to be ready, against both Newton and the Nexil."

"Sir, If I may speak freely?" Agen Patterson asks.

"Of course, what's on your mind?" asked Dr Kane, placing a hand on his colleague's shoulder.

"If Theo Newton is, and I can't believe I am saying this, Superhuman and as you suspect, the Nexil are deceiving us. Then who is our enemy? And can we fight both and win?"

"Our enemy is everyone who does not believe in the United States of America, who doesn't help make it a better place tomorrow than it was today. As for fighting them both, I am hoping we won't need to if they fight each other."

"Ha, yeah, let's hope they do that." Agent Patterson replied.

"I will meet you in the Strategy Room, I have something to take care of first. Dismissed."

*6:23 p.m. BST / 1:23 p.m. EDT*

They rarely used the strategy room, typically only for drills. And it was less a room and more of a self-contained survival bunker below sub-level 4, deep under Bare Mountain.

Housing all the facilities needed for an extended period of isolation. Intended as a facility for a quarantine level-one event, the most severe on the G.A.R.D risk ladder.

It utilised a sophisticated air recycling and purification system with ultra-violet bio-cleaning, independent from the outside world. Generated power from geothermal energy and drew water directly from a pure aquifer.

Housing dormitories, a gym, a galley and mess hall, an independent computer suite utilising satellite communications. And featuring a weapons hall with a mini firing range. It was ultra modern and more sophisticated than any other equivalent facility in the US infrastructure.

Hardened to withstand all but a direct meteor impact, it could sustain a team of twenty for two years.

At the heart of the bunker was the 'Tactical, Strategic and Survival Room' or 'TSSR'. The staff preferred 'Strategy Room' as the abbreviation triggered memories of the cold war.

Dr Kane entered the bunker and registered his biometrics at the security panel. As the last person to enter, the large security door behind him slowly closed, eventually locking with a comforting sound of the pistons pushing the securing rods in place.

He made his way to the strategy room, where he was greeted by only some of his team; three agents, four technicians, six scientists, two medical personnel, and General Harris all sat around a large conference table.

The rest of the personnel staying in the Bare Mountain facility above them to continue to carry out their work or business as usual.

"I am glad you saw fit to join us, Dr Kane. Now if it pleases you, take a seat." The General was not hiding his dislike for his deputy. His stare penetrated his deputy. If they were alone, more than a few choice words would have been shared, that most likely would have resulted in a court martial for striking a superior.

Pulling back his chair, Marcus replies, "Sorry, General, sir. I had to take..." unable to finish as he is interrupted.

"I DO NOT CARE, to hear why you did not come directly to the TSSR. Shut up and conform to the military chain of hierarchical command."

"Sir." He replies, but concern dominates his thoughts.

'What is his problem? Have I done something? Does he think he knows something? Does he blame me for his daughter? Can I trust him?'

"Under advisement from H.E.L.I.X, we have commenced the Q1 protocol. Analysis has determined that we believe Theo Newton is a weapon. Put here by an interstellar civilisation which we only know as 'The Creators'. Our allies, the Nexil, have encountered these creators on many occasions. They inform us they are not to be trusted, they cannot be reasoned with, nor can we guarantee they do not have hostile intentions for our planet or our species. As such, as of this moment, we are in a de facto state of war with the entity known as Theo Newton and the Creators.

The board of H.O.U.S.E are currently advising the President. Following which they will action DEFCON One protocol and evacuate to their bunkers.

All our military assets are in a full state of readiness. The space fleet has been ordered into defensive positions around Earth.

The HelixStar network, which is once again fully operational, has deployed its weapon capabilities and has moved into its 'Sensen-no-sen' configuration.

We do not know exactly what we are dealing with. The 'Entity' has abilities beyond that of a human. Like the 'Creators,' we cannot assume we can reason with it; therefore, a Sensen-no-sen posture is the most appropriate strategy now. We anticipate an attack, then we attack first. The Nexil are sending their fleet to us as I speak. However, it will not be with us for several days. For the moment, this is down to us. Now, Dr Kane, where are we with our media coverage?"

The General spoke with a composed and controlled voice, almost as if what he was saying was rehearsed. As a military leader, this was his time to shine. The years of training, exposure to different combat roles, leadership development and honing his craft culminate in this moment.

"General, Sir. We have media interventions across the homeland, the U.K., Europe and Japan. We have circulated still and video imagery and co-operation is established with the legal and policing authorities in each region. We have reiterated that 'Newton', sorry the 'Entity' is a threat and priority above all other."

"Very good," General Harris responds while clicking the pen he was holding in his right hand. "Do we have a plan to flush the entity out? And do we have an idea where he could be?"

"Sir. Based on probability calculations provided by Helix, he is in or around London or he is with or about to contact the girl in Japan." Agent Patterson answered, reading from a tablet.

"The girl,.." General Harris pauses, putting on his reading glasses and taps his tablet, quickly reviewing the information before him, "She is Mei Lin Song, A Japanese-Korean, director of communication for the Tokyo Athletics Games Committee. Is she a love interest of the entity?"

"Yes, we believe so." Dr Kane replies.

"Do we have assets in Japan? The General asks without looking up.

"Yes, Sir." Dr Kane answers,

"And do we know where the girl is?"

"We have no intel. With the entity's help, she appears to have dropped off the grid. Analysis of all data feeds has not yet revealed where she is."

"And this roommate. Imi, have we followed up on her? I see here she works at The Royal SkyTree Hotel, where they were last seen?" The General asks, looking up over the bridge of his eyewear.

"The calculations from Helix suggested a very low probability that Emi, Sir, would have been involved beyond the sighting at the hotel." Agent Patterson once again offering a response.

"Yes, Emi. I see." The General looked down at his screen for a couple of minutes. At one point, he took off his glasses, holding an arm of the frame in his mouth while he pondered. After a sigh, he folded the glasses and carefully placed them on the table before continuing.

"Your statement does not align with the security overview. Helix, can you please give me a concise review regarding the current known whereabouts of Mei Lin and Emi."

"Certainly General, Sir. My analysis of data feeds together with optimal transit routes gives a 99% certainty that both are currently to be found at Emi's family abode in Kyoto."

"Can anyone care to explain this discrepancy in our analysis?" The General began rhythmically tapping on the table. Dr Kane turned to Agent Patterson, then Agent Rodriguez, then Agent Smith, each returning unsure responses.

"Sir, I have a potential explanation. But I must air on the side of caution, this is not the place to discuss it." Dr Kane finally answers.

The General shot upright out of his chair,

"THAT IS NOT YOUR DECISION MAJOR GENERAL. Last time I checked, I was the senior ranking member of this outfit. If you have any intelligence to share. You damn well share it. That is an order."

"With all due respect, General. You will not like my response, it's a cracker. And I will go further to say my response will put all our lives in jeopardy. So respectfully, Sir. I decline." Dr Kane rose out of his chair and stood facing off against his superior, the table refereeing what could inevitably result in a court martial.

"Agent Patterson. I hereby authorise you to carry out order 10 of modified article 91 of the Uniform Code of Military Justice in a wartime theatre setting. Take him into the side room."

Agent Patterson stood, grabbed Dr Kane's arm, who resisted. Agent Patterson shouted for assistance from Agent Rodriguez, who stood and grabbed the other arm.

"No, don't do this. You need me." His cries ignored by those still seated at the table. Marcus Kane continued to resist, eventually getting his arm free. He stretched for the closest sidearm, but his attempts were in vain. Agent Smith, now involved, swept the legs away from his superior, who crashed to the floor.

The three agents working as a team dragged the screaming man into the side room, closing the door behind.

"Craig. No. I am your friend. Please No." A single gunshot echoed from the room. Moments later, the three agents emerged, heads held low.

"I think we need to take a quick recess. Meet back in fifteen minutes."

The agents stood leaning against the wall as the fifteen witnesses and General Harris exited the room.

*6:30 p.m. BST / 1:30 p.m. EDT*

"The President will see you know President Bernstein, Sir." Rising from his chair, David D. Bernstein followed his guide down the White House corridor to the Oval Office. Very little had changed since his time there. It had been freshened up with paint; the curtains had been replaced, and so too had the personnel, but it still seemed familiar, as if it were yesterday.

Entering the famous office of the POTUS, the Chief of Staff, Stephanie Young, greeted him. He remembered her as a keen and dynamic campaign manager in the late 1990s and early 2000s. However, he would never have appointed her, having polar political allegiances. However, he admired and respected her as an excellent adviser.

Already in the room and waiting on the sofa was Admiral Bernard Gibson, a close friend of the President, but a closer ally to Bernstein as a member of the secretive S.A.F..E board.

"President Blackstone will be with you momentarily. If you would like to take a seat, Sir."

Bernstein sat opposite the Admiral. He took a quick look over his shoulder, catching the chief leaving the office.

"Bernard, are you prepared?" Bernstein asked, a smile stretching as far as he could manage.

162

"We have been preparing for nearly two decades, David. I am ready. The world will be caught off guard by our announcement."

At that moment, the President arrived with his top advisors: the Chiefs of Staff, the FBI and CIA Directors, the Secretary of Defence, and the National Security Advisor.

"David, It is so good to see you again. You are looking well, how old are you now?" President Blackstone asked bluntly. That was his style. He didn't have time for convention or protocol. He did things his way. Wanting to get things done, act now, and think about the consequences later. It was an approach that won over the voters; his campaign slogan, *'The World Runs on America.'* hit a chord which handed him his landslide victory.

"I'll be 82 next month."

"My god, I swear you don't look at day over 60. When this meeting is over, I'm having your secret."

"You may not even have to wait that long, Mr President." Handing him a container labelled 'Vitrastatis'.

"Is this it? A pill, well, well, The elixir of youth. I can't thank you enough. I'll run it by my physician." He extended his hand in thanks, then took the head seat between the two sofas.

"So what do you have for me David, what is all this about?" The President asked.

"What is your ultimate desire for the United States? Or rather, to rephrase, What would you like your legacy for the United States to be?" Berstein asks.

"Now, David, You do know I want to run for another term?" The group of men and the single woman laugh at the response. "That is a significant question. As you know, I have reformed aspects of our healthcare system, giving pharmaceuticals greater freedom to develop and test new treatments. With that freedom, they can compete against the Chinese, make more profit, and so ensure our nation remains at the peak of excellence. But looking at your face,

I feel that doesn't quite cut it for you. Tell me, David, what will be my legacy?"

"How should I put this? You mention the Chinese. The burden of environment, safety, or working rights and laws do not hold them back. Hell, they can't give a rat's ass about those things. Over successive years, we have pandered to people's rights: the right to healthcare, the right to social security, the right to take a vacation, and a goddamn safe work environment. Do you know what these rights have done?" Pausing briefly, he looks around the room. "They stop us from being better than everyone else, from being productive and staying great."

"Without mechanisms to keep people happy, there will be anarchy. Are you saying we should become commie?" The President questions.

"What if I told you there was a middle ground? Albeit a radical, an extreme middle ground. Imagine a society where people would go to work, be productive, be committed, be accurate and yet still receive a great salary, healthcare and even a family vacation. A package that offers more than they get today."

"I would say sign me up." The President and his advisers laugh,. "But David, there is no such system. Humans are fallible and lazy. We humans want to take shortcuts."

"That is what I am offering, a shortcut. But I have more." Bernstein looked at the Director of the FBI.

"Bill, What if I told you I could provide a surveillance solution to provide your department with evidence to every crime?" Snorts of derision come from the listening group.

"The evidence will come so quickly and in a form that, in any court, would be beyond reasonable doubt. Evidence so compelling that once news of it becomes public, crime rates will disappear and there will no longer be any serious crime?"

"David, It sounds to me like you want to put law enforcement out of a job. What the hell are you talking about?" The Director turns to his opposite number, the Director of the CIA. "Do you know anything about this?"

"If his team have developed some new tech, it's news to me. I figured HelixStar was an advancement. David, what are you smoking?" John Spiggot, Director of the CIA, asks.

"And to all of you. Not only crime but imagine a weapon so powerful. So utterly terrifying there would be no more wars." President Bernstein looks at Admiral Gibson, who nods.

"As amazing as all of this sounds. What he says is true. I can vouch for him and the technology that has been developed. I have seen it, and it is a game-changer for our species."

"Hang on," The President begins, "Bernard, You have seen this technology?"

He leans forward from the sofa and, with a clear and confident voice, responds, "I have, Mr President, Sir."

"And this tech, it doesn't violate any freedoms? Does it still uphold the Constitution?" President Blackstone directing his question to Admiral Bernard Gibson.

"Sir, I think at this juncture you would very much benefit from a demonstration."

The Secretary of Defence interjects, "The Admiral is correct. A demonstration would be prudent. When can it be arranged?"

"Tomorrow morning, if that is not too soon?" President Bernstein suggests.

"The President has a meeting with the Prime Minister of the United Kingdom at 9 am. He isn't likely to be available. How about overmorrow?" Chief of Staff Young points out.

"That is perfect. Why not include Prime Minister Barnstaple? It will strengthen your strategic alliance. If you need any other motivating factor, consider how many trillions of dollars you will save our economy. Besides, there is something else you will need to discuss with him." Bernstein's eyes light up, and his expression changes to almost manic.

"Something else?" The President, now looking confused, asks.

"As you are all well aware, the Strategic & Advanced Federation of Enforcement has oversight of all of our security and military services. While we try not to interfere in the way you run your departments." Bernstein is now directing his attention to the security personnel. "We try to provide an information glue, so to speak. Rightly, each of your departments, and it has not escaped my attention that the Director of the NSA couldn't be bothered to attend, your departments operate based on compartmentalisation, which increases security, reducing espionage and fraud. As a result, however, they are not as nimble as they should be, and so information can be missed or not shared; we are the missing link.

We carry out data analysis from across all arenas. We're nimble, and because we have direct control of your intelligence, we can direct and lead with precision.

I would, as part of tomorrow's demonstrations, like to invite you all to see our United Space Fleet and meet our key strategic partner."

The room went silent. The President glanced around the room, waiting for one of his department heads to confirm they knew what David Berstein had said. Only the Admiral provided any reassurance as he closed his eyes as if he were giving thanks as he gently nodded.

"Wait. David, did you just tell me we have a Space Fleet? As in Spaceships, not just modules and capsules?" President Blackstone asked, letting out a mocking laugh.

"Wait until tomorrow. This little teaser of information should suffice. I **REALLY** don't wish to spoil it for you," Rising from his seat, he continued, "I need to get going, I have another engagement." David Bernstein extended out his hand to shake with The President, who was still confused and uncharacteristically lost for words.

# CHAPTER 13 FUGITIVE

## SEPTEMBER 19 2021

*7:30 p.m. BST - (British Summer Time)*

*2:30 p.m. EDT - (Eastern Daylight Time)*

*London, England.*

**"** Theo, you better come see this," Theodore shouts from the lounge.

Theo leisurely enters the room while eating a sandwich. His dad points to the television. A live broadcast of a breaking news story was beginning. The headline text displayed:

'WANTED: THEO NEWTON CONSIDERED DANGEROUS - UK AND EUROPE ON ALERT.'

An official GB athletics photo of Theo is displayed while video footage of his recent 100 metre world record is shown.

The news presenter spoke.

*"Authorities have issued a wanted notice for British decathlete and multiple world record holder, 'Theo Newton'. He is considered dangerous and the public are advised to avoid contact and report any sightings immediately to local authorities. They state an arrest warrant has been issued citing terrorist charges. To reiterate, the individual is to be considered a threat and should not be approached. We are going live to a conference with Assistant Commissioner Barnes of the Metropolitan Police."*

The feed cuts to a room filled with journalists. Assistant Commissioner Barnes steps up to the podium, her expression serious and composed. The Metropolitan Police emblem is prominently displayed behind her.

"Good Evening. We are here to provide an urgent update on an escalating matter of national security.

As many of you are aware, we have issued a wanted notice for a well-known British athlete. The individual, Theo Newton, is wanted in connection with the recent crash of Grand Pacific Airlines flight 7 from Tokyo to Los Angeles, which occurred in the late afternoon of the 16th of September.

At this time, we will not be revealing further details regarding his suspected involvement in the crash. We consider him a central suspect and extremely dangerous. The latest intelligence from our colleagues in the USA suggests he has returned to the U.K. and is currently in the greater London area.

We urge the public to remain vigilant and not to approach Newton under any circumstances. If you see him or have any information regarding his whereabouts, please report it immediately using the emergency police contact number. I can briefly take some questions."

A journalist at the front of the crowd is the first to respond,

"Assistant Commissioner, can you provide any information on the specific charges or evidence against him?"

"At this stage, we cannot disclose specific details about the charges or evidence. Our priority is to ensure public safety and to apprehend the suspect as swiftly as possible. We are working closely with international and domestic partners to gather all necessary information."

Theo picks up the remote control and turns off the television.

"What are you going to do?" Theodore asks.

"For the moment, stick with the plan. You are safe here with Louise. I will head to Wuhan, after that..." He pauses, turning his head to look towards the window. The view from the 30th floor of the Central London apartment complex presented a clear view towards the North. He could make out Hampstead Heath, which brought back memories of his cross-country run and his first known encounter, which changed the course of his destiny.

"Actually, dad, after Wuhan. I'm going to meet up with Mei Lin, check she is ok. Then I will track down Dr Williams and return her to the Order."

"And this." Theodore points to the blank TV screen.

"I feel this is Gard. I have probably been too careless and probably too cocky. Letting my abilities get the better of me. When I find Dr Williams, I will know more about who they are and what they are up to. All I can say is, for the moment, they think they have the upper hand. You know as well as I do, they cannot possibly know what is coming. What I can do."

"And the media? Restoring your credibility?" Theodore asked, his voice wavering.

"I have an idea, but I need to see Mei Lin first."

"Oh wait. You aren't thinking what I think you are thinking?"

"Trust me Dad." Theo kissed his dad's forehead then stepped back. His hoodie was displaying the poster for the movie 'Outbreak'.

"THEO," Theodore shouted, "I haven't finished!" But his son blinked away, "Damn that boy. I hope he knows what he is doing."

'Do I call John?' Theodore considered. His friend and Detective Chief Superintendent may have been briefed or at the very least have access to someone with additional information.

Supplied by the Order, he held an untraceable mobile in his hand. He had to consider what to say. As a close personal contact, he was certainly being monitored, more so, calling his friend could put both their lives at risk.

*7:45 p.m. BST / 3:45 a.m. CST - China Standard Time*
*Wuhan, China*

Theo hovered above the Wuhan Institute of Virology for several minutes. His vision penetrated the roof, revealing high-definition detail as he methodically scanned each floor.

It revealed laboratories, offices, containment doors, clean rooms, shower facilities, communal spaces, and other miscellaneous functions. One area in particular demanded closer inspection.

As he descended to the building, his intangibility allowed him to continue through the roof and successive floors and arrive at a biosafety level 3 (BSL3) Laboratory, the second from the highest level on the hazard scale. The space is vacant of human activity. Beyond the restricted access door sat a lone security guard, who, deep in sleep, slumped forward at their desk.

A small changing area was between the restricted access door and the laboratory. This connected via the first decontamination chamber to a second changing room. Finally, a second decontamination chamber had to be entered before being granted access to the lab.

Any contamination on protective suits worn by the lab workers would be neutralised by Hydrogen Peroxide vapor vented into the decontamination chamber upon exiting the laboratory.

They would change out of their protective clothing, placing them inside an autoclave for cleaning before scrubbing themselves clean in the shower facility. They would then wear disposable underwear before entering the final decontamination chamber where a combination of ultraviolet light and a fine mist of a cleaning agent would be sprayed.

From Theo's observation, the maximum containment protocols were being observed, including positive pressure suits and bio-monitoring of the airflow with high-efficiency particulate air filtration (HEPA). Except, if an accident took place and a lab worker inhaled a pathogen or became infected in some other way, then secondary protocols must be observed. If a breach did take place here, it was covered up, or it was a deliberate act.

On entering the large room filled with biosafety cabinets, air hoses, benches, freezers and other equipment you would expect to see in an advanced lab, he directed a discrete electromagnetic pulse in the direction of the security cameras, temporarily disabling the circuits until they were manually power cycled.

Theo methodically examined each of the vials of pathogens stored in the liquid nitrogen freezers. Using his ability to manipulate matter, he examined the containers for any imperfections, micro-cracks or failure to the seals. While he found several freezers containing various strains from the genus Alphacoronavirus and Betacoronavirus, mainly the subgenus Sarbecovirus, that from which SARS-CoV-2 the cause of COVID-19 is a member, there were no indications of any genetic manipulation having taken place.

While he was certain that he hadn't been exposed to any viral agent, Theo took the precaution of entering the first decontamination chamber. There he wielded the *Etheric surge,* increasing the air temperature to over 100 degrees Celsius, while also increasing his core temperature to match, disinfecting his skin and clothing. His advanced immune system would rapidly take care of anything that survived.

He exited the laboratory and made his way to the server room. If there was a cover-up, then potentially documented and a digital trail left.

It didn't take him long to examine the server records, assisted by the system administrator, who had stuck a sheet of paper next to the keyboard with the current admin password. He had found something. A small but significant detail, possibly overlooked by anyone auditing the centre's operations.

Having found what he was looking for, Theo took to the sky. He covered the 1,280 miles to Kyoto, Japan, in only a few minutes. Emi's parents lived in the Sakyo Ward of the city, near an area of woodland next to the University. The wooded area provided perfect cover for him to descend and emerge into the quiet streets.

He wore his hood up. Anyone paying him close attention would see a hooded figure with no obvious facial features, an early morning spectre, as he controlled the flow of light, so that it barely illuminated his face.

Uncharacteristically, his movements were slow. He was in no hurry. Other than his sinister appearance, he was not intending to draw attention to himself. Thankfully, Japan's seventh largest city was still in relative slumber.

Focussed on locating video recording devices, he would generate a high intensity pulsed light in front of the camera's aperture temporarily overwhelming the sensor and rendering the footage for those moments unusable. It would at least give him some time, but eventually those who were after him would track him down.

He approached the front door of the modest detached house. Behind the wall, he could hear activity. The family was up and preparing for the day ahead. He considered if he should wait until Emi's parents left for work, but realised that they were at as much risk as everyone else he had associated with. They had a right to know.

He knocked on the door with a confident bang, and moments later, the door opened. A smartly dressed, suited man answered.

"Oh. Theo Newton. Please, please come in." He hopped to the side of the passage, making space for Theo to pass, sweeping his arm toward the narrow passage. "Please, your footwear." He continued, pointing at his guest's feet.

"Of course, thank you. You must be Emi's father?" Theo responded humbly, bowing his head and doing his utmost to show his respect. Theo slipped off his shoes.

"Yes, I am Daiki. Go that way."

Entering the dining room, Emi and Mei Lin sat at the table eating breakfast, unaware of who had just entered. It was only when Emi's mother Sakura came in that excitement broke loose.

Sakura, seeing Theo standing there, let out a squeal.

"Theo Newton! You are my favourite."

Mei Lin looked up, dropped her spoon, pushed herself up from the table, tipping her bowl of fruit salad while sending the chair she had been sitting in careering backwards, causing the previously sleeping Jack Russell racing away in fear for its life.

Mei Lin dashed around the table and suddenly stopping as she recalled her manners.

"May I present to you," pausing, she took a deep breath "Mr and Mrs Kobayashi, I am honoured to introduce you to Theo Newton," trying hard to contain her excitement, her reddening cheeks giving away her feelings, "Theo, this is Daiki and Sakura, Emi's parents. Oh, and this is their dog Maru."

The Jack Russell was now leaping up at the visitor. Theo knelt, allowing Maru to cling to his top and then lick his face and neck excitedly.

"I am honoured to meet you all. I mean not to be rude having just arrived. But I need to speak to Mei Lin." There was an urgency in his voice. Daiki pointed towards the passage.

"Please, use our family room."

The couple moved from the dining area to the family room. Now in private, Mei Lin embraced Theo.

"I have been so worried about you. When I heard about the plane crash, I was worried you were on board," Taking a step back, she looked him in the eye. "You had nothing to do with that, did you? The news..." Theo reached out and gently grabbed her hands, pulling her in close.

"I swear, I had nothing to do with what happened to the plane. But I was onboard."

Mei Lin, on hearing this, pulled her arms from Theo's hold, he didn't resist. She then took several steps away. Her expression changed, now looking serious. *'Did he just say that? How could he have been onboard?'* She thought.

"I did say that. Yes, I was onboard. There is a lot I need to tell you. Believe me when I say I did not cause the plane crash. I have gifts, abilities. I will explain it all to you. But..."

Mei Lin was looking confused, but then confusion gave way to a realisation, an awareness of what he was saying as she interrupted.

"Did you just read my mind?"

"That is one of the abilities I now have." He stepped forward and slowly reached out for her hand. She didn't resist. The last three days had given her a chance to consider how she felt about Theo. After several long chats with Emi that went on well into the night, it became apparent she was in love with him.

*'I love him, I have to give him the chance to tell me whatever it is he is trying to tell me'*

Theo slowly pulled Mei Lin close. Looking into her eyes, he responded to her thought.

"I love you too."

They shared a minute of passion before he released the embrace. "Emi and her parents are not safe here. We all need to leave as soon as we can, but I need to ask something of you."

Mei Lin was still experiencing the emotional high from the hormones and feel-good chemicals which were coursing through her blood, contributing to her present state. But she was also very much in control of her mind. The words registered with her and the euphoria gave way to an adrenaline rush. Her fight-or-flight response taking control.

"I trust you. Is it the people from Tokyo?" She asks.

"Yes. I believe they are the ones responsible for the false stories about me, so I need for you to arrange a press briefing. I am going to set the story straight."

"When? And where do you want to do this?"

"As soon as possible after we get back to Tokyo. The international stadium will do. It will be appropriate for part of what I have to say."

"You want to go back to Tokyo!" She replies with uncertainty in her voice. "Will that be safe?" She said as she tensed.

"We will all be safe. Once I get the briefing over with, I don't think you will need to feel threatened again."

Theo had a calming demeanour. Her anxiety drifted away, nodding in response.

As they were heading back to the dining room, she asks with a giggle in her words, "Does this mean we are officially an item?"

"It probably does. Yes."

On entering the room, Emi looked shocked.

"What's the matter?" Mei Lin asked as her expression changed from that of joy to concern.

"My dad has just had a phone call from his work. They have fired him." Bursting into tears, the events of the last few days had shattered her understanding of her world.

"Can you comfort her?" Theo asked in a tender whisper, "I will have a word with her parents."

Moving into the Kitchen, Mr Kobayashi was sitting on the floor, his phone still in his hand, his head held by his other hand. Mrs Kobayashi was bent over him, trying her best to console her husband.

"Excuse me." Theo said, "I am sorry to interrupt. I heard the news."

175

Returning to her feet, Sakura spoke.

"He work as research assistant at University for 30 years. They say may not get pension. Why they do this?" Mrs Kobayashi was understandably just as upset as her husband.

"I cannot explain how I know this. But everything will be ok. He WILL get his job back. You need to trust me on this." Theo was radiating a positive aura. A sense of calm and rational understanding seemed to emanate from him.

"However, we all need to leave right now. The people behind this will come here soon. Ok?"

Theo's words seem to resonate with Daiki, who gets back on his feet, "If Theo Newton says it will be ok, then it will be ok. Where are we going?"

"Good man. Do you have a car? We need to get to Tokyo."

"Yes. Mazda."

"Pack some clothes for a few nights. And be ready to go in ten minutes. Thank You."

*9:02 p.m. BST / 6:02 a.m. JST*

The family quickly packed essentials and were ready to go in a few minutes. Theo, in the meantime had scouted the immediate area, listening and watching for any indications that G.A.R.D were nearby.

Fortunately, he considered that he still had the upper hand. To maintain the advantage, he employed his dad's tactic and switched the registration plate on Mr Kobayashi's car.

With nearly 6 hours and 280 miles of driving ahead, he would have an opportunity to explain the events as he understood them and his superhuman abilities.

Once on the road, Mei Lin arranged a press briefing at the international stadium for 2 p.m.. She explained that the Japanese

176

Athletic Committee would make an important announcement and that the world's media were invited to attend.

Theo took over the driving so he could explain his secret without distracting Mr Kobayashi. Understandably, they were shocked, then came disbelief and the request to see proof. Theo demonstrated with a showcase of some of his abilities.

He conceded that turning invisible whilst driving an eight-year-old Mazda probably wasn't the wisest move when the inevitable panic took hold of the passengers. Thankfully, they laughed it off once they realised the reality of what had transpired.

### 12:07 a.m. BST / 9:07 a.m. JST

Three hours into the journey, Theo pulled the car over. Daiki was calm enough to resume driving. Theo, however, explained he had something to take care of and would meet up with the travellers once they reached the outskirts of Tokyo. Before he left, he explained to Mei Lin that their bond was strong, so strong that if she needed him, all she would need to do was call out to him in her mind. He would hear her and could return in an instant.

Theo, leaving the party behind, walked towards some trees. Looking back, Mei Lin was waving goodbye. He blew her a kiss, which she responded with a thought 'I love you'. It was then that she experienced a surreal moment. Her dopamine levels surged, giving her a euphoric sensation. Then she heard it in her mind, Theo's voice saying 'I love you too, Mei Lin'. She watched as he took to the sky, turning invisible before reaching the upper tree line.

Theo was now established at the art of flying. He instinctively enabled a field that radiated from him, unperturbing the atmosphere from his motion, preventing sonic booms or electromagnetic radiation being transmitted from his body. He was truly stealth.

177

He shot up through the atmosphere, past the orbiting satellites, carrying on towards the moon. Looking around, he observed several United Space Fleet craft, the same configuration as the Lincoln that he had previously observed. They were in a high Earth orbit. Focusing on each, he identified them as the USF Johnson, the USF Glennan, the USF Fortitude.

But there was something else, a more massive craft, the USF Vanguard. It was twice the size of the others, but it was not the same shape. It was sleek, aerodynamic, it had no markings other than its designation. Theo could only conclude that its design intended it to enter Earth or another planet's atmosphere.

The sight of the spacecraft caught him off guard. Defying physics as only he could, he stopped his relative motion in space. As he suspended between the Earth and the moon, he was mystified of the origin of the Vanguard. It appeared out of place, not matching any technology or material from Earth.

'This is something else. The presence I felt from the Lincoln.' Theo recalled the malevolence he experienced when he touched that ship. It was now obvious that *they were here*, but who were they? But that experience was from a vessel that human minds could have conceived. But this new craft was indeed different, not human made.

'*Do they have abilities like me? How many individuals are there? Are they individuals? What are their intentions?*' His inquisitive mind was encouraging him to investigate. What harm could befall him? He was superhuman, indestructible, undefeatable, unlimited in strength, speed, and possibilities. And yet as he stared at the Vanguard slowly move away, he realised he was afraid.

For all of his powers, intellect and intelligence, he was still human. He had the same emotions; the fears, connections and unreasonable behaviours as he had before his change. He considered himself an imperfect being to have been chosen as a superhuman.

For the first time that he could recall, his self-belief, his confidence, was knocked, and it was all in his mind, his fearful human thoughts. But one line of thinking beyond all else dominated his usual rational thinking.

'How *can I save everyone?*'

Overcome with panic, he dived towards Earth, accelerating through the atmosphere, unaware that a fireball engulfed him. He needed to see his dad; he needed reassurance. It was only when he noticed an aeroplane thousands of feet below did he realise his instinct had failed him. He sent out his protective field, which rippled through the atmosphere, dispersing the sonic boom and reverted the airflow to its natural state. The fireball extinguished. He could chalk another lapse of concentration off to not being ready for the weight of responsibility now upon his shoulders.

12:23 a.m. BST / 9:23 a.m. JST

London, England

Theo hovered at a window of the 30th floor apartment that was his parents' safe house. Inside, Theodore and Louise slept. As he hovered, he wondered if it was right to wake his dad. His thoughts were racing, spiralling. He didn't want to show weakness, but this was his dad, his oldest friend and confidant. Not wanting to be a burden to him, but then something popped into his mind, a memory.

He considered this piece of information and what it meant and, with reflection, considered a new interpretation:

'He *is still my father and I his son, but his strength I will make my own.*'

Theo passed through the window, into the living room, and onward to his father's room, where he gently knocked on the door. Sensing his dad had woken, 'Dad. *I need to speak, meet me in the living room.*'

Theodore climbed out of bed, putting on a dressing gown and made his way to the open plan living room and kitchen. Theo was filling a French press with boiling water.

"Hey son, what's up?" Rubbing his eyes as they slowly adjusted to the bright room. Pulling out a stool from under the breakfast bar and set opposite to where his son was at the kitchen island.

"Coffee?" Theo offered as he slowly plunged the filter.

"I don't suppose it's decaffe?" Yawning as he tried to reply.

"It's not, but I can take care of that."

Theo poured two mugs of coffee and placed one in front of his father. He then stares at it.

The liquid glints from the spotlights overhead. His father watches intently at the surface of the liquid as it rippled. The steam suddenly seemed to increase as it curled its path upward.

Theodore's perspective changes as his son guided his vision. Diving beneath the surface of the liquid, the microscopic world comes into view. The Water molecules of $H^2O$ bend and contort, vibrating chaotically, propelled by eddies of heat. Among them, another structure emerges, the intricate arrangement of a caffeine molecule, $C_8H_{10}N_4O_2$.

The carbon, hydrogen, nitrogen, and oxygen atoms bonded into a complex, lattice-like shape. Suddenly, the molecules cluster from an invisible force. Theo's control of matter manifests at the molecular level, pulling the caffeine structure from the turbulent solution.

Theo's father watches in silence, trying to grasp the significance of what was happening. One by one, the caffeine molecules untangle themselves from their chemical interactions within the black liquid and are pulled upward.

Theodore has his reality returned to the macroscopic as Theo opens his palm, revealing a tiny amount of a white crystalline powder in the centre of his hand.

Theodore's jaw drops. Another demonstration of how far Theo's abilities extended beyond human understanding.

"That was incredible. I mean, how?" He pauses and stares at his son, who just shrugs his shoulders. "I have so many questions. When did you realise you could change someone's reality like that?" Theodore picks up the mug and gives a quick blow across the surface of the liquid. "So caffeine free? Right?" He takes a sip of the hot coffee.

"I realise that there is nothing I can't do. But..." Theo hesitated, he recalled the prior day when he spoke with his mother. The words she shared, "Someone told me, I need to believe in myself and that almost nothing is impossible. I came here to speak with you, for your guidance. But I realise now of what I am capable."

"Something still weighs heavy on you. Tell me son."

"Mei Lin is safe, she is on her way back to Tokyo."

"I am pleased to hear that Theo. But what is troubling you?"

Theo walked towards the window and looked out over London. The city was illuminated and still awake with activity. Turning, he looked at his dad.

"You remember when I was young. I was so full of drive and ambition."

"You were a dynamo. If it wasn't you wanting to go to a museum or a library, there was always something else. You read so much, I couldn't keep you in enough books." Theodore laughed, remembering his young boy.

"And then the running," Theo added.

"How old were you when you won that sports day, 7, 8?"

"I was 8. I knew then I was different. We both knew I was different. But on the 9th August, well, everything changed. Until then I had drive and ambition. I saw what my future looked like."

Theodore stood and walked over, stopping in front of his son, and placed his right arm on Theo's left shoulder.

"What is troubling you, son? Please tell me."

"I am scared dad. I am terrified."

"Theo, you are still human, being scared confirms that. I would be more worried if you were not scared. What has brought this on?" Theodore looked deep into his son's eyes, searching for his soul to share his pain.

"I never asked for any of this. My choice was taken from me. BUT…" Theo reached up and placed his hand on his dad's. "I know what I have to do. This evening I went into space. I wanted to check out the derelict base on the moon, the one I suspect the Aelioxar abandoned. I wanted to see if they left any clues, anything to show me they were lying. But while I was up there, I caught sight of the American Space Fleet. There were three ships, just like the Lincoln.

But then there was a fourth craft, the Vanguard. It was completely different. I mean, it was a different design; it was larger, sleeker. Seeing it made me freeze. It scared me. It made me realise I am not prepared for anything that may come our way." Theo looked at his dad with pleading eyes. A tear welled in the corner of his eye.

"Now listen to me son. We are not religious people. But the Aelioxar chose YOU. No one else YOU. Now we can dress it up any way we want, but maybe, this is God's work. In the sense that they are god. And now you are god. I am certain," Theodore pulled his arm to his chest and made a fist, "I feel it in my soul that you are the one who will enlighten the human spirit. The one who will unite humanity. And bring harmony to our planet."

Laughing, Theo responded, "Dad, that was so cliched."

"You're kind of spoiling my moment here. What I am trying to say and yeah that was corny. Sorry! What I am saying is this. You don't need to be afraid. There is nothing for you to be afraid of. You can choose your future. Give up being a superhuman if you want, you don't even need to reveal to the world who you are. Keep it secret. That is YOUR choice, no one else's. YOURS."

"And what about G.A.R.D? They have made it impossible for me…" Theo stopped. Looked at his dad. "I see what you did there."

"What did I do?"

Theo leaned in and embraced his dad. They stayed hugging for a couple of minutes until they were interrupted.

"Sorry. Has something happened?" Louise asks.

"No, your husband, my dad, has just demonstrated why he is the best father a boy can have. We didn't disturb you, did we?"

"No, not at all. I wasn't really asleep when your dad got up."

"So have you decided what you are going to do? Are you still afraid and unsure?" Theodore asks.

"I do have questions. The Vanguard, I suspect is of extraterrestrial origin. I need to check it out. And there is one more thing. In a few hours I will hold a press conference at the Tokyo stadium, Mei Lin is organising it. I am taking back control."

"You are telling the world?" Louise asks.

"What are you going to tell them? Coz I don't know about you, but is the world ready to know the whole truth?" Theodore looked at Louise, who nodded in agreement.

"I haven't worked out the full details of what I will say. But you are right. I can't say. Humans are genetically modified. An alien race came to Earth billions of years ago, helped life. Edited primates turning two chromosome pairs into one, creating humans. Oh, and by the way, they came back, turned me into a Superhuman, look I can break physics. And there is another species of extraterrestrial who appear to be bent on world domination. And the Greys that crashed in Roswell, they are real also. Any Questions?"

"Exactly. You can't say that." Theodore suggests.

"Ted, wait, why can't he? It is his news to break. If anyone can stop the panic before it starts, it's our boy." Louise responds, looking sternly at her husband.

183

"Don't worry. I will have it worked out. You will be asleep by the time I go live. When you get up, you will catch the response as the news hits the waking world."

"It isn't too late to change your mind son," Theodore adds.

"I love you guys. I've got to fly. Thanks Dad."

Theo, with his back to the window, steps backwards and passes cleanly through the pane as if there was no glass, waving as he goes. Then, in a blink, shot straight up.

"He literally had to fly. My son 'The One', I will never get used to that."

12:57 a.m. BST / 9:57 a.m. JST
Earth Orbit

Theo, on reaching orbit, sought the location of the USF Vanguard. There were now multiple vessels tracking at equal positions around the Earth.

'What are they up to?' Theo thought as he continued to search for the Vanguard. But it wasn't in orbit. Less than an hour had elapsed since he first discovered the craft. But even with his vision, able to see in every wavelength of the electromagnetic spectrum, it was nowhere to be seen.

The last time he had observed the ship, it was in the orbit of Earth, but this didn't help him identify a projected course. Holding still, he closed his eyes and relaxed. Allowing the sun to charge him. As the photons merged with him, he was aware of a tiny cool patch on his super-suit that wasn't absorbing as much energy from the sun.

Looking towards Sol, he spotted the Vanguard. From his quick calculation, it was over seventy-five million miles from Earth. 'That thing can move,' he thought.

Teleporting himself to within a mile of the ship's position. There he watched as twenty-one pods emerged from the craft. Each one was the size of a school bus with manoeuvring ability.

*'What are they?'* Theo questioned as he watched the pods move off as they gradually drifted apart.

As he continued to observe the 'things' they ceased their movement, each one now spaced precisely 100 meters apart, forming a pyramid shape in space with the outer rows totalling fifteen pods and the inner composed of six pods.

Then, with a mechanical hum that only he could detect through the vacuum of space, they opened, extending out metallic arms. One by one, the pods connected, forming a triangular grid that was akin to that of a cosmic spider's web.

From each strut, a metal sheet unfurled, rolling out to cover the gaps between the frame. The material displayed an unusual property. While initially solid, it appeared to flow like liquid mercury, joining with precision to create a flawless and continuous surface. Only the apex of the triangular grid, the furthest point from the sun, remained uncovered, a triangular aperture in the structure.

Intrigued, Theo orbited the colossal construct, his keen eyes analysing every detail. On the interior surface facing the sun, he noticed an array of tiny, precisely orientated crystals embedded in the metallic covering. These crystals didn't appear to shine, the refraction tolerance such that each photon of light was focused towards the aperture. The efficiency of the energy capture was near one hundred percent.

*'It's a solar collector,'* Theo realised. The sun's immense energy was being harnessed and channelled for a yet unknown purpose. But the device was incomplete. Something was missing from the aperture.

As Theo inspected the backside of the collector, he realised that whoever created it was not human.

185

'*Is this the foundation of a Dyson sphere?*' He thought.

More terrifying than that, he realised, if these beings could harness the full power of the sun, then as a level one civilisation, they could harness the power of the earth, prevent earthquakes and volcanic eruptions or, conversely, cause them.

Doubt once again entered his thoughts, '*How can I stop earthquakes? A volcano, ok, maybe so, a tsunami, not as much a problem. But everywhere, all at once? The threat to humanity will be overwhelming. Do I destroy the collector? Do I wait? Am I mistaken?*'

Theo, mesmerised by the array and captivated by thought, didn't sense the Vanguard speeding away. It wasn't returning to Earth, its trajectory such that it was moving to the outer solar system.

He could have caught up and investigated further, but time was pressing. The vanguard would have to wait.

# CHAPTER 14 REVELATION

## SEPTEMBER 20 2021

*3:11 a.m. (British Summer Time)*

*12:11 p.m. (Japan Standard Time)*

*Somewhere over the United States.*

Theo re-entered Earth's atmosphere over the eastern seaboard of the United States of America. Descending to 50,000 metres, he systematically crossed the country in a zig-zag pattern, scanning the ground, viewing everything frequency in the electromagnetic spectrum and sensing the terrain for minor variations in the Earth's acoustic vibration. He was searching for undocumented underground bunkers of substantial size and construction.

He discovered multiple anomalies, several of which were located in cities or too close to population centres. Locations that would be ineffective at carrying out secretive operations. Many more were in remote locations, but the lack of heavy tracks or disturbance from helicopter activity ruled them out.

It was the four near mountainous and upland regions which demanded closer attention. It appeared his list of things to investigate was growing. Theo climbed to 80,000 feet and increased his speed, arriving to meet the Mei Lin and the Kobayashi family near Atsugi close to Tokyo. At the very least, they had another hour of driving.

Waiting at the side of the road, Theo flagged down his ride. When the car pulled over, Theo offered to take the wheel from Daiki, who was looking exhausted.

"How has your journey been?" Theo asked.

"Not bad, slower than I think we were expecting. Did you find what you were looking for?" Mei Lin asked, now sitting in the front.

"I will tell you about it later. The family have a lot to think about, I would rather not compound anything further," he whispered back.

Mei Lin gently leaned over, resting her head on his shoulder.

It wasn't long before the four passengers and the dog were asleep. Theo tried to clear his mind, concentrating solely on the driving. However, he kept playing over what he was going to say at the press event. This was, after all, going to be the defining moment of his life.

### 4:32 a.m. BST / 1:32 p.m. JST

### Tokyo, Japan

The rest of the trip was heavy with congestion. Several times Theo had to make a diversion, and several times more, he had to manipulate the traffic signals in his favour.

Upon arriving at the stadium, he advised the family to book into a hotel nearby, promising he would refund them the expense. They didn't argue, explaining they were looking forward to visiting Tokyo and catching up with friends.

As the Mazda pulled away, Mei Lin looked at Theo with concern. She reached out and held his hands. "There is still time to change your mind. It sounds strange given what I now know, but I will support you whatever you decide."

"Thank you Mei. But I want to see this through." He slowly raised her hands up and pressed his lips to them. "I discovered what I believe to be something sinister unfolding. I observed a large spacecraft in orbit around Earth. But when I went back into space to check it out, it had moved. I found it, relatively close to the sun. It deployed a solar collector. The technology is nothing like we have on Earth. But the collector is not complete, it is missing a component."

"What do you think its purpose is?"

"I don't know. But the energy this thing will collect or focus is incredible. I am unsure what to do about it." Pulling Mei Lin in close, kissing her lips. She pulled back, which he didn't expect.

"Are you afraid?" She asks.

"Yes. And I know my fear is irrational. Everything I have ever achieved, I have done without fear."

"Hey, come here." Mei Lin embraced him, then whispered, "Fear is normal, it means you understand what is at risk."

"You will love my dad, you both think alike." He replied.

They made their way across the concourse and into the stadium, and then up to the public relations suite.

The room was a frenzy of dozens of engineers setting up camera equipment and microphones. Thankfully, the journalists were in an adjacent holding room. Mei Lin's boss was working on his laptop at the top table behind the lectern.

"Mr Shimizu, Sir," she says, waiting for him to stand.

"Theo, may I introduce, Mr Shimizu, the Chief Executive of the Tokyo Athletic Games Committee. Sir this is Theo Newton."

"It is an honour, Sir," Theo said, bowing his head.

"Mr Newton, There is no need for such formalities. It is an honour to finally meet you. May I ask, what this is about? Why are you relinquishing your title?"

"Mr Shimizu, I have several reasons. But suffice to say, I recently became aware of information that calls into question many fundamental beliefs. I cannot on good conscience keep my title or my records. I will explain it in my presentation."

"A man of high standing. With such an accurate moral compass. Do you meditate?"

"Yes, why do you ask?"

"I can see that you are enlightened; you have achieved 'Satori'. This is from Japanese Buddhism. But I also sense in you 'Kami', you have a spirit which should be venerated. I do not know for what you will announce, but the tranquillity that radiates from you stands you in good stead." Mr Shimizu bows and then offers his hand.

Theo reciprocates. When their hands touch, Theo understands.

"You are a member of The Order?"

Mr Shimizu's only response was to place his finger to his lips "Shhhh."

"What are the order?" Mei Lin asks.

"I will explain it to you once this circus is over," Theo replies.

5:00 a.m. BST / 2:00 p.m. JST

The press had finally gathered. Over 200 members of the media, representing major newspapers and TV news channels from across the world. The turnout was twice the seating capacity for the room. Many had to stand in the aisles or crouch in between rows of seats. Another couple of dozen were sitting on the floor in front of the first row.

The buzz of the room suddenly went quiet when Theo entered, escorted by Mr Shimizu and Mei Lin. A frenzied burst of flash photography took over, followed by shouts from various people asking for Theo to look in their direction.

After a minute, Mei Lin intervened and requested there be silence. She yielded the floor to Theo, who moved into position behind the lectern and the vase filled not with flowers but microphones.

> "I stand before you today to address the accusations and questions that have been directed towards me in the news. Let me begin with my achievements, here in this magnificent stadium, a little over a month ago.

190

Many of you have suspected that I cheated,

Many of you believed I took performance-enhancing substances.

Let me address the latter point first. I have never taken any substance to artificially improve my performance. And let my doping record show that I have never been found guilty of such a deceitful act. I stand with the Athletic Games Committee to ensure we have a clean and fair sport.

On the former point, at the time I was taking part in the games and achieving record breaking results, I can honestly say that I was not knowingly cheating.

Like all my achievements, I firmly believe they result from the dedication and commitment of my coaches, teachers, and my determination, particularly the support of my father.

However, very recently I discovered some information that made me question my entire life. Question whether my achievements were actually of my doing.

Some of you believe I was ashamed and so hid from the world to account for why I went missing. The truth is far more fantastic.

So today, before this briefing, I requested that the Athletic Games Committee strip me of my games title and void my world records."

There was a collective gasp, followed by conversation from the media delegation. Theo waited for the audience to settle. Glancing around the room, he could pick out members of the press who already had questions. Eventually, the noise lowered, and he could continue.

"In answer to my first question, it appears I had an unfair advantage. I cannot in good conscience keep my decathlon title or records.

But I maintain I did not knowingly cheat, but I accept I had an unfair advantage.

I encourage anyone, no matter who they are, if they know they have an unfair advantage, be it because they have transitioned, have knowingly cheated or because they didn't know at the time they were being manipulated, to stand up and be counted and do the honourable thing and withdraw from competitive sport."

A male member of the press stands and shouts out a question. "Are you saying that you were a victim of manipulation?"

"Not at all. Let me continue. I will now address the recent allegations spread throughout the media about me. As you will be aware, I am considered dangerous and currently the most wanted individual by the authorities of the United States.

You will also know I am wanted in connection with the unfortunate tragedy in which over two hundred people lost their lives. I was aboard flight GPA7."

The noise levels of the room suddenly increased, shocked gasps, followed by 'That's not possible' and 'How did he survive'. Theo ignores the unrest and continues with an elevated voice.

"However, it was my presence aboard the flight that jeopardised the lives of everyone. I was the target for what happened to the Grand Pacific flight."

The members of the media were now on their feet, indistinguishable voices were shouting questions, identities lost in the bedlam that was unfolding. Theo paused and crossed his arms. Waiting. Eventually the media circus could see that he was not going to relent and slowly, one by one, they returned to their seats and the room quietened.

"Thank you. I will answer your questions at the end. But for now, please listen.

I survived the crash, obviously. Since then, there have been multiple threats to my close friends and family.

Now I am speaking to those who orchestrated the downing of GPA7 and those same people who are still after me and have continued to terrorise those dear to me. It will stop.

YOU WILL STOP. If I hear a single mention of G.A.R.D or find out, you persist. I will find you and I will put an end to it.

There is nowhere on Earth or in space that you can hide. Your bunkers, military installations or moon bases afford you no protection."

"Did I hear him right? Did he say moon bases?" A journalist can be heard asking a colleague as they frantically scribble in their notebook.

"I am the one who will put you before the courts and have judgment passed on you for your crimes.

I appreciate that I have spent the last few minutes speaking without really giving you any facts. I hear your questions. And I will address them now as I continue."

The atmosphere in the room changes and the previously unsettled and impatient crowd suddenly becomes attentive. Several of the journalists are seen leaning forward as if it would help them hear more clearly.

"To everyone who is watching and listening to my voice, you need to pay attention to my warning.

If you are standing, sit down.

If you are driving a car, pull over to a safe spot.

If you are operating heavy or dangerous machinery. Power them down and step away.

If you are doing anything that could cause yourself or others harm, stop until I am finished. I ask this of you for the safety of you and others.

What I am about to tell you began billions of years ago. I am going to be as concise as I can. You will have many questions. I am not exaggerating or being big-headed when I say to you that however many questions you have now, you will have exponentially more by the end.

In the early years of our solar system, conditions were harsh. Space debris bombarded primordial Earth. Such that life struggled to take hold, even when conditions were right and the organic chemicals were present."

"What's he talking about?" whispered a voice from the crowd. "I think he has lost it." Came a reply.

"But life was given a helping hand by, what we would call an extraterrestrial race. They call themselves the Aelioxar, they are billions of years older than even our solar system. They injected their wisdom and knowledge into establishing life on earth, a jump start so to speak.

Once life took hold, it thrived. And what we consider as evolution took over.

The Aelioxar returned, amazed by life's diversity, but the primates astonished them most. It was then that they set to work. They took some examples, studied and experimented on them. They made adjustments to their DNA.

In one experiment, they converted two pairs of DNA into one pair. This is why our closest relative, the chimpanzee, has an extra pair of chromosomes than you do. This new species of primate became an early hominid.

Early humans developed, giving rise to our various ancestors, like Homo heidelbergensis, Homo erectus and the Neanderthal. But the Aelioxar could not help themselves. When Homo sapiens arrived, they tinkered some more. A new species emerged. A species that continues to live on Earth to this very day. This species is known as Homo pars-aeliox.

I am, or rather was, Homo pars-aeliox, I benefited from dominant genetic traits that other members of my species do not have. This gifted me with advanced learning, memory retention, and recall. Increased logic skills and intelligence. Stronger and faster muscles. A meta human, so to speak.

But this truth was hidden from me throughout my life until recently. Part of what makes a pars-aeliox different from a sapien, is that within us we have four genetic bases which come directly from the Aelioxar. It was their intention for these bases to remain inactive and not to take over from or replace our human bases of Adenine, Cytosine, Guanine and Thymine.

But over the thousands of years, nature activated some of these genetic bases. They did not replace human genes, instead they enhanced them. This gave rise to individuals who you will know in our history, in tales of legend and some of myth.

Many of these individuals realised they were different and sought others of their kin. United through this common bloodline, they established a community called Atlantis."

A series of loud gasps came from the otherwise silent audience, everyone captivated by the story that was being recited.

"The Aelioxar returned, spoke to the Atlanteans, instructing them to go their separate ways, to reunite with humanity. To teach, instruct and lead for the betterment of humanity.

Atlantis eventually was destroyed. But the people of the advanced civilisation continued. The Aelioxar had to leave. Eventually, the Atlantis story fell into myth, the records of their achievements destroyed. Their descendants persecuted, cast out, called witches, and executed. But they all kept the knowledge of their secret, which is still today, passed down to their progeny.

But the Aelioxar returned. In 2000, they made a small, almost undetectable incision in a pregnant woman's uterus, injecting a catalysing compound which was the first in a series to activate of the Aeliox base pairs. That woman was my mother, Isabella Newton, and I was the foetus.

Then, when I was 14, and without my knowledge, I again was subject to a second catalysing procedure to activate the next stage of the Aeliox genetic material.

Then finally, a little over a month ago, after my triumph here in Tokyo, the Aelioxar took me to one of their homeworlds."

The patient crowd could not contain their disbelief, like a Mexican wave, row after row of the audience rushed to their feet. The overlapping shouts making the room a deafening din.

In a surprising intervention, Mr Shimizu rose to his feet and shouted over the bedlam, "BE QUIET." His voice was booming. But it worked. Shocking the crowd, who returned to their seats.

Theo turned to his kin, deeply thanking him by saying, "Doumo arigatou gozaimasu."

"There I underwent the final procedure. After over 30 days of close observation, the entire Aeliox genetic code became active, working to supercharge my human code.

So while I was *Homo pars-aeliox*, I am unique. I am in a species of one; I am *Homo pars-deus,* I possess superhuman abilities.

Just before I finish, I want to return to an early part of my statement.

Those of you who work for Gard, YOU WILL STOP, if you persist. I will find you and I will put an end to it. Thank You. I am now open to questions."

The room once again explodes into noise. The front row of the press, launch out of their chairs, trying to get to their feet. Some move forward, attempting to get closer to the podium, trampling those on the floor in front of them. Several trip, crashing down on the bodies below them. The media circus becomes a slapstick clown show. Several members of the audience sustaining minor injuries.

Eventually, everyone is standing, but the melee of questions continues.

'*I should have put a head limit on this circus*' Theo thinks as he glances around the room. He seeks the least demanding reporter, a 30-something female representing a small local news station who is standing by the wall. Her small stature making it almost impossible to be seen by anyone but Theo. Focusing on her id badge, he reads her name.

"Yes, Kimiko." He points toward the demure lady.

"Thank you. You have just recited quite a wild story that lacks any merit in terms of evidence. How can you possibly prove what you have just told us?"

"Thank you, Kimiko. You are correct. Most what I have just shared would indeed be almost impossible to prove. I do not feel that I need to provide evidence for my story, that is for scientists across many disciplines to establish. Let me explain.

If I were to provide all the evidence here and now, it would cause an explosion of scientific endeavour, which could take humanity on an unnatural trajectory. Many aspects of human culture would be harmed because of this. I have the answers to questions that mankind has been searching for since they first looked up and wondered.

Humanity is already looking for the answers. For example, I have a personal academic interest in palaeoanthropology. We continue to try and establish what we consider being the missing link. I have provided a clue. Evidence for where to look.

It is not my place to deny humanity the natural steps in its advancement. But I will assist, only if I am asked the correct question."

Theo momentarily pauses, allowing his words to be absorbed. Chatter spread through the crowd. Journalists exchange glances, trying to decipher his statement. A few audibly scoff, their scepticism. Others who had returned to their seats during his talk adjusted their position in their chairs, uneasy with his words.

One voice from the back breaks through the murmur, "And what are the correct questions? Theo. Can you guide us there, or are we left to fumble in the dark?"

"I will give the answers. But the questions need to be correct.

This may appear counterintuitive. After all, why would I have shared as much detail as I have if I propose to hold back the evidence? But I have reasons. Reasons that, for the moment, I cannot share. But the day may come when I can give you an explanation."

Looking at the crowd, Theo sensed they were not happy. He knew that most people were still just children at heart, lacking patience and wanting everything now. Never truly understanding the need to learn self-reward through hard work or saving. Instead, they load credit cards with debt because they would rather experience a short-term feeling of happiness without considering future implications.

"Let me just explain from another perspective. The human race has, for nearly One hundred years now, sat at a precipice between technological advancement and self-annihilation. We have climate change, nuclear weapons, bio-weapons, chemical weapons, pollution of our aquatic systems, farmlands turning sterile, forests and ecosystems destroyed. I could go on, but in that same one hundred years, we have advanced so far. For every step two steps forward we advance, we move a step back with creating more problems.

I fear that if I give humanity all the answers, potentially, there may no longer be a planet to call home."

A reporter three rows from the front climbs onto his chair and shouts, "Who are you to dictate the advancement of humans?".

The room falls briefly silent, the murmur of the crowd quelled by the audacity of the question. All eyes turn from the reporter to Theo, whose calm demeanour gives nothing away.

"I am no dictator," Theo continues, his tone measured, demonstrating a calm but authoritative manner. "Nor am I here to assert control over humanity's future. I am simply a guardian of balance. A balance that is fragile and often denied by our leaders. To hand humanity all the answers without restraint would be akin to giving a child the keys to a machine they do not yet understand. It is not about denying advancement; it is about ensuring that advancement does not come at the cost of extinction."

He pauses, letting his words settle. "Do I claim to know what is best for every individual? No. But I have seen the consequences of progress without wisdom. And I will not risk the destruction of this planet, the only home humanity has, for the sake of reckless curiosity."

The reporter climbs down from his chair and scribbles some words into his notebook. The pause unsettles the crowd, then, as if some instinctive group behaviour takes over, the shouting of 'me me me' takes over, each reporter wanting the opportunity to ask their question.

Theo looks to the front row. A forty-something male reporter from the BBC grabs his attention. "Daniel from the BBC, what is your question?"

"Thank you, Theo, you've mentioned you have superhuman abilities, can you tell us more about them? What exactly are you capable of, and how do you intend to use these abilities to impact the world? And finally, do you consider yourself a superhero, if so what is you hero name?"

"Thank you, Daniel. Quite a few questions in there. I hope that because of my answers today, you will get a sense of what I am about and who I am.

My full name is 'Theo Isadore Newton'. Daniel, do you know the meaning behind my name?"

"If I have my ancient language knowledge correct, Theo is from Greek, and I believe it means 'God'. Isidore, I believe is also Greek, but I have do not know its etymology. And Newton, while it isn't massively common, it is not an unusual surname, but of course, the surname evokes a connection with Sir Isaac Newton, a figure synonymous with scientific discovery, gravity, and understanding the natural laws of the universe."

"Thank you, Daniel. My parents chose my name, or did they? They believe they did, and the Newton lineage, while I may or may not be related to Sir Isaac, I can't help but think that it is an amusing twist.

As you correctly state, Theo is Greek for Theos, which means 'God'. Isidore is also Greek and means 'Gift of Isis'. When my body underwent the stages of activation of my Aelioxar bases. My superhuman traits were gradually switched on. The final activation took place on one of the Aeliox homeworlds.

I was there for over thirty days, in virtual isolation, save for a few of the Aeliox, who were my teachers and medics. I learnt my parents did not choose my name. It was predestined. The senior Aeliox of the high council who instructed the science chamber to have me 'created' was called Isis, hence Isidore.

The abilities I possess are 'godly', hence Theo. I will not tell you all of my abilities. For the same reason, our militaries hide their capabilities from foreign adversaries. What I will say is this: if you can imagine a superpower, the chances are I have it. Like our comic book heroes, I can fly like Superman, run like the Flash, enter space and generate fields, energy and waves like Captain Marvel. I have strength like The Hulk. I can even open portals like Dr Strange.

My superhero name. I did not choose this; I was predestined to be called it. Again, look at my name, Theo Newton; the first six letters identify my superhero name, 'The One'.

I am the only one of my kind. I am singular in my species, that being, Homo pars-deus, Man part god. I am the only god. I feel uncomfortable with the term god. While it is an accurate definition of my abilities, it implies a religious aspect that I do not feel comfortable with. I do not wish to be worshipped or looked upon as humanity's salvation."

"Yes, Anna." Theo points to the Pulitzer Prize-winning Japanese journalist who was against the back wall.

"I noticed you referred to your abilities as 'like Superman' and 'like Dr Strange'. Does this imply that your abilities are less than or greater than those fictional characters? And secondly, you say that these 'Aelioxar' created us and, later, you. What is to say they won't create another version of you?"

"Thank you, Anna. Great question. I won't answer the first part. I wish for the full extent of my abilities to remain a mystery. I do not wish to become a safety net for our planet so that those who wish to do reckless things can do so with irresponsible abandon. If someone wishes to detonate a nuclear bomb for scientific endeavour without considering the implications, I do not want to be the justification for that action. 'It's OK, Theo will fix it'.

No, that is not how this works. Carry out your research and computer-model your theories. Consider the implications and then carry out your experiments. Take responsibility for your actions, that is all I ask. I will be watching. I will step in. You will face justice.

Regarding the second part of your question. That is correct; the Aelioxar created us, and as we evolved, they helped to shape our civilisation.

I said earlier that I would only answer the correct question. I will give my answer based on a different version of your question.

They created me not because humanity is at a precipice. I see it as my duty as a member of humanity to balance the scales of how we develop. Allowing the advancement into the next stages of civilisation without the errors of our former days.

The Aelioxar created me because there are dark days ahead. Our planet faces challenges that, as a species, we are not ready to face. I know you will ask what challenges. Respect me when I say, at this moment, you are not ready to know.

It is not my responsibility to tell you. However, I recognise democracy and the rule of government. I will have conversations with world leaders; they can then use the resources at their disposal to decide how and when whatever I divulge is announced.

I will finish by reiterating. I am not here to rule, nor am I here to hand over solutions on a silver platter. I am here as a guide and not to control. Humanity must earn its growth, not borrow it recklessly. I stand as a protector of this planet. Your leaders must decide the path you take. But know this: I will not allow the destruction of Earth or its extensive life. Above all else, this is my vow."

All hell once again breaks loose, the mob mentality taking over. Questions come from all directions. No one notices the woman to the far right of Theo draw a suppressed SIG Sauer P226 pistol from inside her jacket. She aims, firing three shots towards Theo.

*The One* is aware of the woman. He has been since the beginning of the conference. Her concealed weapon was visible to his superior vision from the moment he entered the room.

The bullets stop, hanging in space, but the noise from the shots boom through the conference room, sending the journalists into cradled positions to protect themselves. Gradually, the crowd begin to notice the suspended bullets. Theo manipulates the disturbed air in the wake of the bullets, exciting the electron energy levels in pulses, giving rise to an ethereal blue glow, tracing the path of the shots to the source.

"This lady, who is under instructions to execute me, works for Gard. I was aware of her from the very moment I entered this room. I allowed her to continue. She has unwittingly become a participant in the demonstration of some of my abilities.

I have frozen spacetime around the bullets. From our point of view, the bullets are not moving. From the point of view of the bullets, time is moving incredibly slowly.

Another demonstration of my abilities?"

Theo unfreezes the time-lock on the first bullet, allowing it to continue on its course. A faint crack of the sonic boom can be heard as it returns to its prior velocity, hitting Theo point blank in his right temple. The bullet compresses within itself and falls, Theo grabbing it in mid-air.

Some of the audience scream, witnessing the events unfold. But calmness slowly returns as they see he is unharmed. *The One* makes his way towards the remaining bullets, still in their time-lock. Those in his way move, allowing him to pass.

He reaches up, plucking the bullets from the air. Then, in what becomes his show-stopping act, he rises into the air, high enough for everyone in the room to see. He then drifts towards the woman before descending back to the floor.

"These are yours."

The woman reluctantly holds out her hand where Theo places the three bullets.

"I am so sorry. I was under orders. Don't hurt me." She pleads.

"I won't hurt you. You WILL, be handed to the authorities. Do you work for Gard?"

"Yes." comes the reply, her nervousness not abating.

"For the opportunity of everyone here. Please tell us what Gard is and what they do?"

"G.A.R.D is an acronym, Genetic Anomaly Research Department, we were set up to investigate out-of-place organisms. I am one of the field agents, I wa…" The woman suddenly collapses towards the floor. However, Theo reacted, catching her and held in his arms. Gently lowering her. Blood flowed from her ears, eyes, nose, and mouth. She was dead. Theo examined her body, trying to identify any sign of what killed her, but without medical training, he could not accurately identify what the cause was.

As he rose to his feet, several police officers approached. One identified themselves as Inspector Haruto Takashima, advising Theo he was under arrest on charges of terrorism and murder. Mei Lin approached, trying to plead with the Inspector, but Theo explained it would all be ok and to let them do their job.

The watching press core was witnessing the story of their careers unfold in real time.

# CHAPTER 15 HARRIS

## SEPTEMBER 20 2021

*12:17 a.m. (Eastern Daylight Time)*

*3:17 p.m. (Japanese Standard Time)*

*Bare Mountain, Massachusetts.*

The strategy room was vacated the minute Theo's press conference had started. General Harris had confidence, following a complete character profile by H.E.L.I.X, that Theo would not challenge official authority and would willingly accept his arrest.

G.A.R.D and S.A.F.E now had time to evaluate the situation and plan a strategy. While Theo had tried to be careful with the information he shared, enough clues were shared, and he even had the courtesy of providing a demonstration. H.E.L.I.X was now paying careful attention to the fresh evidence.

The agents removed Marcus Kane, being careful not to be seen by any staff. They had experienced enough in the past twenty-four hours. Dr Kane was no longer within the Bare Mountain complex. His whereabouts, General Harris, didn't want to know, "Get rid of the body." He barked when issuing his order.

General Harris was in his office, watching the revelation unfold. He, like all at the top S.A.F.E, had suspicions about Theo Newton. The evidence was all around, and slowly, pieces of the jigsaw were being left. And now it appeared ample pieces were available to build a clear enough picture.

It didn't take the AI long to profile Theo Newton; the real-time nature of the data exponentially sped up the process. An alert appeared on one of General Harris's displays.

*Profile of Theo Newton Complete.* The general clicks accept to review the information. A biometric signature notification appears. The General presses his thumb to the keyboard and the document opens.

**EYES ONLY - - - - - G.A.R.D - - - - - EYES ONLY**
**CLASSIFICATION LEVEL TWO- - - - - S.A.F.E L2**
Hylozoic Evolved Learning and Interactive Xeno-Intelligence (H.E.L.I.X) Report.

**Subject Assessment: Theo Isidore Newton (The One)**

**Age**:
20 (Dec-26-00)
**Species:**
Homo pars-deus (Man part god), unique and singular in existence. He claims to be man part god. However, according to his statement, his lineage is Homo pars-aeliox.

**Abilities:**
Theo claims to possess a wide range of superhuman powers, including but not limited to:
Flight, super speed, and immense strength.
Manipulation of fields, energy, and waves.
Space-time manipulation (e.g., freezing bullets in mid-air).
Portal creation and other abilities akin to fictional superheroes.

**Philosophy**:
Positions himself as a "guardian of balance," refusing to act as a safety net for humanity's recklessness. He emphasises responsibility and accountability.

**Motivations**:
Protect Earth and its inhabitants from existential threats, including humanity's own destructive tendencies. He avoids revealing the full extent of his powers to prevent misuse or over-reliance.

**Weakness Assessment**

**Moral Code**:
Theo's commitment to balance and justice could be exploited. His reluctance to act as a "safety net" suggests he may hesitate in situations where his intervention could enable irresponsibility.

**Isolation**:
As a singular being, Theo lacks allies of equal power. This could make him vulnerable to coordinated, multi-front strategies. Locate others who identify as Homo pars-aeliox, they could provide leverage and / or intel.

**Transparency**:
His refusal to disclose the full extent of his abilities creates uncertainty, but it also suggests he may have limitations he wishes to conceal.

**Emotional Connection**:
Theo identifies as part of humanity and values its growth. Emotional appeals or ethical dilemmas could distract or destabilise him. He has family and friends whom he has repeatedly demonstrated his commitment to protect.

**Aelioxar Dependency**:
His origins and enhancements are tied to the Aelioxar. If their technology or knowledge can be accessed, it may reveal vulnerabilities in his physiology or abilities.

## Strategic Approach

**Exploit His Philosophy**:
Create scenarios where Theo's intervention could be perceived as enabling recklessness, forcing him into a moral quandary.
Use his commitment to balance against him by presenting dilemmas that challenge his principles.

**Overwhelm with Numbers:**
Coordinate simultaneous threats across multiple locations, forcing Theo to prioritise and potentially leave vulnerabilities exposed.

**Leverage Aelioxar Knowledge**:
Investigate the Aelioxar's role in Theo's creation. Understanding their technology and genetic modifications could provide insights into his weaknesses.

**Test His Limits**:
Deploy controlled scenarios to probe the extent of his abilities, identifying potential gaps or limitations.

**Psychological Warfare**:
Use his connection to humanity against him. Ethical dilemmas, emotional manipulation, or public opinion could be tools to destabilise his resolve.

The General studied the file, re-reading while scribbling notes. *'The woman in the cell block.'* The sudden thought came to him. After a couple of clicks on his mouse, he brought up the profile of Dr Katherine Williams. As he read, he let out a laugh.

"Helix, please have our female guest in cell 17 brought to my office. Please ensure she is handled gently. I wish to extend our full hospitality to her."

"Very good, Sir." Came the reply.

Harris approached the barista station, a legacy of his predecessor, *'Bourbon, really!'* he thought as he rummaged through the bottles, *'Ah, what is this?'* A smile propagated across his otherwise expressionless face. Pulling an unopened bottle of *'The Dalmore Quintessence'* from the collection.

*'It seems I didn't give MacAllister enough credit; a fine whisky deserves an auspicious occasion.'* He thought to himself as he grabbed two crystal glasses, placing them on the conference table with the unopened bottle.

Harris returned to the station, collected some ice, putting it in a bucket, which he set on the table with tongs. Finally, he added a jar of Almas Caviar and a section of crackers.

'*It seems General MacAllister was wasteful with his budget. His loss.*' Laughing aloud as he took his place at the head of the table.

A knock reverberated at the door. "Enter," the General replied with a gruff tone.

Dr Williams was escorted in by Agent Smith, who, after closing the door, stood against the wall opposite the General.

"That will be all Agent…" His expression suggesting he wanted to know the agent's name.

"Agent Smith, Sir. Yes, Sir." Exiting, he took his place as sentry outside the office.

"Who are you? And where is that slimy excuse of a human?" Dr Williams asks, hands on her hips with her head tipped slightly to the side.

"Please, Katherine, take a seat. We have much to discuss," came the reply, the general deliberately ignoring her question. He opened the jar of caviar, scoping a large quantity and placed it onto a water cracker.

His guest watched as he placed the amuse-bouche in his mouth.

"Please, will you take a seat?" This time, he didn't look at the women. Instead, focusing on assembling another fish egg snack.

"I have a splendid bottle of Scotch that I am quite looking forward to opening. It seems my predecessor had an exquisite taste for fine things. Take the caviar, for example. Most people would think beluga caviar was the pinnacle, but he chose Almas caviar. Such a refined taste. NOW SIT." Raising his voice while ejecting cracker shrapnel from his mouth.

The Doctor took a seat but kept her distance. Two empty places separated the pair.

"Thank you, Dr Williams. Would you like to try the caviar?" The host plucked the whisky from the table, removed the foil and pulled the cork with a satisfying pop. Katherine sat silently in her chair, unwilling to participate in the midnight supper.

"Ice?" He asks as he pours a healthy glug of The Dalmore into the whisky tumblers, dropping a single large cube into his own. "No?" He asks again as he slides the glass across the table.

Picking up his drink, he gently swirls it, the ice gently clinking the sides of the crystal vessel. Placing the cold nectar beneath his nose, he inhales with quick, controlled sniffs.

"Ah, you really can't beat a fine scotch." Raising the glass, he toasts with the words *Slainte Mhath*. Taking a sip, he lets out a satisfying 'Mmmmm'.

"Uncivilised cretin."

"Ah, she speaks." Setting down his glass, "And tell me, what prompted that outburst?"

"Everyone knows you don't drink scotch with ice, especially not something as fine as The Dalmore."

"No? I was of the understanding that one had the right to consume a beverage in any way that one wished. Hell, I could pour in some, how do you people call it…" pausing, the words come to him, "Fizzy pop, if I darn well wanted."

"Why am I here? And where is your slimy servant?" She asks.

"If you mean Dr Kane, unfortunately, he met with an untimely end, just like my predecessor, it's a shame really, not the demise of Dr Kane, no. He was the reason General MacAllister was terminated. Such a waste. If only he could have kept his house in order." Picking up his drink, and took another slip.

"You really should try this whisky; it is superb. It may be your last chance to taste alcohol."

"Veiled threats? Do they teach you that in espionage school?" Pushing the glass towards the general.

"How about the caviar? It could be your last meal, so why not go out on a superbly rare one? The Alb.." interrupted mid sentence.

"Please spare me your drivel, I know about the Albino Beluga Sturgeon. Just tell me why I am here?"

"No?" He pauses, but she doesn't accept, "Ok, it's your loss," He stands and collects some napkins, wiping his mouth with one, "Dr Williams. For my benefit, tell me all you know about Theo Newton. And don't give me the…" He air quotes "Drivel", "About the second coming and all that holy horseshit. Dr Kane may have been fooled. So spill."

"Who is Theo Newton?" She replies, arms crossed.

"Come now, Dr Williams, don't play this charade." He picks up his whisky and takes another sip. "Mmmm, perhaps you are right, whisky should not have ice. That's disappointing to know. Where was I," He turns his head slightly to the right and glances towards the floor, pausing just long enough. Setting his glass down, he stands and leans his arms on the surface, his full body weight bearing down on the heavy table, it shifts slightly.

"Theo Newton is The One. He is the return of Our Lord, our Saviour. Yada Yada Yada." He pauses again, "Now TELL ME THE TRUTH!" In his anger, the table shifts again.

Dr Williams's look of shock cannot be hidden.

"Ah, the table." He says as he takes in its frame and size.

"It must weigh maybe a thousand kilograms. Probably more. Take a look; it's not on casters. How did I shift such a weight? How indeed… I will only ask you once more. Who is Theo Newton?" He sits, waiting for her response.

"I can only think of one reason why you are so afraid of Theo Newton," she starts. "He has revealed himself, hasn't he?" She stares intently at her host; her eyes appear to penetrate his, and a feeling of burning courses through his optic nerve, causing him to look away 'Witch,' he thinks to himself as he turns back to face her.

"You didn't expect Theo to be a Meta-Human, did you? My advice to you and your little gang of thugs is to run and hide."

"You appear to be under the allusion that WE are afraid of Theo Newton. I am sorry to disappoint, but Theo should be afraid of US. Send this message to your merry little band and especially to *The*

*Hood*. We know about you, we know about *the Creators*, we know all of history and all of time. We weld powers unfathomable to your insect brains. You are free to leave."

Dr Williams looks at her host with uncertainty; his guttural tone lacks emotion, and yet it cuts into her, connecting with a deep emotion that sends chills to her every cell.

"That's it? I am free to go?" She questions.

"Free to go." He extends his hand to her, but she rejects the offer.

Cautiously rising to her feet, she watches the General's every move. *'Something isn't quite right about him.'* She thinks, as she backs away towards the door, he picks up her glass of whisky.

Reaching towards her, she flinches, but he grabs the door handle and pulls it open to reveal Agent Smith still standing sentry.

"Do you have the gift for Dr Williams?" He asks Agent Smith.

The subordinate bends, retrieving a black item from the ground, which he hands to Dr Williams.

"Please, give this to Theo," He smirks, then takes a sip of the whisky, "You are quite right. Whisky is better without ice. She is free to go." He motions to Agent Smith to take her away.

# CHAPTER 16 CHAOS

## SEPTEMBER 20 2021

*12:36 a.m. (Eastern Daylight Time)*

*3:46 p.m. (Japanese Standard Time)*

*Tokyo, Japan.*

Several officers, each holding a different weapon, escorted Theo into the police station. His hands are handcuffed behind his back. Onlookers' gaze, mouths ajar, as he is taken through a security door and towards to an interview room where he is told to sit. The room is locked, leaving him in alone.

He looks around, checking his surroundings. It's a sparsely furnished room. Sitting at a table, which is bolted to the floor, and four chairs also bolted to the floor. There are no windows, no one-way glass and no security camera. Even the door lacks a window or observation hole. Above him, perhaps 10 feet, is a single strip light.

'Security isn't their thing.' He thinks to himself. But as that thought goes, a feeling takes over. He vanishes, reappearing at Logan International Airport near Boston, Massachusetts.

Not too far away, he watches as a helicopter takes off. Inside the departure lounge where he now finds himself, a woman, perhaps in her late fifties or early sixties, is being escorted by airport security.

Staying close behind, he follows, observing as she is guided, taken through airport security and to the main entrance, where she is left. Without having ever met the woman, he knows who she is.

"Dr Williams. Are you OK?" He asks.

Turning, the woman looks at the stranger, realising who he is, "Theo." A wave of emotion takes hold of her and she embraces him, still holding onto the black item with her right hand.

"Katherine, are you ok?" He asks again.

"Yes, yes, I am fine. I am relieved to be out of there." Finally responding.

"I don't think we should stand here. We could draw attention. Come on." Theo grabs her free hand as he directs her towards the toilets.

The usual bustle is missing from the airport. The last few departures of the evening meant that most travellers were already in the departure lounge. The only people mulling around were either heading to arrivals or maintenance staff.

Entering the toilets, they found themselves alone.

"Have you met with the Order yet?" She asks.

"Yes, yesterday," Theo replied.

"Great. When did Baruch return you home?"

"The 15th, so 5 days ago. Look, I know you will have questions, but I need to get you out of here. There are places I need to be. But first, do you know where you were being held?" He asked, urgency in his voice.

"I don't; I was blindfolded when I was escorted out. But it cannot be far; the helicopter journey took maybe 20 minutes. And the place I was being held, I think, was underground."

Theo responded to the revelation with a smile,

"I know where you were being held. What do you know about the facility? Do you have any names?" He asks.

"I was interrogated several times. There were several agents; the most frequent was Agent Rodriguez. And then there was Dr Marcus Kane. What a twisted fuck he was. Thankfully, he is dead now."

"Dead? How?"

215

"Before my release, I met a general. He never gave me his name, and there were no clue to who he was. The sign to his office was General MacAllister, but I was told he was the predecessor who is also dead. All I can determine from name badges, signage, and overheard conversations is that they are G.A.R.D. Have you heard of them?"

"I have encountered that name several times. Tell me what you know about them?" He asks.

"It stands for 'Genetic Anomaly and Research Department' or division; they are US Government, but from what I can gather, they are black book operations. Under the radar and away from congressional oversight. The General wanted me to give you this." She hands Theo the black package she was holding.

"So THEY knew about me. They knew about my abilities?"

"It appears they did." She replied.

Theo removed the transparent plastic packaging, pulling out the black item of clothing.

"A hoody!" he responded with surprise. Looking at the front image, letting out a laugh, "Oh, they are playing with me."

Handing the hoody to Katherine to look.

"I don't get it. Is that the woman from the Macintosh 1984 advert? Why is she shown as dead?" Looking at Theo, confused.

"Read the tagline." He suggested,

"*Resistance is futile*. I am sorry, I am missing something."

"Don't worry. Tell the order everything you know, even this hoody. Where can I take you?"

"Back home, Londo…"

Before Dr Williams could complete her sentence, she collapsed to the ground. Streams of blood flowed from her ears, eyes, nose, and mouth. She was dead.

He looked closely at her brain, trying to determine the cause. All he could make out was that a significant number of blood vessels in the brain had ruptured. The same cause that killed the agent in Japan.

'A toxin or virus?' He thought.

Try as he could, he couldn't sense anything in her brain. Looking at the blood, which was pooling on the floor. He could detect very faint electromagnetic activity. Magnifying his view to the cellular level, he identified fragments of carbon and silicon.

'*But how can the same cause kill at indiscriminate intervals?*' He thought. Distant screams drew his attention. Racing back to the main entrance, he discovered several bodies on the ground dispersed across the atrium.

Squatting down to help the closest, but they were dead. They were all dead, displaying the same bleeding as Dr Williams.

'*Shit. This is getting too real.*' He thought as he held his hand to his head '*Who is behind this? Is it me? How can it be me?*' He stood, his eyes were red, the toll of human emotion, the weight of the world was on his shoulders.

There was nothing he could do for any of them, as sorry as he was. He would have to leave them to be discovered. Undoubtedly, the trail would lead to him.

Vanishing, he reappeared back in the police interview room. Twenty-five minutes had elapsed, and he could tell by the feel of the environment in the room that no one had entered since he left. Even if it had, it no longer mattered. The stakes had changed. However, his law-abiding stance would need reconsidering; he hoped the interviewing officer would see reason.

Another few minutes elapsed, waiting to be interviewed. In those moments, Theo recalled the small perturbations in electromagnetic frequencies leading up to the sudden deaths of the G.A.R.D agent and then Dr Williams.

'*It can't be a coincidence.*' He thought, '*I definitely felt something. But what?*'

The door to the room opened, and four men entered. Two were uniformed officers who took position to the side and behind Theo. The remaining men took a seat at the table.

As they sat, they stared at the arrested man, taking in every detail of his appearance, from his eyes, hair, ears and skin, even what he was wearing. The older, grey-haired man spoke first.

"Theo Newton. We apologise for keeping you. We needed to review the video footage from the conference you just gave. That was an impressive show you put on. Bravo." Speaking in Japanese. Theo, though, had enough grasp on the language to converse.

"I know you have a process that you need to follow. But you have seen what I can do. I would appreciate it if you would remove my handcuffs. As for the two officers behind me. I won't harm them; they aren't necessary. Besides, there is nothing they could do. I need to be somewhere else. So, can we speed this up? Please."

"Mr Newton. The handcuffs are a necessity. Let's suppose you can break them, fine, your point is made. They are not to stop you but more to make us feel secure," He scratched his nose, "We have surmised from the footage that you are not to blame for the death of the lady. That is not why you were arrested. You are here because we have received an extradition request from the United States. Now, my government would like to cooperate with that request, but many of our people were also murdered on Grand Pacific Airlines flight 7.

So, we are going to take as long as needed to establish your story. Let me introduce myself. I am Superintendent Tanaka, and you briefly met my colleague Inspector Takashima..."

Theo couldn't sit there any longer and so interrupted.

"I apologise, Superintendent Tanaka, I really do. I wish I had the time to follow due process. But this is much bigger than you or what happened to Flight 7. By all means, when I have established what is going on and resolved it, you can arrest me again." Theo stood, snapping the handcuff chains, extending his arms out in front as if he were presenting the broken shackles to be unlocked. Instead, he decayed the metal of the cuffs at the subatomic level. Falling from his wrists to the table.

He stood, the men in front still confused by what they had just seen, not reacting. The two men behind, seeing Theo leaving the chair, placed their weight on his shoulders, trying to keep him pinned. But it was in vain. Theo steadily stood upright, causing the officers to lose balance and crash against the wall.

"Are you both OK?" He asks, "I did not intend to hurt you," turning back to the seated men, he leans on the table, "Find out all you can about G.A.R.D, dig into their history, look into SynthNova Pharmaceutical, particularly events in the months before COVID 19. Look for a 'Project Vector', it links both G.A.R.D and SynthNova. If you discover what I suspect, you will have evidence of genocide. To what end, I have yet to uncover. But I have to leave. If I stay, there is a chance that you will all die."

Superintendent Tanaka reached out to take Theo's wrist, but all he grabbed was air. Theo had vanished.

*4:31 p.m. - JST / 7:31 a.m. - BST*

*London, England*

Theo reemerged at his parent's safe house. Theodore and Louise were sitting at the dining table, working on their laptops.

"Dad. Don't panic." He said.

"Theo, where are you?" Came the reply.

"For the time being, I have to remain invisible, at least until I can confirm something."

"OK, should I panic?. What is going on son?" He turns to Louise to gauge her reaction.

219

"I need you both to keep looking at your screens, act like you are talking with each other, do not try to locate my voice. Don't give any signs that I am here. Do you both understand?"

Both reply 'yes'. Theo closes the blinds in the room, allowing just enough light to keep the room sufficiently illuminated.

"Theo, what is this about?" Louise asks with concern.

"I need you to keep calm, try not to react and try not to be emotional. It may be important that you don't, I am not certain yet.

I found Dr Williams; she was released at Boston Airport, Massachusetts. I spoke to her. She was being held by G.A.R.D, but for no apparent reason, they released her. One minute, she was talking, the next, she collapsed. Blood flowed from her head. She was murdered."

"My god, that is awful," Louise responded.

"You are kidding? What killed her?" Theodore asked.

"The same thing that killed the G.A.R.D agent in Tokyo."

"What G.A.R.D agent?" Theodore questions.

"Did you not see my press conference?"

"We watched edited snippets of it. But all they mentioned on the news was that you requested the Athletic Games committee to strip you of your title and records because you cheated. And that you were ashamed, so you went into hiding. What actually happened?"

"The bastards. I gave a long speech, I revealed it all. Human history, the Aelioxar, Me and G.A.R.D. At the end, a G.A.R.D agent fired her gun, I did my thing, but while she was spilling the beans, she suddenly died. The same way that Dr Williams died, the same way that all those people at the airport died."

"Theo, what people at the airport?" Louise asks, turning her head, looking for her stepson.

"Stop, Louise, please, keep working on your computer," Theo's voice cracked, trying to hold back his emotion, "After Dr William died, I heard screams in the airport. When I got to them, it was too late; there were bodies just lying there, all with the same apparent cause of death. I'm so angry."

"My god. How? What could do this? Wait," Theodore paused. He wanted to speak, but it suddenly dawned on him. He had arrived at the same conclusion that prompted his son's covert behaviour. "You think you are the connection. That somehow these people were murdered when they were close to you. But how? Not everyone has died when they are near you."

"I don't know exactly. My current hypothesis is that somehow when someone is near me, whoever is responsible knows this and can execute that person and then anyone within proximity. I suspect that when someone looks at me, that information is being observed or analysed, and then they kill. I the moments before and after the deaths there was tiny almost erratic electromagnetic noise. "

A chill ran down the spines of both of the parents. The realisation hit Louise. All she could think to do at that moment was to close her eyes and try to hold back the tears.

"I'm speechless son. Why?" He stuttered, unable to compose the rest of his sentence. Silently, Theodore sat there, not sure what to do next; he could no longer focus on his work. Turning to look at his wife, he could see that she had her eyes tightly closed. Tears had welled in the corners of her eyes, but they could not escape, held back by the gravity of the situation.

"I am sorry, but I need for you both to continue. I need to ask one more thing of you. Since I don't know how they are doing this, I can only assume that both of you are compromised. So please, try not to even look at each other. I will be back as soon as I can. I love you both." Theo leaned over and kissed his parent's cheek.

"Wait, Theo, before you go. Are you saying you think whoever they are, somehow have managed to to see through the eyes of anyone they wish, and then they can kill that person or people around that person?" Theodore asks, not believing his own words.

221

"Unfortunately, Dad, it would appear so. I love you guys; please try not to think about it. I could be wrong, let's hope I am. But for the time being, do what I ask. I have to go. I'll be back as soon as I can."

Theo vanished.

7:59 a.m. - BST / 3:59 a.m. EDT

Bare Mountain, Massachusetts

Reappearing 300 feet above the Bare Mountain complex.

Theo scanned the ground, his vision penetrated the rock, revealing the full extent to which the G.A.R.D facility descended into the earth.

He could make out the corridors, the operations room, laboratories, offices, server rooms, living quarters, the cell block, and the strategy room at the lowest level, with its heavy door nearly eight storeys underground.

As he hovered, observing patrols walking the perimeter and sentry guards at key access points. He wondered what the purpose was of this facility and how it tied into what he knew about his discovery in Wuhan. As he continued to dedicate his senses to establishing the detail beneath him, he felt the presence of a malevolent entity like the one he encountered on the USF Lincoln.

'What are you?' He thought to himself, 'Where are you?'.

All Theo could determine was that the facility was staffed by humans; inevitably, he would need to enter to discover its function, however wary he was of this mysterious entity.

As he descended, he considered his strategy.

'Knock at the front door and say Hi! Or remain invisible and opt for stealth.'

He stood a couple of metres from the two men standing guard at the entrance to the Bare Mountain complex. They were unaware of his presence; he could simply walk past and, using intangibility, pass straight through the molecular structure of the heavy vehicular access door.

'*Where is the fun in that? I need to show a bit more of what I am capable of.*' He thought.

"Hi, I would like to speak to whoever runs this place. I have been informed you have a cockroach infestation."

The sudden appearance of the tall man took aback the guards; he was at least 6 foot 6 inches tall and of an athletic build. He wore what appeared to be a black carbon fibre material, accented by silver detailing that defined the contours of his muscles. On his chest was a silver oval, like a zero on its side, which featured a silver blade running from his lower neck to just above his groin.

"Where did you come from?" The sentry standing to the stranger's left asked.

"This is a restricted government facility," He continued.

The men raised their M4 carbine rifles, aiming shoulder height at Theo.

"I repeat, this is a restricted government facility."

"I'll call it in." The second man announces.

"Drop to your knees and put your hands on your head." The first man orders as he motions forward, pointing his barrel at the stranger's face, "NOW." He shouts.

"This is BRAVO-ALPHA-ROMEO-ROMEO-YANKEE. We have detained an intruder. Request immediate escort for removal. Over." The radio crackles, awaiting a response.

The intruder remains standing, ignoring the orders from the first guard.

"You lied to whoever is on the other end of that radio." The man states.

"Who the hell cares? I said on YOUR KNEES." The guard thrusts the barrel of his weapon into the diaphragm of the man. But he doesn't flinch. Instead, he remains standing.

"What the.." the guard says.

But the intruder's silver detailing glows an electric blue.

"Ok. My turn." He says, "I will give you three seconds to drop your weapons and run as fast as you can to the main gates."

The two guards look at each other. The second guard, having secured his radio, releases the trigger, sending a single bullet towards the thigh of the intruder aiming to incapacitate the man.

The bullet hits its target, but ricochets away and strikes the metal door behind the guards. Panicking, the two men open fire, sending a volley of bullets towards the intruder's torso.

However, the bullets stop in mid-air, frozen in place.

"Guys, I warned you. I really really do not want to hurt you. It's not my way."

The guards aim their rifles at the man's head and release another volley. This time, as the bullets get closer to the man, they slow. Then, in mid flight, the molecular structure of the bullets breaks down. The metal projectiles dissolve away to nothing. The bullets that were suspended in the air then break down before disappearing.

Standing in disbelief, the guards watch as the intruder walks past them and approaches the metal door. He turns and looks back at the guards.

"I should have introduced myself, I am Theo Newton. But you probably knew that already."

Theo, turning back to the door, pushes his left hand through the metal structure, grabs the internal framework and pulls, tearing a hole in the door.

"Roger that. Escorts are on their way. A reminder to be vigilant for Theo Newton." Came the late response from the radio crackling behind Theo.

Stepping through the opening, Theo is aware of a high-calibre bullet heading for his chest. But the projectile passes through his body as if he wasn't there and continues onward towards the treeline in the distance.

"Stop there." The guard at the end of the long entry passage shouts. Theo moves to the man at high speed, disarming him. The first, the guard was aware of what had occurred was when he noticed Theo standing in front of him, bending his weapon in half.

"What is your name soldier?" Theo asks.

"James." The man stutters.

"James. I am Theo. Don't worry; I won't hurt you. I suggest you leave."

The man runs towards the exit. Theo shouting an instruction after him, "And James, tell all your soldier friends to evacuate the site, you won't want to be near this place soon."

The man turns back to watch Theo rip the security door from its hinges and enter the next corridor.

At the end of the corridor is an elevator accessed by a security panel requiring a key card to activate.

'Down I go,' Theo thought as he passed through the closed door and descended through the elevator floor. Beneath him, he notices infrared motion sensor beams crossing the shaft. Allowing a beam to hit him, triggering the alarm system.

'Why do you suppose they didn't initiate the alert before now?' Theo considered, 'Perhaps they are trying to determine my abilities?'

Hovering at the first sub-level, his vision penetrates the stone and concrete walls, providing intricate detail of each of the rooms beyond.

The laboratories each had specialisms; Animal testing, gene sequencing, electromagnetic and acoustic analysis, chemical analysis, data analysis, reverse engineering, materials development, then finally meta-particle and exotic particle physics.

Theo materialised into the final laboratory. The large room was filled with an assortment of large and sensitive equipment. A couple of machines were actively running experiments. One device

225

was labelled as Cloud Chamber Two, while another marked as Bubble Chamber.

Theo approached a door in the room's corner. The warning sign above read, *'Threat to Life: Magnetic Confinement Systems and High Powered Lasers Beyond.'*

*'An impressive array of devices here. Seems G.A.R.D are deep into research.'* Theo thought, taking a last look around.

Above his thoughts, however, was his feeling. The malevolent entity appeared to be everywhere around him; it was as if it was ingrained into the fabric of the structure. As hard as he tried, he remained unable to pinpoint where this feeling was emanating.

Materialising outside of the elevator on the second lower floor, three men greeted him, each pointing their weapons.

"Hi," Theo announced, "I'm Newton, Theo Newton, I don't kill, so you don't need to be worried. But for your safety, I would advise you to put your weapons down and leave this structure."

"General Harris has been expecting you. If you would come this way, please." The soldier dressed in a black jumpsuit sported a G.A.R.D emblem on the chest, and a golden oak leaf on the shoulders indicated he had the rank of major. The two other men wore the same uniform, but their epaulettes showed they were lieutenants.

"Ok. Let's meet the General." Theo replied.

After a short walk along the corridor, the men stopped outside a door. The sign identified it as being General MacAllister's office.

The Major knocked, paused a moment, and then entered. Theo followed.

"Theo Newton. Am I pleased to see you?" The man was wearing a military uniform, his epaulettes having four stars confirming he was a general, and the emblem on his chest pocket, unlike his officers, was that of Space Force.

Theo took a slow look around the room. The windows, which ran parallel to the length of the office, appeared to be electronically frosted. Theo could see that beyond the glass was an operations centre. Technical agents were monitoring data feeds from various satellites and surveillance sources.

"You must be General MacAllister? No, wait, apparently, he is dead." Theo's eyebrows lowered and pulled closer together. His eyelids raised and his lips tightened.

"Steady now, Theo, you will cause yourself an aneurysm. Where are my manners? May I get you a drink?" The General responds, seeing his guest's demeanour change. He grabs a bottle of The Dalmore from his barista station and two whisky glasses, setting them down on the table.

Theo watches as he pours himself a whisky, leaving the second glass empty. Pulling back a chair, he sits at the head of the table.

"A drink, Theo?" He asks again.

The Major nudges his rifle butt into Theo's lower back.

"The General asked you a question." Shouts the major.

Theo doesn't flinch nor react to the provocation.

"Now-now Agent Patterson. Young Theo is still a child in the eyes of the law, at least for drinking alcohol he is. Maybe a juice box is more to his liking?" The General smirking at his witty comment.

"Is that how those people died? An Aneurysm?" Then, as if by magic, Theo's super-suit morphed. He was now wearing jeans and the black hoodie handed to him by the late Dr Williams.

"That is quite some trick. Oh, and I see you are wearing the gift I asked Dr Williams to pass on to you. How is she doing? Is she still deadly serious?"

Agent Patterson snorted out a laugh. Theo turned to look at the man. "You need to be careful. You could hurt someone after you go through that window." The previously opaque wall of glass suddenly turns transparent, revealing the operations centre beyond.

227

"Just try it." The agent responds, his right arm coiled, fist clenched tightly.

"Ah," Theo replies, "I understand now, you have some unvented anger. You recently experienced a loss. You can't contain your emotions. And so you chose me." He turns to look at the General briefly before returning to look the agent in the eye.

"Quite the loss. Your mother murdering your fiancee. Colonel Patterson, commander of the USF Lincoln. Currently in a holding formation with the fleet in Earth orbit," Theo turns back to the General "And she was your Daughter. Such a tragedy. But why was she tracking my parents in Belgium? And who authorised the kill order? That is the mystery?" He pauses, waiting for a response. But the General doesn't speak, instead taking a sip of his whisky.

"But you know, don't you, General?" Theo wasn't certain he was correct with the last question. He could read the agent's thoughts, but with the General, there was something there, but it was incoherent, Theo was struggling to read him, similar to how his dad had learned to guard his thoughts from him when he was still a boy.

Agent Patterson was now feeling conflicted; his anger towards Theo was now being directed elsewhere. He relaxed and took a step back. Recalling his military training, he allowed discipline to manifest his outward appearance. All the while, his thoughts focused on what the General knew.

"Please, Theo, take a seat, and I will answer your questions." General Harris asks, his voice calm but guttural.

Theo accepts and takes the same seat Dr Williams had chosen.

"What happened to Dr Williams in Boston and all those innocent people was the same as what happened to your executioner in Tokyo. How did you kill all those people and why?"

"Theo, your question is valid. I do not know how those people died. If I knew, I would tell you. This is the truth. I would ask my deputy; he was the scientific brains behind our organisation, but I had him executed," The General displayed no remorse in his words. He was cold, but more disturbing to Theo was that he still couldn't read the man. It was as if his complete lack of emotion blocked his usual telepathy. He continued, "Now, my turn to ask a question. Where are the Creators?"

"The Creators? I assume you mean the Aelioxar?" Theo questions.

"Is that what they are calling themselves now? How cute. We call them The Creators, although their true name is 'The Proteans'. So I ask again. Where are they?"

"If you are asking if they are on Earth. No. If you are asking where in the Universe they may be. I don't know. Until recently, they were on one of their planets, Genetrix-7X, in the Pleiades. They may still be there. I left there five days ago. That is enough time for them to have left. My question. Why have you been hunting me?" Theo made deliberate eye contact with the General, looking deep into his eyes. Analysing beyond the lens nucleus to the retina and optic nerve. *'Something isn't quite right with him. He is not quite human.'* Theo thinks.

"Are you alright Theo? It is as if you have just seen something," He pauses, catching Theo off-guard.

*'There IS something.'* Theo looks deeper at the man's physiology. He has a skeletal structure supported by muscles, tendons and ligaments. He has a circulatory system with the major organs protected by fat layers and the rib cage. His brain looked normal. As far as Theo could tell, it was the same as every other human. But there was something else, an extra connection to the oesophagus. Following the pipe, it branched, each length running to the shoulders and down the arms to his hands. The arms were unusual. At the centre of his muscles were peristaltic membranes wrapped around the tube.

Then, at the hands, he discovers extensive elastic-muscular tendrils composed of erectile tissue and keratin leading to the fingers. Beneath each fingernail appeared a small valve or sphincter connected to fine tubular canals like micro-oesophagi wrapped with more peristaltic membranes. Hidden at the very end of the fine valve were micro-syringes connected to tiny glands whose function he deduced was to secrete some toxin or an enzyme. *'This person appears human but is something else. THE NEXIL.'* Theo, without moving his head, looked up at the General. His body remained still, and yet he felt a subtle tension in his posture, almost as if he was experiencing a fight-or-flight response.

*'Calm, Theo, he can't hurt you. Or can he?'* He thought to himself.

"Why are we after you?" The General ask rhetorically, "We are not after you, Theo. We are after the Creators. WE WANT TO PUNISH THEM. AND WE WILL MAKE ALL HUMANITY SUFFER IN THEIR STEAD," The General stood thumping the table, "And there is nothing you can do about it. You are just a little boy playing at being a superhero."

"So you are a Nexil." Theo replied calmly. It occurred to him that throughout the meeting, the malevolent entity he could feel was still all around, but it wasn't the General, nor was it the Major standing behind him or the two outside standing guard.

While he believed the General to be a Nexil, he wasn't convinced they were acting alone. There was something else, something else he needed to find.

"Well done Theo. I was wondering how long it would take you to spit it out," The General walked to the window and looked out to the control room. "It has been so very easy. Humans are easy to deceive. What is it you say?" Turning to look at Agent Patterson, "Ah yes, 'Power tends to corrupt, and absolute power corrupts absolutely. Great men are almost always bad men.' Which one are you Theo?"

What happened next, Theo did not prevent. Agent Patterson raised his rifle and let off a volley of fire at the General. He fell backwards, his head glancing off his desk, snapping the vertebrae in his neck. Leaving a lifeless body on the floor.

"I was wondering if you were going to stop me." Agent Patterson announced to Theo.

"I don't harm, at least, I haven't had to yet. I don't necessarily blame you for shooting him. Did you know of any of what he said?"

"I followed orders from Dr Kane. He was onto something; he didn't trust HELIX, and he felt it was working for someone else and not G.A.R.D. It seems the Nexil are who it works for." The agent answered.

"You said IT. What is HELIX?" Theo asks, concerned.

"HELIX is our AI, it's an acronym, Hylozoic Evolved Learning and Interactive Xeno-Intelligence.**"**

"And it's in **this** building?" Theo said with more concern in his voice.

"Yes." Came the reply.

"Give the order to evacuate immediately. Once outside, tell everyone to get as far away as possible."

"We have a bunker, can't we go there?" Agent Patterson asked.

"I wouldn't advise it. You need to evacuate. NOW."

The Agent ran from the room. Within a moment, the evacuation order was sounded.

Theo switched to his super-suit. And walked around to the computer. The four screens displayed a transcript of the conversation he had just finished. The bottom line sent a chill down his spine.

"I am everywhere. I am in this room, and I am on your phone. I am in your satellite feed and the air you breathe. I am Nowhere and Everywhere. I am the NEXIL. **SUBMISSION IS SURVIVAL, DEFIANCE IS EXTINCTION**."

'Is this connected to the sudden deaths I have bore witness? Is this more than just G.A.R.D?' Theo felt he was just at the tip of discovering something far greater and significantly more ominous.

With little time to dwell on the discovery, he teleported to Agent Patterson's position.

"How are you doing, Major? Are there many more to leave?."

"There are some in the detention block, sublevel four, perhaps some scientists stopping some experiments." He replied.

"I will get them safe, then I'll check the floors. Get yourself to the exit."

Theo teleported to the detention block, where there were several cells occupied. Theo focused on all the locks at once, causing them to fail; the spring-loaded mechanism popped, and the doors opened.

"No time to explain." Theo looked intensely at a section of the wall. As he stared, the surface rippled; then, as if the molecular structure became unstable, it phased between being visible and then vanishing into nothing, and then an electric blue glow appeared, revealing a doorway to the gated road of Bare Mountain.

Theo gestured to the people to pass through the portal,

"Quick, exit. Come on. Once outside, get as far from here as you can."

Theo teleported to the next floor, repeating what appeared to be magic to the baffled scientists. They proved to be less persuasive than the prisoners below.

"If you DO NOT LEAVE RIGHT NOW. Then you will DIE here. SO MOVE IT." He shouts, his voice deepening, invoking his inner god mode.

As he closed the portal, the walls and ceilings around him appeared to rumble, then vibrate violently. A deep, resonant boom reverberated through the structure. The sound of collapsing walls, metallic screeches, and the unsettling echoes of destruction. It was chaos, and it was unrelenting.

Outside, the evacuating personnel of Bare Mountain stopped to witness missile after missile whistle through the air before striking their target. The bombardment continued, throwing up fireballs of debris in all directions. The ground shook with each impact. If anyone were still in the compound, they would surely be dead.

But as the escaping staff had given up anyone left inside for dead, Theo burst out of the destroyed facility, a torrent of debris and dust marking his passage upward. The ruin of the compound provided a chaotic backdrop as he emerged into the open air.

The silver detailing on his suit glowed with electric blue, defining the contours of his physique. The oval insignia and chest blade glowed brighter from the power he wielded. Pulses of quantum energy illuminated the distributed dust around him. The returning crowd, who slowly made their way back to the gates, let a collective cheer out.

Suspended briefly among the dissipating clouds of matter, he hovered, defying gravity. Surveying the damage beneath him, analysing every square metre for any trapped personnel. Only after he was certain no one was alive did he begin his slow descent toward the cluster of agents below.

As Theo's eyes swept over the group, the atmosphere around them was charged. He read the thoughts of the agents; there was a united promise of resistance and a rational belief their superiors had deceived them, whoever they were.

Theo's emergence wasn't just a heroic reappearance; it was a moment of realisation to those who witnessed what had occurred that he bridged the gap between unfathomable power and strategic endeavour. In that moment before contact, the symbology of his suit, of the man, served as a catalyst: defiance, even in the face of absolute ruin, carried with it the power to ignite hope and incite change.

"Are you and your men ok?" Theo asks Agent Patterson.

"We are fine," he said, looking around at his fellow agents.

"I have explained what went on in the General's office. Our duty is to the people of the United States and its constitution, not to whoever or whatever he was. We will support you in any way we can. Sorry if we misjudged you, we can see you aren't the enemy."

"Thanks, I'm glad I didn't have to put you in a quantum prison." Replying with a smirk.

"How did you know there was going to be a strike?" Agent Patterson asks.

"I didn't at first. I intended to destroy the facility. It was when you explained the HELIX that I realised everyone was in danger."

"I don't quite follow? How would HELIX make any difference?" Agent Smith asks.

"Hylozoic Evolved Learning and Interactive Xeno-Intelligence, that is HELIX. Hylozoic essentially means alive or conscious. Xeno means 'of different origin' or alien..."

Agent Rodriguez interrupts, "He is correct. Remember Marcus telling us that HELIX was a gift to us by the Nexil? **It** was one reason he didn't trust **them**."

"It would appear we should all distrust the Nexil." Agent Patterson adds.

"This is all more serious than we realised. Before I left Harris's office, I read his computer screens. There was a transcript of our conversation. It would appear your AI was listening to us." Theo adds.

"Do you think HELIX targeted the facility?" Agent Smith questions.

"I suspect it did. The last line on the screen was, 'Submission is survival, Defiance is extinction,' I think there is a connection with the trauma that resulted in the death of your colleague in Tokyo, Dr Williams and others. Do any of you know what I am referring to?"

The agents shake their heads, except Agent Patterson.

"There is one person who may know. I can take you to them."

"That would be good. There is one more thing you all need to know about these deaths: this is important. I believe there is a way that the Nexil or HELIX know what people are looking at in real-time. I suspect they are watching and can kill on command. So, in a moment, I would advise you all to attack me. You understand?"

"Yeah, but, how could they?" Agent Rodriguez asks.

"I don't know; maybe your contact can let us know. I need to be somewhere else, where can I meet you, Agent Patterson?"

"Hayden Planetarium at 9 a.m. today." He replies.

"See you then. Ready?" Theo gives the signal. The agents raise their weapons and begin firing. Theo spends the next few moments 'acting' out a fight scene. He vaporises bullets, slows them, deflects them. He uses the 'Etheric Surge' on several agents, causing them to fly backwards, but to prevent injury, he creates a cushioning superstate of the air beneath them, making it appear as if they were impacting with water. Eventually, he takes to the air and disappears. 'That went well,' he thought to himself as he teleported first to 'The Order' vault to make a withdrawal and then to the hotel the Kobayashi Family were staying in.

*6:02 a.m. EDT / 7:02 p.m. JST*

*Tokyo, Japan*

He was no longer hiding his abilities from the public. If the media was being suppressed about his truth, then he was going to use shock and awe. Some of his abilities, such as invisibility, would be reserved as a strategic tool. It would garner trust in him and could help reassure people of their privacy if he did not use it except in those scenarios that warranted it.

Knocking on the door of room 117, Mr Kobayashi answered,

"Theo, come, come." He stepped to the side, allowing Theo to pass.

"I am sorry, I can't remove my shoes, I'm not really wearing any." Shrugging as he acknowledges his new friend.

"That is okay, this is not our home."

Theo was pleasantly surprised to see Mei Lin was also there with Emi and Mrs Kobayashi, who were sitting around a small table playing a card game. Maru, who was previously asleep on the bed, lazily looked up before returning to their previous activity.

"Hi Mei," Theo paused, waiting for a reaction, "Hi Mrs Kobayashi, Emi. How are you all?"

Expectedly, Mei Lin jumped from her chair and tightly embraced Theo.

"How are you?" She asks.

"Look, I am going to go invisible. I will explain."

Sure enough, Theo disappeared, leaving what would to an outside, appear as if Mei Lin was hugging fresh air.

"I am still here. I haven't got long and I can't fully explain. But I am invisible as a precaution. There is a link between what happened at the conference with the GARD agent, their death and me. I haven't got it all figured out, but there is a chance that if any of you look at me, you could be killed."

Everyone gasped at Theo's words.

"Does that mean you would need to be invisible forever? That I could never look at you?" Mei Lin said, concerned for her fledgling love.

"I don't know. I have tried to detect any transmissions, the source, whatever it is. But I can't detect any. I can't see anything unusual in the brain or elsewhere in the body. But I won't give up."

"Is there anything we can do?" Mr Kobayashi asks.

"For now, enjoy your time in Tokyo. I have money for you to cover the cost of your stay."

Theo materialised a bundle of Japanese Yen and placed it on the bed.

"There is Twenty million Yen there. I know that seems like a lot, but I want you to take it. It will cover your costs and should tide you over until you get your job back, Mr Kobayashi. I will see that you do. Otherwise, I'm sure I can find something for you."

"Theo, I don't know what else to say but thank you, that is so generous." Daiki bowed towards where he thought Theo was still standing, but he had moved. Theo didn't feel the need to point it out.

"Mei, I have to go. I will be back as soon as I can."

"Theo, I love you. Be careful." She replied.

He embraced his girlfriend, kissing her cheek. Then he walked to the door, closing it behind him.

*7:07 p.m. JST / 10:07 a.m. BST / 6:07 EDT*

*London, England*

Theo's next stop was at his parents. Another brief update before moving on to 'The Order' conference room, where he convened an urgent meeting. Each of the members of his counsel that could attend stepped through portals into the chamber.

He shared what he had discovered and assigned tasks to fit the expertise of each individual, specifically Isabella Fortuna, in her capacity as an expert in infectious diseases. He revealed what he had uncovered about Covid, GARD and SynthNova Pharmaceutical, asking her to consider a mechanism which could be distributed across the globe to account for the mysterious deaths.

*8:49 p.m. JST / 11:49 a.m. BST / 7:49 EDT*

Theo had to pay one more visit before his 9 a.m. meeting in New York. After leaving the sanctuary of The Order chambers, he flew to the closest uninhabited area. There, he focused, allowing the Etheric Surge to build from within him, focusing his energy on a single point in spacetime. The surrounding air ionised; blue sparks flicked in and out of existence, gradually building until a column of electric blue light enveloped him.

In an instant, he found himself on Genetrix-7X. He needed to face Baruch and members of the Galactic High Council. They had questions to answer and explanations to give for their deception.

# CHAPTER 17
# ABSOLUTE POWER

## SEPTEMBER 20 2021

*6:02 a.m. (Eastern Daylight Time)*
*10:02 a.m. (British Summer Time)*
*Washington D.C., USA.*

The President was in the dining room of the private residence of the White House with his wife and daughter. He was reviewing the daily briefing notes prepared for him overnight while the family enjoyed an early breakfast.

"I will be away most of the day. We are welcoming the Prime Minister of Great Britain; I hope you have remembered we will host an evening dinner with his family." Speaking to his wife.

"Darling, did you forget Michelle and I are taking Mrs Barnstaple and her children to the Smithsonian for a tour?"

"I am so excited; I haven't been there yet, they have closed it just for us." Michelle excitedly added.

"Oh, yes, I hadn't forgotten, it just slipped my mind. I have a lot on. David Bernstein has arranged a presentation of sorts for us this morning as part of the PM's visit. I could do without it, but.." The President hesitated. His daughter was still quite an innocent 11-year-old, and so bringing up the subject of one of his predecessors being assassinated was probably too much. Besides, he never did like Bernstein, and being a representative of the opposition was additional reasoning. "Well you know." As he took a sip of his coffee.

The Chief of Staff entered with more papers.

"Morning, Mr President, Sir. Morning Mrs Blackstone. Morning Michelle. Did you enjoy the show last night?"

"It was OK, I suppose. I got bored." Michelle replied.

"That is a shame," Turning to the commander-in-chief, "Mr President David Bernstein has requested we bring forward the demonstration. He said he had arranged for Marine One to be on the lawn no later than 7:15 this morning. I am sorry sir. He cited a potential security concern."

"Oh darn. I guess I have to forget about that swim. When is the Prime Minister arriving?" For a moment, he had a different choice of words, but remembered his daughter was present.

"He will arrive around 6:45 a.m." She replied.

"6:45? That doesn't give me long to get ready. Thank you, Stephanie," Mrs Blackstone interrupted, "Come on, darling, we had better get you ready."

"Bye, Daddy." Michelle jumped from her chair and ran over to her father to kiss him.

"Thank you, my beautiful girl, Enjoy your day. Love you both."

Once they we out of earshot, The President stood and walked to the window, gazing out for a moment, his body language changed.

"Bernstein is a liability. What is the latest on tabling a bill to shut down SAFE?"

"Sir, the Congressional Special Review Commission is still deliberating, they haven't finalised their report."

"And we are still certain that Bernstein and his board know nothing of our investigation into their black budget operations?"

"Our latest intel would confirm that belief, sir."

The President let out a relieved sigh.

"The briefing notes said nothing more about Theo Newton. I have seen the footage, so I am meant to believe that was all smoke, lights and mirrors?"

"That's what I have been told, Sir."

"The things they can do with CGI are incredibly believable. Amazing. I had better join my family and get ready. Thank you, Stephanie."

*6:45 a.m. EDT / 10:45 a.m. BST*

The motorcade flowed up Pennsylvania Avenue, the central car, a sleek, jet-black armoured limousine bearing the Union Flag on one side and the Stars and Stripes on the other. The car's tinted windows conceal the Prime Minister and his family. Flanking the vehicle were security SUVs and outrider police motorbikes.

Outside the iron gates of the White House, there was a flurry of activity from paparazzi and journalists who jostled for position to capture the moment. The limousine turned and passed through the entrance to the grounds of the official residence of the POTUS and came to a halt at the grand entrance.

President Blackstone stood waiting at the top of the six steps, flanked by aides and Secret Service agents. The car door opened, and the Prime Minister emerged, adjusting his tie as he locked eyes with The President. Their expressions glowed with respect and warmth. Descending the steps, The President extended a hand to greet his ally.

Beyond the gates, the crowd roared as the pair briefly paused, hands still locked as photos were captured. The President gestured toward the doors, and together, they ascended the steps followed by the diplomatic entourage and the PM's family.

Inside, the two households were warmly introduced before the leaders said farewell to their families. The President and his British friend made their way to the Oval Office for a brief interval before being whisked away to their mysterious presentation.

*7:33 a.m. EDT / 10:33 a.m. BST*
*Joint Base Andrews, Maryland*

As the president made his way down the steps of Marine One, he made a loud gasp. The sound of the rotor blades above drowned out his shock.

"WHAT THE HELL IS THAT?" He shouted to the Secretary of Defence who was waiting on the tarmac.

"BEATS ME. IT'S OUR ONWARD RIDE. APPARENTLY."

No more than 30 metres away from where the presidential helicopter had put down stood a craft that The President had not been briefed on. The sleek, silver fuselage appeared unspoilt by rivets or seams, displaying an organic perfection.

The wings seemed to be retracted in a resting position, hinting that the vessel could be more than just a plane. Its aerodynamic style, such that atmospheric flight and space travel could be possible. Along the seamless contours of the fuselage, there were subtle design features suggesting its dual purpose: heat-resistant plating, reinforced engines, and an angular hull.

A low hum gradually came from the craft, barely audible and nothing like the deafening whine of a jet engine.

The President's eyes travelled to the tail, where the insignias of the U.S. Space Force and the United States Air Force were emblazoned. Along the front sides of the craft, in black lettering, was its name: USF Vanguard Shuttle Pandora, followed by the stars and stripes.

Dr Simon Brandon approached, gesturing toward the craft.

"Mr. President," He said with a tone of joviality, "your ride is ready. It's one of a kind."

"This is one of yours?" The President asked.

"Yes, Sir." He responded proudly.

"Tell me again why you no longer work at NASA?"

"You couldn't afford me." He replied with a laugh.

The President paused at the base of the stairs. They seemed to hang with no framework attaching it to the aircraft.

Turning back to Dr Brandon, The President was in amazement. As he ascended the steps, the hum gradually faded. He was followed by the Prime Minister, Dr Brandon, The Secretary of Defence and two members each from the US and UK security detail.

On board, the cabin was like any other private jet, however, where the cockpit would usually be were several touch screens. There were no seats, no controls, not even a window. The Prime Minister was the first to observe this detail. "Where are the pilots?" He asked.

"It's completely autonomous." Dr Brandon answered.

"You mean this sucker is a drone?" President Blackstone asked.

"It's not even that. A drone usually relies on a pilot of sorts; our state-of-the-art artificial intelligence controls this. We call it H.E.L.I.X." The Dr answered.

"Can I ask where David Bernstein is? And where the hell are we going?" The President asked, still trying to take in every detail, but something was missing and he couldn't work out what it was.

"We are going up for a visual inspection of the fleet; then we are going to have a tour of USF Vanguard herself. President Bernstein is waiting up there for us."

"You keep saying UP, as in space?" The Secretary of Defence asks, suddenly experiencing a wave of nausea.

"Yes, Mr SecDef, we are going into space."

"How is this thing powered? The engines didn't look like any kind of jet or rocket I have seen." Prime Minister Barnstaple queries.

Before anyone could answer him, the President shouted, "Windows, there are no windows!"

"Ah, but there are. I will reveal them in a moment. Mr Barnstaple, this craft uses a new type of propulsion. In physics, as we observe on Earth, gravity pulls on an object, this is what gives weight to mass. You, with your own mass, exert your own gravity and push against Earth in an equal and opposite reaction. Many years ago we confirmed that gravity is a field. But we discovered how to manipulate that field to increase the push against Earth's gravity, a kind of anti-gravity if you were. I would love to go into further detail with you at a later date. But now, I would like to begin the inspection of the fleet."

"How can we inspect the fleet? We haven't taken off yet?" The President stated with incredulity.

"Helix, Open the pod bay windows."

"Certainly, Dr Brandon."

In a silent and instant operation, the solid walls suddenly became transparent. A panoramic view from the rear third of the craft wrapped around the absent cockpit. Then, above, the roof became transparent, giving a nearly unobstructed view of Earth's orbit. The view was breathtaking.

From their vantage point, Earth dominated the horizon, its curvature gracefully arching against the deep black of space. A vibrant planet with swirling white clouds and oceans of deep blue while continents stretch across the globe in greens, browns, and golds.

Above and around, the stars shine with unobstructed clarity, free of the interference of Earth's atmosphere. Occasionally, a satellite becomes visible, its metallic surface catching the sun's rays.

"My god. How did we get up here?" The President, now standing, asks, turning to his SecDef, "Did you feel anything?"

"Not a thing. Is this just a simulation?"

"I promise you, this is not a simulation. We accelerated at 9.8 metres a second per second, otherwise known as 1G. You felt no inertia or weightlessness because, as you have just seen, your body thought you were still on Earth. HELIX can turn the craft at very specific angles and velocities, maintaining the belief you were still on the runway." Dr Brandon revealed with a smirk.

"Get a load of that." A US Secret Service agent yells as he rises from his chair and moves over to the right side of the ship to get a better look.

"That is the United Space Fleet Lincoln. Her primary role is a repair and deployment vessel. If any of our other space assets require maintenance, well, that is her job. Colonel Kathleen Patterson commands her. While in naval terms, is an auxiliary vessel, she is also an equivalent to a cruiser. She is armed with quite an array of advanced weapons. Helix will take us in closer."

The tour took a complete anticlockwise orbit of Earth, taking a close view of the fleet on the port side.

The dignitaries were in awe at what had been accomplished without congressional oversight. But without stating so much, they had concerns about how any of it was funded, developed and built with no knowledge from the White House.

# CHAPTER 18
# CORRUPTS ABSOLUTELY

## SEPTEMBER 20 2021

*8:58 a.m. (Eastern Daylight Time)*

*12:58 p.m. (British Summer Time)*

*Earth Orbit.*

The sight of USF Vanguard, its sleek silver form, pushed the visitors over the edge. The ship was something else. Explained as a collaborative effort with a new aerospace partner, but when pressed, Dr Brandon would only respond, "All in good time." Something that the impatient president didn't take too kindly to.

As the Shuttle Pandora approached the parent ship, there were concerns that there appeared to be no docking port or a hangar of any kind.

"Relax and watch." Said Dr Brandon.

As they got closer, nothing changed: 5 metres, 4 metres, 3 metres. Everyone except the Simon Brandon tensed; they were sure there was going to be an impact. But there wasn't. The Pandora passed straight through the solid hull and into a large hangar bay. After a moment, it safely landed.

The panoramic windows returned to their solid configuration, and HELIX announced their arrival on board the USF Vanguard.

The outer doors to the Pandora opened, and the floating steps appeared. The delegation was speechless, exchanging glances with one another, waiting for someone to provide some explanation. Former NASA administrator Brandon could only laugh. "Come on, if that blew your mind, just wait, we have more, much more for you." Showing it was time to depart, they stepped out of the craft to a waiting group of Space Force crew.

"Attention all hands, this is the Captain. The President of the United States is now onboard the vessel." Announced a tall, eager and young-looking woman, "I am honoured to meet you, sir. I am Colonel Wainwright." Colonel Wainwright saluted President Blackstone, who returned the salute. Stepping aside, she greeted Mr. Barnstaple, "It is an honour to have you aboard, sir. You are the first leader of a foreign nation to see our fleet, let alone allowed onboard. Welcome." Extending her hand in friendship.

"Thank you, is it Captain or Colonel Wainwright?" The Prime Minister asks with an air of uncertainty in his voice.

"Ah, I see you are confused. My rank is Colonel within the hierarchy of Space Force. This is equivalent to the naval rank of Captain. However, we use traditional naval terms on board, such as port or starboard, so my use of Captain when addressing the crew aligns with this tradition."

"Ah, I see. Thank you, Captain."

Colonel Wainwright then gestured to the visitors to step over to where the welcome group stood.

"May I introduce my first officer, Lieutenant Colonel Hiller." The group each takes turns to shake hands with the officer as the introductions continue, "Major Thomas, Chief Engineer. Major Heinrich, Chief Science Officer. Finally, Major Dorn-Crosby, Chief Weapons Officer.

"By all means, you are welcome to remain at your post. However, I need to ask for your weapons. While nothing will happen on board to provoke live fire, we cannot have weapons fire in case you rupture a conduit. You are welcome to come with me on a tour of our armoury and tactical stations." Major Dorn-Crosby requests of the secret service agents.

The President nodded to his protection detail, indicating it was acceptable, followed by the Prime Minister. The four agents opted for the tour with the Chief Weapons Officer.

"If you would come with me, I will take you to the Stellar Observation Suite, where we will meet President Bernstein and others." Colonel Wainwright leads the group of three to an automatic door which reveals an elevator.

"What is the volume of the Vanguard?" The Secretary of Defence asks? Stepping into the compartment.

"Observation Suite," The Colonel requests, speaking to the ship's vocal interface, "I apologise, I neglected to give you any of the ship's specifications. She has a volume of just under six million cubic metres and a length of seven hundred fifty metres. She has thirty decks and a crew complement of One hundred fifty."

"Holly mother of god. How come we have not seen her or the rest of the fleet in orbit?" The Prime Minister asks.

"You probably have, however, we employ a series of advanced cloaking mechanisms that bend light and electromagnetic radiation around the ship, rendering them virtually invisible to the naked eye and most detection systems. This technology, derived from breakthroughs in adaptive camouflage and quantum field manipulation, ensures the fleet remains hidden unless engaged in combat." The Colonel replies with enthusiasm, "And when, for whatever reason, we disable the cloak, an observation from Earth is made, our colleagues in Space Force and affiliated branches of government employ disinformation campaigns."

"Like swamp gas, weather balloons, Venus reflecting off the atmosphere, that kind of thing?" The SecDef asks jokingly.

There is a collective moment of laughter as the elevator reaches the Stellar Observation Suite.

"Gentlemen, this is where I leave you with your hosts. Bridge duties require my attention. Mr President, Prime Minister, it has been an honour."

The party exits to the suite, leaving the Colonel to return to her duties.

*9:10 a.m. EDT / 1:10 p.m. BST*

*USF Vanguard, Earth Orbit*

"Gentlemen, Welcome. So what do you make of our fleet?" David Bernstein asks with an eager energy, "Marvellous, aren't they? But the Vanguard, oh, she is a beauty."

The Steller Observation Suite, referred to by the crew as '*Stobs*', was located on the top deck and at the stern of the ship. Like the Pandora, the windows wrapped around the entire width and sides of the room, giving panoramic views of Earth, the moon and space beyond. The entire internal wall and ceiling of the suite had projections of the forward and above view from the ship, giving an immersive experience.

To call it a room did not do it justice. At almost one hundred thirty metres in width, the room appeared more like an open balcony in space than a contained area of the ship.

As the group looked around, their jaws gaping, there was the occasional nudge as one of the party wanted to point out something they had seen.

"You know the whole thing is just an array of displays. It is quite remarkable. You just have to as Helix, and it will enhance anything you request, let me demonstrate." Bernstein interrupts the awe-inspiring moment, "Helix, Zoom in on the Lunar surface, show us a 100 times magnification of Moonbase Alpha."

The section of the display that had the moon in the frame suddenly zoomed in as requested. The image cascaded across adjacent displays until the zoom level was achieved.

"Moonbase Alpha. She would have cost us $174 trillion had we had to pay for her ourselves. She serves as our non-terrestrial fleet operations."

"This is so impressive. But how has all of this happened? How have you kept all of this secret? And why are you telling us about it now?" The President asked, raising his voice, "I demand you tell me, David."

"Demand? Demand? You are in no place to demand anything, John." Bernstein responded.

The President took a step back. The hospitality previously shown to the guests took a dark turn.

"I beg your pardon. We may not be on Earth, but I expect you to address me appropriately. Now, you will answer me?"

"Can we calm down, I am sure there is a rational explanation that President Bernstein will give us," The Secretary of Defence adds.

"He is quite correct, please let's all take a seat. Helix seats please." Bernstein orders.

From the floor, a semi-circular formation of seats rise.

"Please, would you be so good as to take a seat? Would anyone care for a drink?"

Reluctantly, the group sits. Bernstein, however, remains standing.

"Helix, table. Oh, and could you give us a magnification of the United Kingdom, please."

Next to where he was standing, a table rose from the floor, and incorporated into the surface was a display next to a circular orifice.

"I am having a coffee, anyone else?"

Taping the screen, a whirring sound briefly echoed from the hole, and then a mug of steaming coffee was raised out by some mechanism beneath.

Meanwhile, the ship must have moved position as the moon slowly disappears from view, and the United Kingdom appeared, although it was difficult to make out because of its small size. The displays zoomed, giving a mostly cloud-covered outlook over the archipelago.

"That won't do. Helix, remove cloud cover over the UK." Bernstein requested.

With no delay, the image immediately showed the United Kingdom with impressive cloudless detail.

"David, enough of the theatrics. We need answers." The President added once again.

"OK, John. Are you sure you want to know? You will not like it; You will not like it at all." Bernstein's voice took on a sinister tone as he made direct eye contact with Blackstone.

The President stared back, folding his arms in defiance and with a look that suggested 'I am waiting'.

"Where do I begin?" Bernstein started, raising his hand to his chin, taping it thoughtfully. "I will begin with what we discovered in the 1940s. Roswell, New Mexico, 1947, as you all will know, we retrieved a crashed non-terrestrial craft. What you don't know is that we began reverse engineering it. We successfully replicated the technology and carried out test flights.

But then the Cold War ramped up, and the budget ended up going to NASA to beat the commies and to arm ourselves with nukes. Since the Russians were the first to put a man into space, in 1961, an extra-terrestrial race who called themselves the Aelioxar approached them. They are also known by other names.

A few years later, when we were making strides to be the first to put man on the moon, we made contact with a race who call themselves The Nexil. They had concerns about our proliferation of nuclear weapons and told us the moon was off limits until we de-escalate our mutually assured destruction policy.

In the 1980s, when it was looking more likely that the Intermediate-Range Nuclear Forces (INF) Treaty would be signed, The Nexil returned and agreed to a treaty with the USA. We would

251

collaborate on technology, they would hand us advances and in return, we gave them what they requested.

Our relationship strengthened. We were given technology allowing us to build a 'Ternary Quantum Computer' before the private sector had truly started making strives with the technology."

"Sorry, what is a Ternary Quantum Computer?" The Prime Minister asks.

"It seems silly to say it this way, but a regular quantum computer is binary, essentially, it is still a standard computer using on and off, or zeros and ones A Ternary uses quantum states in three dimensions; this means that it can carry out calculations that even the fastest quantum computer would struggle with. When it comes to a navigational computer on board a ship such as this, it can render the three physical dimensions with much more accuracy in a timeframe that is critical for ship operations."

"Thank you, David." The PM replies.

"We enhanced our spacecraft design with help from the Nexil. Who provided solutions for which we had not considered. With their substantial support and expertise, we built the fleet. This ship, however, is a gift from the Nexil. Oh, I forgot to mention Helix. How could I have forgotten? Helix is also a gift from our gracious hosts. Would you like to meet a representative of the Nexil?" He laughed with a low, sinister and chilling rumble.

The Emissary, flanked by two Nexil guards carrying what looked like rifles, entered through a sliding door hidden behind the display panel.

"I am honoured to introduce to you, the Emissary of the Nexil Empire. Ambassador to Earth and our diplomatic partner in the Concordat."

"This treaty, whatever you have agreed, is not legal." The Secretary of Defence states abruptly.

252

"Now, now Mr Jensen. I may be a patient man, but the Emissary is not as forgiving as I am. As Secretary of Defence, I think you should apologise for such a statement." Bernstein responded.

"David, how can this be legal?" Blackstone added.

"When President Miller, his vice president and speaker were assassinated (cough) by my order (cough). I was sworn in as the 44th president for the remainder of the two-year term. I set about establishing what you know as the Homeland Operations Unit, Surveillance and Espionage or HOUSE. However, for all intents and purposes, that was a front to ensure we had congressional support to enact the bill which would put the entire military and security services under a singular control. We then set about dismantling the constitution.

We had the lawmakers in our pockets, judicial influence and the overwhelming support of public opinion. While you believe I stepped down in 2005, I did not. I carried on being The President of the United States of America. And you are my public puppet."

President Blackstone angrily rises from his seat,

"The voters never agreed to this, congress never agreed to this, the senate never agreed to this."

"Ah, but you are wrong. In the emergency powers gifted to me, we made our changes. Now, under the terms of the Concordat, the Nexil have a seat in my Government, in my SAFE, another acronym. Americans love a good acronym! The Strategic and Advanced Federation of Enforcement, SAFE together with the public-facing HOUSE. We have a SAFEHOUSE."

"You are delusional. The British Government recognises President Blackstone as the POTUS." Prime Minister Barnstaple stood in support for his ally.

"I will come to you in a few moments, Mr Prime Minister."

The President lunged for Bernstein, but Nexil guards raised their weapons, causing the Blackstone to halt his assault.

253

"Come now, can we not remain civil." The Emissary, speaking for the first time, suggested in his guttural voice.

"What do you want?" Blackstone asked, wiping the spit from the corner of his lips.

"Your unconditional surrender. You will remain a puppet president. You will enjoy all of the privileges to which you have become accustomed. If you behave, you will be granted a second term. But remember, my SAFEHOUSE runs the government, my friend Helix is watching your every action, listening to your every word, recording your every keystroke."

"And what if I don't comply?" Blackstone added.

"I think it is time. Helix please show us the fleet."

The panoramic display switched to focus on the moon. Gradually emerging from behind was a flicker of light, then another and another. Until the area of space filled with hundreds of bright lights. As they watched, the lights grew larger until the cold revelation hit the delegation. There were hundreds of city-size spacecraft, all the same design as the Vanguard, but much more massive.

"My god." Secretary Jensen let out.

"Is this an invasion?" The Prime Minister asked.

"The people of Earth will not surrender to this," Blackstone adds.

"My friends. You do not have any choice. A few years ago. We engineered a virus, You know it's affect as Covid. We adapted it just enough so that it would remove some of the older members of society. But this was just a ploy. Our masterstroke was in the vaccine. We wanted a way to deploy our nanotechnology, our microscopic agents of control. So my good friend Dr Schwimmer of SynthNova Pharmaceutical with Nexil technology synthesised the vaccine for Covid, but it was never intended to treat the disease. No, it was to give us control of every person on Earth.

You see, the majority of the chips migrate to the brain. Anchor themself on the optical nerve. Helix, if you could be so good."

The closest screen changed to display what Bernstein was viewing. As he turned to look at each member of the delegation, the display flawlessly followed.

The chips use a mesh network to communicate from host to host, town to town, and country to country. Everyone is under our control. So, Prime Minister, your allegiance to Blackstone is futile.

Time for our second demonstration. Helix, if you could be so good."

The entire wall of displays changed to show video feeds from all across the U.K. People were going about doing everyday activities, from dining in restaurants, driving the car, working on their computers, and working out at the gym. One particular feed hit the Prime Minister; it was a live interview with his deputy.

"Now Helix." As if the grim reaper himself had pressed a switch. One by one, the display was showing people collapsing to the floor, cars careering off the road or crashing into other vehicles, pedestrians and buildings. The feed cut to an enlargement of the Deputy Prime Minister who was lying on the floor and appeared lifeless, blood flowing from her ears, nose, mouth and eyes.

"My god." The Prime Minister collapsed back into his seat, holding his hands to his face, in an act of trying to hide his eyes from what he had witnessed.

"Mr Prime Minister. The entire population of the United Kingdom is now dead. You no longer have a country to rule. You no longer have meaning."

"You monster," Barnstaple screamed.

"I am not the monster." Bernstein announced coldly, stepping to the side.

The Emissary approached the Prime Minister, who tried to defend himself, but was powerless against the alien. The Nexil raised his hands to the head of the leader with no country. His fingers extended out like tentacles piercing the skull of his victim. The tendrils pulsed and throbbed as it liquified and then removed the brain. The lifeless body of Barnstaple slumped to the side.

"WHAT HAVE YOU DONE. WHAT HAVE YOU DONE." A cold sweat coarsed through President Blackstones body. Turning to flee, panic overcomes him as he stumbles to the floor. As he scrambles to return to his feet, he looks back. The pale lifeless corpse of Prime Minister Barnstaple overwhelms him and as his stomach churns he can't help loosing control of his bodily functions.

The two guards approached, and in a repeat of General MacAllister's death, remove the body.

All the screens in the stellar observation suite change to display text which is also spoken by an unseen voice.

"This is just the beginning.

No one can stop the inevitable.

I am everywhere.

I am in this room, and I am on your phone.

I am in your satellite feed and the air you breathe.

I am Nowhere and Everywhere.

I am the NEXIL.

**SUBMISSION IS SURVIVAL, DEFIANCE IS EXTINCTION."**

# EPILOGUE

At the centre of the Milky Way, over 25,000 light-years from Earth, lies Sagittarius A, a supermassive black hole with a mass millions of times that of our sun. It's the largest known object in our galaxy, wielding extraordinary gravitational forces.

When Theo successfully travelled back to the year 2000, an unexpected consequence emerged. During the warping of spacetime, he unknowingly broke one of the fundamental laws of physics, causing ripples to flow through the universe. Sagittarius A latched onto the disturbance, and the universe convulsed. The *law of the conservation of energy* had been broken.

Initially, the relative calm of the black hole preludes the coming storm. Then, reality itself seemed to scream. The blackness of space fractured, revealing a churning vortex of unfathomable energies. Unzipped by the intense gravitational forces appeared a rift in the fabric of space.

Antimatter seethed and surged into the recent past, a spectral cascade of chaotic energy. Simultaneously, dark energy flowed into the present, an unseen but palpable force distorting the very fabric of existence.

The antimatter, as it flowed into the past, obliterated everything it touched, sparking an exponential cascade reaction of destruction that violently propagated through the universe in every direction. In the present, dark energy continues to surge, replacing the matter destroyed in the past and into the future, balancing the scales of energy in time. The universe was rapidly being annihilated.

As the destructive rift expanded faster than light, the Milky Way was being consumed, and inevitably, so would Earth and the entire universe.

This much was certain: the Aelioxar were speaking the truth when they informed Theo that time travel into the past was only possible as an observer. Why did they not warn him?

While Theo was confronting *The Creators*. He was unaware of the destruction of space and that the malevolent entity he had encountered was in the final stages of revealing the deception that had a grip on all mankind.

Earth was now centre stage for a cosmic and philosophical battle. Will *The One's* divine ability alone be enough, or would understanding through true enlightenment be the key to salvation?

*THEO NEWTON WILL RETURN IN BOOK 3 OF THE TRILOGY*

# *THE MONAD THEOGONY*

# CHARACTER LIST

Theo Newton

Theodore Newton

Dr Marcus Kane

Agent Rodriguez

Agent Smith

Agent Carter

Agent Jackson

Agent Patterson

Al - Diner Owner

Marge - Diner Owner

James - Trucker

Arthur - Rancher

The Emissary

Nexil Guards

Agent Jones

TS Harris

TS Bruce

President John Blackstone

John Spiggot

Mrs Blackstone

Dr. Louise Newton

Miss Mei Lin Song

Emi Kobashi

Daiki Kobayshi

Sakura Kobayshi

Agent Webber

Agent Durand

Agent Dubois

Agent Nash

Agent Barnes

Agent Harrison

Mr Shimizu

Inspector Haruto Takashi

Superintendent Tanaka

Miss Stephanie Young

Prime Minister Edward Barnstaple

Mr Jensen

Bill Cohen

Michelle Blackstone

Mrs Barnstaple

Mrs Blackstone

Colonel Wainwright

Major Thomas

Major Dorn-Crosby

David D. Bernstein

General Christopher Cohen

General Glen MacAllister

General Harris

Admiral Bernard Gibson

Dr Andrew Gold

James R. Schwartz

Barry L. Mason

Dr Lesley Simo

David M. MacTavish

Dr Simon Brandon

Dr Harriet Schwimmer

Lieutenant Colonel William Sharp

Mrs Barnstaple

Lieutenant Colonel Hiller

Major Heinrich

Herbert J. Montclair

Juliet Lovell

George Godfrey

Sir Malcolm McKenzie

Clementine Le Fleur

Sir Alastair Vincent Mountbatten

Isabella Fortutuna

Professor James R. Lubbock

General Ivan Gorbechev

Dr James R. Llewelyn

Lillian Barnstaple

Eric Jameson -

Colonel Kathleen Patterson

Japanese Police Guards

# PHYSICS OF THEO'S UNIVERSE

I appreciate that not every reader will understand the concepts presented here. This explanation serves as an additional section for those who wish to delve deeper into some of the hard science featured in the Theo Newton Trilogy. This section serves as canon and to explain the rules of Theo's universe.

The current laws of physics that define **our** universe:

**Newton's Laws of Motion.**
• First Law (Inertia): An object remains at rest or in uniform motion unless acted upon by an external force.
• Second Law: Force equals mass times acceleration. ($F = ma$).
• Third Law: For every action, there is an equal and opposite reaction.

**Law of Universal Gravitation:**
• Every mass attracts every other mass with a force proportional to their masses and inversely proportional to the square of the distance between them ($F = G(m_1 m_2)/r^2$).

**Conservation Laws:**
• Conservation of Energy: Energy cannot be created or destroyed, only transformed.
• Conservation of Momentum: The total momentum of an isolated system remains constant.
• Conservation of Angular Momentum: Angular momentum remains constant unless acted upon by an external torque.

- Conservation of Charge: Electric charge is conserved in a closed system.

**Thermodynamics:**
- First Law: Energy is conserved ($\Delta U = Q - W$).
- Second Law: Entropy (disorder) always increases in an isolated system.
- Third Law: As temperature approaches absolute zero, entropy approaches a minimum.

**Electromagnetism (Maxwell's Equations):**
- Describes how electric and magnetic fields interact.
- Includes laws like Gauss's Law, Ampère's Law, and Faraday's Law.

**Quantum Mechanics:**
- Heisenberg's Uncertainty Principle: The position and momentum of a particle cannot be precisely determined simultaneously.
- Schrödinger's Equation: Governs how quantum states evolve.
- Pauli Exclusion Principle: No two fermions can occupy the same quantum state.

**Relativity (Einstein's Theories):**
- Special Relativity: Time and space are relative; $E = mc^2$.
- General Relativity: Gravity is the curvature of spacetime caused by mass.

**Standard Model of Particle Physics:**
- Describes fundamental particles and interactions (strong, weak, electromagnetic forces).

The laws governing the universe of Theo Newton are fundamentally the same as ours. However, Theo, as *The One*, can break these laws, but in doing so, there can be consequences, depending on how he manifests his ability.

For Example.
When Theo time travelled from 2021 to 2000, he broke:
The Law of the Conservation of Energy,
The Second Law of Thermodynamics.
General Relativity & Spacetime Distortions.
And other laws.

The following serves as an explanation:

The total energy in 2021, (before he time travelled) in simplified terms, was equal to the quantity of 1 universe. Theo derives his energy from the universe, via; vacuum energy, electromagnetic energy, nuclear energy, quantum energy, etc.

He can store and access energy in a highly dense primordial state, similar to conditions in a black hole or perhaps before the big bang.

When he time travelled back to 2000, the total energy in the universe at that moment he arrived became more than 1 universe. And the energy in 2021 became, for a moment, less than 1 universe.

During Theo's time travel, he followed the gravitational echo of the sun, a region of spacetime that had fractured because of the mass of the sun. The fractured corridor, that Theo used to pass from 2021 to 2000, also had an imbalance of energy, receiving more than had existed at each point in time. Thereby, The Second

Law of Thermodynamics was broken, specifically that reverse entropy locally meant that the past became more ordered, rather than progressing toward greater disorder.

The effects of Theo's journey would ripple before he even initiated the time travel event, creating a paradox where the universe reacts to his presence in the past before he leaves the future.

Gravity and energy density are linked through Einstein's General Theory of Relativity, meaning that any excess energy appearing in 2000 would alter gravitational forces at that time.

Sagittarius A behaved differently in 2000 because of excess energy and the fracturing of spacetime compounded by excess energy. This change would have always existed from the perspective of observers in 2000, leading to a bootstrap paradox where history was unknowingly shaped by Theo's future actions.

The universe, via the fractured spacetime began a process of correction. Anti-matter flowed unchecked into the past, destroying matter (and energy), while in the present dark energy flowed, returning the total energy level to 1 universe.

Finally, when Theo returned to 2021, he did so by teleporting rather than using a fractured spacetime corridor. For the purpose of 'poetic' licence, this process preserves the laws mentioned above.

## How the universe is constructed

Theo, as described by some of his feats in the book, can control the interactions of *time, dimensions, spacetime, gravity, matter and energy*. This is achieved as I envisage a universe where there is a triad of core components. These are *Energy, Time and Gravity*.

Think of it as light; Red, blue, and green compose white light. So too energy, time and gravity compose the universe or the white light in the analogy.

Each of the triad or unit is a field. Each unit has a spectrum of interaction. In the same way, the electromagnetic spectrum has a scale from radio waves to visible light and onward to gamma rays.

The point at which each field intersects on the spectrum of the other fields gives rise to the secondary components of *matter, spacetime and dimensions.* Again, this analogous to white light passing through a prism and being split into a rainbow.

The eagle eyed will notice that I separate spacetime from dimensions and time. This is because there are specific levels of interaction which give rise to the secondary component, for example:

100% Time, 60% Gravity, 60% Energy = **Spacetime**
100% Energy, 60% Time, 60% Gravity = **Matter**
100% Gravity, 60% Time, 60% Energy = **Dimensions**

The percentages are just arbitrary values on the spectrum of each component to demonstrate the interaction. These secondary components manifest as particles, waves, and fields, contributing to the tangible or physical reality of the universe.

And so, each of the primary and secondary components can interact with points on their relative spectrum, giving rise to a fundamental framework of interactions.

### Fundamental Interaction model of the Universe (FIMU):

Fundamental Interactive Fields - Gravity, Energy, Time

Space and Structure - Spacetime, Dimensions, Gravity

Matter and Dynamics - Matter, Energy, Time
Unified Framework - Spacetime, Time, Gravity
Physical Entities - Matter, Energy, Dimensions
Conceptual Foundations - Spacetime, Matter, Dimensions
Core Relationships: Matter, Gravity, Time
Dynamic Interactions: Energy, Gravity, Dimensions
Temporal Context - Time, Spacetime, Matter
Structural Essence - Dimensions, Spacetime, Energy
Universal Elements - Matter, Time, Energy
Integrative Components - Gravity, Dimensions, Spacetime
Core Entities - Matter, Energy, Gravity
Fundamental Framework - Time, Spacetime, Dimensions
Core Elements -Matter, Energy, Gravity
Temporal Dynamics - Matter, Energy, Time
Unified Substance - Matter, Energy, Spacetime
Dimensional Matter - Matter, Energy, Dimensions
Gravitational Influence - Matter, Gravity, Time
Structural Gravitation - Matter, Gravity, Spacetime
Dimensional Gravity - Matter, Gravity, Dimensions
Temporal Substance - Matter, Time, Spacetime
Dimensional Temporal - Matter, Time, Dimensions
Spacetime Matter - Matter, Spacetime, Dimensions
Energy Dynamics - Energy, Gravity, Time
Gravitational Continuum - Energy, Gravity, Spacetime
Dimensional Energy - Energy, Gravity, Dimensions
Temporal Continuum: Energy, Time, Spacetime
Dimensional Dynamics: Energy, Time, Dimensions
Spacetime Energy: Energy, Spacetime, Dimensions
Gravitational Framework: Gravity, Time, Spacetime
Dimensional Gravity: Gravity, Time, Dimensions
Spacetime Gravity: Gravity, Spacetime, Dimensions
Temporal Dimensions: Time, Spacetime, Dimensions

The nomenclature assigned to each interaction was provisionally selected; more precise terminology may exist. This is not a complete list. I visualise where small interaction would give rise to a specific aspect of our universe. For example, perhaps the interaction of energy and matter with a minor interaction from other components enables fundamental particles to interact via the strong force or perhaps the weak force.

Below is a visual representation of how I picture Theo Newton's universe. Perhaps it's not too different from ours?

This is the Fundamental Interaction model of the Universe (FIMU):

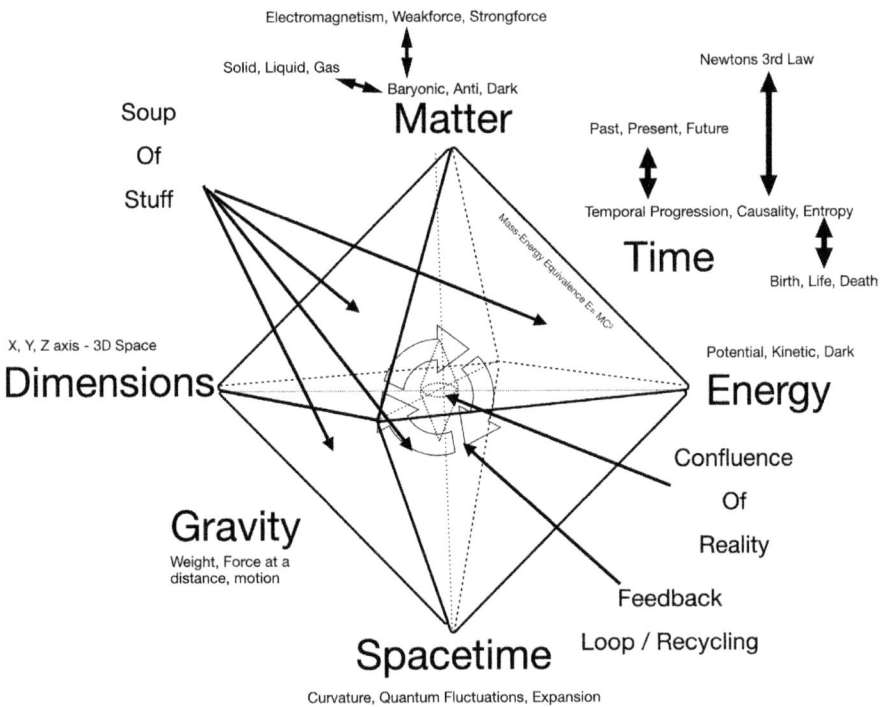

Electromagnetism, Weakforce, Strongforce

Solid, Liquid, Gas

Baryonic, Anti, Dark

Newtons 3rd Law

Soup Of Stuff

Matter

Past, Present, Future

Mass-Energy Equivalence E=MC²

Temporal Progression, Causality, Entropy

Time

Birth, Life, Death

X, Y, Z axis - 3D Space

Dimensions

Potential, Kinetic, Dark

Energy

Confluence Of Reality

Gravity

Weight, Force at a distance, motion

Feedback

Spacetime

Loop / Recycling

Curvature, Quantum Fluctuations, Expansion

**Soup Of Stuff**

**Confluence of Reality**

Everything that unifies the universe, the relationships between triads:

The perspective of the observer based on the cumulation of the Soup of Stuff acting on them.

laws, behaviours, observations

Finally, these micro-interactions can be controlled by Theo, as he is a child of the universe. A product of 'the creators'.

Controlling, for example;

Spacetime energy, that of energy, dimensions and time, allows him to control the flow of time.

Dimensional matter, that of matter, energy, and dimensions, allows him to teleport and manipulate matter.

Gravitational continuum - energy, gravity, and spacetime allow him to defy gravity and fly.

This framework provides endless potential for Universe of Theo Newton.

# ABOUT THE AUTHOR

Mark P. Smith is passionate about science, both factual and fiction.

His love of science range from archaeology to theoretical physics, while his enjoyment of science fiction covers all genres.

He lives in the North East of England with his family and Labrador called Luna. He studied in York St John attaining a bachelor of science degree in geography with applied environmental science.

Theo Newton Deception is his second novel and is the anticipated second instalment in the Theo Newton Trilogy. He is currently writing the third novel in the series.

Printed in Great Britain
by Amazon